Love on LEAVE

Printed in the United States of America

First Printing, 2019

ISBN 978-0-578-60605-7

Publisher: LMCD Contact info available upon request.

For More Information Visit: www.LeahMcDonnell.com

In Loving Memory of My Dear Friend, Kristen

I will always keep our adventures close to my heart,
And our friendship embedded in my soul.

"Many people will walk in and out of your life but only true friends leave footprints in your heart."

~ Eleanor Roosevelt

LOVE
ON
LEAVE

Leah McDonnell

CHAPTER ONE

I close my eyes and step on, too afraid to look down as the numbers begin to climb. 186…187…188. *Oh, come on!* I groan as I stare down at 188.3 pounds. The number silently laughing as it beams up like a Times Square billboard. I fling my towel off and jump back on, praying we own the heaviest towels ever made. I watch as the number on the scale spins to 188.2. *What the hell am I doing wrong?* It's probably a curse for calling the hundred and twenty-pound version of myself, fat in high school. Now I have the pleasure of battling the never-ending female "chub rub." *Yes, because nothing screams sexy like constantly digging shorts out of thigh fat!*

Defeated and slightly bitter two weeks in the gym hasn't budged the scales, I carry on with normal morning rituals. Plucking grays and my daily Easter egg hunt for anything new growing, sagging or wrinkling on my face. "You've *got* to get this new 10x magnification mirror I've been using," Lana said. "You'll just love it," she said. "It's the greatest thing since men discovered the g-spot!" *Blah, blah, blah! This thing is the damn devil!*

I'm pulled from my mid-life pity party as a traffic alert dings from my cell phone. My morning drive is going to be easy-breezy now that the tourists are gone. I smooth the front of my navy blue pencil skirt and slide on my uniform-required beige pumps.

I hold my head proudly as I snap the top gold button of my suit jacket and straighten my Katherine Vines name tag. I take one last glance in the mirror and smile. *See! I may be forty-four, but I've still got it! You can kiss my lily-white butt, Father Time!* I won't mention the fact my feet are already killing me and I've had two hot flashes before I've even made it to the car.

Pride and Prejudice on audiobook, spills from the speakers of my Tahoe, as I make the thirty-minute commute to Del Ray Island, Georgia, where I work as the General Manager for The Sun Crest. An upscale, all-inclusive beachside resort, boasting every over the top luxury money can buy. I pull into the parking deck just in time to catch Elizabeth Bennet turn down the douchebag, Mr. Collins.

It's late October and the final slew of peak season vacationers have checked out of their suites, leaving a battered hotel and exhausted staff in its wake.

"Ah, Cody, it's so nice of you to join us. Seagulls blocking the island bridge again?" I say, shaking off how annoyed I am at his tardiness.

"Sorry, Ms. Vines. It was actually pelicans this time."

"Well, perhaps the pelicans can help you empty the ashtrays in the smoker's lounge after we're finished."

A huff escapes as he takes a seat. "Yes, ma'am."

The group makes a sad attempt to control their snickers as I pull out my notes and begin our weekly team meeting.

"Now that we are all *finally* here, I'd like to congratulate everyone on a job well done. We made it through another crazy season!"

A round of applause, high fives, and praise carries across the room. "Unfortunately..." I shout. The room settling. "Y'all know what's next." Their smiles falling.

"Ugh!" Landen throws his head back. "Freaking, inventory."

I lift my finger in the air and smile. "Ding, ding, ding! *And* Joe, I'd like you to head up the exterior year-end inventory. Start with large items… pool and beach loungers, umbrellas, and clam shades."

I take a sip of the overpriced coffee the resort provides, as the eyes of my management team gaze up from the massive conference room table.

"Thanks to old man, Gibson and his love for the all-you-can-eat seafood buffet, we definitely have three loungers that'll need replacing," Landen teases, blowing out his cheeks to resemble the Stay-Puft Marshmallow Man.

"You'd think with all that money he makes, he'd invest in a personal trainer," Stewart, the catering manager chuckles.

As hard as it is, I refrain from joining in on the employee banter. I lean back in my chair and give a knowing smile. "The housekeeping team will log any items in rooms that need to be repaired or replaced. Stewart will work on food and beverage. In the meantime, I'll be buried in my office working on next year's budget and will make all necessary orders we need before Spring Break season begins."

"Whoa!" Brad's eyes widen. "I know I'm still learning the ropes around here, but I thought we'd at least have a chance to catch our breaths from the summer and fall insanity before we start working on the next one."

The room erupts in laughter as Joe places his large, calloused, hand on Brad's shoulder.

"Welcome to the world of hotel management, Newbie. There are two things we do here… peak season and preparing for peak season."

After combing through the laundry list of to-do items, relief floods the team's faces as I stand and stretch the ache out of my back. "Unless there are any further questions or issues we need to address, I'll bring this meeting to a close."

They glare at each other and give the silent *don't you dare ask another question* look.

I grab my notepad and cell. "Well, alrighty! Have a good day everyone."

My sales manager, Shelby, the only person I don't have to wear a "boss hat" with, and I walk out of the conference room and into the lobby of the grand Sun Crest exhibition hall.

"How are group sales looking for next year?" I ask.

She beams. Her dimples on full display. "Pretty darn good, actually. After the writer's conference grabbed the open August date, it left us with only one weekend available. It's Easter weekend, so I doubt a convention group will snag it up, but maybe a wedding party will."

"Sweet! One more reservation away. It doesn't get much better than that! The higher up's will be thrilled."

"Not to mention putting us one step closer to our bonus!" Her ginger waves bounce as she lifts her hand for a high five.

I smack it. "Amen, sister!" Congratulating her on a job well done as I pile in my office to begin the daunting chore of year-end reporting.

I'm three cups of coffee in when my office door creaks open. "Ms. Vines, I'm sorry to bother you when I know you're crunching budget numbers…" Landen grimaces when he sees me lift a brow over my computer screen. "But there is a Mrs. Santos holding on line two.

Says she's a friend of yours."

I soften at the mention of my childhood friend's name. "I'll take it."

I place the phone to my ear. "And how exactly is my oldest and dearest friend in the world doing?"

"Oh, Kate! It's so good to hear your voice! I feel like it's been ages since we last talked."

"I know! Texting isn't the same as a good old-fashioned phone call. How have you been?"

"Well-LL," Ashley draws out. "I have exciting news I wanted to share with you before it gets slapped all over social media. Our oldest, Savannah, got engaged Saturday night!"

"Oh, congratulations, Ash! I can't even imagine how excited you and Nick are."

"Thank you! We couldn't be happier for her. Tim is just a gem. Heaven-sent after the jerk she dated in college."

"So have they set a date yet?"

She chuckles. "That's actually the reason for my call. Savannah wants to have a beach wedding next spring and we couldn't think of a more perfect place than The Sun Crest. We are going to invite the whole gang and make it a mini-reunion! Doesn't that sound amazing?"

Thirty minutes later Shelby's bubbly voice echoes across my ocean view office. "Kate?"

"Uh-huh?" I squeak out between long, slow breaths into the white paper bag I rummaged out of the trash.

"Ummm...," confusion setting in as she rounds the corner of my desk. "Do I dare ask why you're hiding under your desk, hyperventilating into a McDonald's bag?"

I pull the crumpled bag from my mouth. "You know that open date we had for Easter weekend?" I ask, straight-faced.

"Yeah?"

"I filled it," I say in disbelief.

An ear-to-ear smile stretches across her face. "What!?" Her arms fly in the air as she turns a little happy dance. "Best. News. Ever!"

"Yeah. Great." I force out as I slowly crawl from my makeshift hole. "Just fantastic."

"Oh, try to contain your excitement."

I look up at her, unable to speak.

She throws her hands on her hips. "Seriously, Kate. What's wrong? You should be doing cartwheels with me! Instead, you look like you've seen a ghost."

"No ghost. But, my past is definitely coming back to haunt me."

CHAPTER TWO

"You've been staring at that reservation calendar for months now," Shelby says, breaking the torment the March 20th date has brought me every day since October.

"Are you going to tell me who or what has you in this ridiculous state of anxiety?"

"It's a long story, Shelby."

"Yes. I know," she groans. "You've been giving the same lame excuse for months. Now we're only a week away and you could have told this *so-called* 'long story' fifty times already."

I jump, startled by the sound of "Girls Just Wanna Have Fun" blaring from my cell phone.

"Saved by the bell!" I shout as Shelby gives an irritated side-eye.

"Hello, Lana," I grin, thankful for the interruption.

"Busy?"

"I'm *always* busy. Because us little people *actually* have to work for a living."

"I thought maybe you were drowning in your sorrows since today marks exactly one week until a certain 'you know who' walks through those doors."

I roll my eyes. "Ugh! If I'm reminded about this wedding one more time, I'm going to lose it. Besides, how can you be so cavalier about it? I believe there is a certain skeleton in your closet who was invited to this little shindig too."

"Ha!" she shouts. "Unlike you, I'm off the hook. My skeleton RSVP'd he couldn't make it. So he's staying in the closet, right where he belongs."

I fling my hand over my open ear. "Huh? I didn't catch that."

"I said… HE'S. NOT. COMING!"

"How many times do I have to tell you, Lana? I can't hear you when you have the top down. It sounds like you're driving through a hurricane!" I shout over the noise coming from her overpriced, Mercedes SLC.

"Oh, Kate! Stop your bitching! I can't help it that I get to enjoy this glorious spring day, while you're stuck in…" Coughs, chokes, and spits blast through the phone.

I laugh. "A bug just flew in your mouth, didn't it?"

"These fucking Georgia flies!" she chokes out.

"You know they call that karma, right?"

"You're an asshole!" she spits.

"Yeah, but you love me."

"I'm pulling up to the gym, so I need to run. But I was calling to see if you wanted to meet at The Docks for dinner?"

"If it will get me off this wind-tunnel of a phone call, fine!"

"See you at six!" she shouts, hanging up before I have a chance to preemptively parent her on the importance of timeliness.

Our favorite seaside restaurant is buzzing with vacationers; their stress-free chatter carries through the room as our server, Collin, pours us each a glass of Pinot Grigio.

"I can't believe it's Spring Break already," Lana says, giving Collin undeniable bedroom eyes.

"Yep, off-season flew by," I agree, letting out a heavy sigh as he walks away. "It was almost as fast as your fling with our, oh so, attentive server."

"I know, I know! Two weeks was a little fast to end it, even for me. But he wouldn't stop trying to put his fingers in my butt."

I choke on wine. "Oh dear God, Lana! Ever heard of a thing called TMI?"

She snarls her nose. "I'm all for games… but damn! He serves my food."

I shake my head as we both keel over in laughter. "I think I've lost my appetite."

After finishing off our bottle of wine and an appetizer, we'd caught up on all the latest island gossip, the scoop on my ex-husband's new 'lady friend,' and how the college term is going for my daughters, Olivia and Gentry.

Lana leans in, her face unflinching. "So changing the subject to one you are so clearly trying to avoid. Are we going to talk about this big reunion of sorts, or are we going to continue to ignore it?"

"No." I shrug. "I'm hoping I will wake up and realize this was all a terrible nightmare."

"No such luck, my friend. It's definitely happening. And the sand is quickly running out of the hourglass."

I throw my head back. "I know I'm being ridiculous," I groan. "It's just… it took me so long to finally put that chapter of my life behind me, the mere thought of having to open it back up, downright scares the hell out of me."

Her eyebrows raise. "But you have to admit, Kate." Her perfectly manicured hand lifts an empty glass in the air. "It was one helluva chapter."

An uncontrollable smile begins to grow as I raise my glass to hers. "It most certainly was."

CHAPTER THREE

"How was dinner with Lana last night?" Shelby asks as we sit on the floor of my office, stuffing plastic visors into Sun Crest welcome bags.

I chuckle, a vision of Collin popping in my head. "Oh, you know Lana. It's never a dull moment."

"Y'all have been friends since you were little, right?"

"Yep! She has more dirt on me than a colony of ants. You wouldn't believe the crazy stuff the two of us used to get ourselves into when we were younger."

"Well, ya know… now that inventory is complete, budgets are finished, the hotel is pristine and ready for the weekend, you're officially out of excuses." She gives a shit-eating grin. "*And* since we're just sitting here filling bags, I can't think of a more perfect time to tell me about one *particular* story." Her eyes pleading for the scoop.

I shake my head. "*Fine!* You win. I'll tell you. But it's a long roller coaster ride, so you better buckle in."

"*Finally!*" she shouts, kicking off her beige heals as she settles in for the proverbial stroll down memory lane.

I crawl off the floor and slide into my black leather chair; unsure where to even begin. "It all started after the spring term of my sophomore year in college. I'd been back in Alpharetta for two weeks after completing semester finals at the University of Georgia…"

"Wait! I didn't know you went to Georgia. I thought you were a Cornell grad?"

"I was." I glance at the 1996 Cornell University diploma proudly displayed on my office wall. "But I did my core classes' in-state."

I stand and slide my suit jacket off. "Although academics came naturally, I was in no way, shape, form, or fashion, a bookworm. I was driven but didn't let it consume me. I had goals, but didn't let them strip me of the best years of my life. I was responsible, but didn't let it stand in the way of having some good ole fashion fun every now and then."

"So how old were you when all this happened?" she asks.

"Well, unlike the chubby mom bod I have now, I was a lanky, string bean, twenty-year-old. I've always been tall like my dad, but got the brown curls and hazel eyes from my mom. I guess you could say I was above average in the looks department, but I was never branded as a head-turner. I was excruciatingly flat-chested and after spending years incessantly trying to hide it with padded bras, I finally learned to embrace it. Unfortunately, it didn't stop the guys from calling me 'Fried Eggs and Ant Bites.' And of course, I was a card-carrying member of the 'Itty Bitty Titty Committee.' My only hope was one day I'd marry a man who had plenty of money to buy me a set, or at the very least he'd be an ass man."

Shelby lips purse. "Boys could be such dicks! I was called 'Speckles' in middle school because I had coke bottle glasses and a face full of freckles. It haunted me for years.

I grimace. "That's awful!"
I pull us each a bottled water out of my mini-fridge and settle back into my chair.

"Luckily for me, I wasn't easily offended and could rock a dirty joke or throw out a dig as fast and funny as the guys did."

She points. "I *knew* it!"

"You're always so serious at work. But I knew deep down there was an inner wild woman hidden in there!"

I laugh. "Nah. Being the wild woman was more Lana's speed. She was Lana Mathews back then. Or 'the bombshell' as guys called her. She had a runway body and boobs that could land her straight in the middle of a Snoop Dog video. The total hot girl cliché, all the way to the blond hair and blue eyes. One of those girls you wanted to punch in the face just so they'll look bad for a few days. She had that loud over the top laugh of hers and never took herself too seriously. She was always up for a party and typically the first one drunk. Clearly, she hasn't changed much, even after all these years."

Shelby leans back on my file cabinet. "Oh, how I love that crazy lady!"

"I'd been in love a few times, or at least I thought I had. I'd had a mostly 'off again' relationship with Wayne Stewart, the town bad boy who was one of those, *I don't want her but I don't want anyone else to have her either*, type of guys."

She crosses her arms. "I knew there had to be a guy."

"Oh, there was a guy all right. But Wayne definitely wasn't him." I admit as memories of twenty-five years ago begin to flood my mind…

Memorial Day Weekend - 1994

It's 1994. The days of grunge, rap, and good ole boot-scootin' country. *Mtv, The Fresh Prince of Bel-Air,* tanning beds, acrylic nails, and *Guess* jeans are all the rage. Of course, everyone who's anyone has a beeper. I wouldn't put Lana and me in the spoiled category. We're way too down to earth for that. We have part-time jobs, have chores, and shop second hand like everyone else our age. But thanks to our upper-middle-class parents, who are all happily married and successful, we've both grown up in a bit of a "white picket fence" life. Lana is a few years younger than me, but always holds her own when it comes to the older crowd. She graduated high school last night with my little brother James and is heading to college with me in the fall.

"Lana! Would you hurry the hell up? We should have been on the road an hour ago!" I honk the horn repeatedly, knowing good and damn well it won't make her pack any faster. "We've got a beach full of guys to flirt with and an obscene amount of beer waiting for us a few hours away," I yell from the front seat, hoping the thought of boys and booze will hurry her up.

"Calm your tits, Kate! I'm coming!" she snips, bouncing her large blue polka-dotted overnight bag on her shoulder.

"It's about time!" I grumble, annoyed how off schedule we are.

"Ugh! You and that damn schedule!"

"*Now* where are you going?"

"That bag is just makeup and shoes. Duh!"

My head falls against the headrest. "Oh for Pete's sake!"

She gives a devilish smile. "Like you said, we have a beach full of hot guys waiting on us. I have to look my best." She flips her hair as she spins back towards the house.

"Finally on the road and only one hour behind your precious schedule," Lana teases, opening the bag of M&M's I'd brought for us to snack on.

"Give me some of those!" I say, snatching the bag. "I wanted to get the hell out of town before Wayne and his Merry Band of Assholes get on the road. I don't want to take any chances of running into him on the way down. And to help ensure it, I didn't tell a soul when we were leaving or where we're staying. Not even James."

"Your brother's already there, why wouldn't you tell him?"

"Because! You know how Wayne is. He gets things out of people. He's like a walking lie detector. The less James knows, the better. I have no doubt we'll run into Wayne at some point, but I want to enjoy as much time free from his insanity as we can. I refuse to have a Spring Break repeat."

"Please, God! Don't even mention the cold, rainy, trip from hell!" She groans. "I was about ready to kill him by the time the week was over. He was one step away from peeing on you when other guys were around."

"One of these days he's finally going to get it through that thick, stoned, skull of his that it's over."

She slides her yellow wayfarers down her nose. "And, let's not forget the whole Jenn debacle."

I laugh. "How could I? She spent the first two days of the trip piled in the hotel room, having loud porn star sex with the guy she met from Auburn. Then she spent the final two days in total hysterics after she realized he'd given her crabs."

Lana cringes. "A midnight run to Walgreens for a RID Kit was not my idea of a fun vacation."

I slam my fist against the wheel. "Come hell or high water, this *will* be the 'do-over' weekend we deserve!"

I proclaim as we wave goodbye to Alpharetta, in pursuit of fun, sun, and if we're lucky... a little love.

An hour into the drive, with the wind whipping through our hair and singing every song from Prince's *Purple Rain* CD, Lana has had enough of the silence.

"I still can't believe you convinced your dad to let us take his car." She runs her hot pink nails along the front dash of my dad's brand new, cherry red, BMW 325i convertible.

"He was kind of forced into it. His old Honda they gave me is a stick shift," I say, reaching for the case of CDs in the back seat. "I've tried for weeks to teach myself how to drive it, but I still suck. There's no way in hell I would have made it in all the beach traffic."

"You are pretty damn awful at it."

"Oh, gee thanks!" I chuckle. "I had to beg him to let us take it. He finally caved after hours of pleading in my best daddy's girl voice. James was beyond pissed."

She pulls out my Green Day disc. "Well, thank you, Mr. Carpenter and your mid-life crisis!"

I turn the volume up as "Basket Case" begins to play. "I have a feeling this is going to be a trip for the memory books!"

We live outside Atlanta, Georgia, so it's only a few hours' drive to the coast. A trip Lana and I had taken so many times we know the route like the back of our hands. Palm trees slowly appear as we inch closer to the state line. Wooden, spray-painted signs advertise roadside stands selling watermelons, tomatoes, and peaches, while the scent of hot boiled peanuts fills the air. A burst of excitement rushes through us when we spot the big blue "Welcome to Florida - The Sunshine State" sign.

Lana pops up and down in her seat. "I gotta pee!"

"I need to get gas anyway, so you're in luck," I say, laughing. Creeping the car as slow as possible into the Shell station.

She crosses her legs back and forth. "Hurrrryyyy!"

"Grab me a Dr. Pepper while you're in there!" I yell as she bolts from the car.

She only acknowledges me by shooting the bird over her back as she double times it to the door.

"Whoa! Nice wheels!"

I load the pump back into its cradle as I glance around for who said it among the caravan of cars.

A scruffy, shirtless guy in swim trunks and dollar store flip-flops pops out from the pump behind me. "This your car?"

"I wish. My dad let me borrow it for the weekend." I admit, smiling more than I probably should.

His eyes widen as Lana rounds the car with an arm full of drinks and a large bag of barbecue chips.

"You ladies headed to Panama City?" he asks, more intrigued with Lana in view.

"Hell yeah, we are!" she flirts, quickly chiming into the conversation. "It's not a real party unless we're there!"

"Oh, really? So are we." He points over to his buddies in the red Jeep Wrangler beside us. "Where are y'all staying?"

"Um, we're staying on the north end of the beach… uh… The Best Western," I interject.

"Well, two beautiful babes in a hot car like this. You'll certainly stand out in the crowd. I'm sure we'll have no trouble finding you." He gives a cocky wink as he walks back to his friends.

Her brow furrows. "I thought we were staying at the Sea Blue Motel?" she asks, sliding back into the car.

"We are! *You idiot!* We aren't even there yet and you're already trying to hook up! You better put that thing on lockdown!" I say, pointing between her legs.

She pouts. "But he was hot and it's been far too long since I had a good shag." She wiggles her eyebrows. Her frown growing to a mischievous smirk.

"Gross, Lana! He had a dip in his mouth!"
We bust out in loud laughter as we make our way back onto the small Florida highway.

I smell the salt in the warm air as soon as we turn onto Front Beach Road and catch glimpses of the emerald blue ocean between the hotels. Yellow flags are flying, cautioning beachgoers of the surf conditions. The shops and restaurants are buzzing, as guys with cases of beer on their shoulders and girls in triangle top bikinis pop across the road like a game of Frogger. Excitement radiates from their faces, all eager to know what the weekend has in store for them. We pull into our hotel in time to watch the sunset in the distance. Both of us taking a moment to appreciate it before we unload the car and insanity commences.

"I know you said you were running low on money, but damn! This may have been pushing it." Lana scoffs, looking around the dingy hotel room. "This is one step up from a by-the-hour!"

"Oh, it's not *that* bad!" I say, hoping to hide my own concern. "It's only the two of us splitting the cost this time. I had to go cheap. Besides, we've partied in a lot worse places."

She opens the drab curtain to our parking lot view. "I knew I should have been worried when it had the word 'motel' in the name. You better get some beer in me quick or you may find me sleeping in the car."

"Speaking of…why don't you go get ready? It'll take you longer to get dressed than me."

Lana's inability to be on time has been an ongoing battle we've had since we were kids.

"I'll finish unpacking while you're in the shower."

"Well, don't put any of my stuff on the floor. God only knows what's been crawling around this room!" she yells from the bathroom.

Sadly, I have to agree with her. Perhaps I had gone a tad overboard on my choice of cheap accommodations, seeing as how I'm pretty sure this is where they filmed the movie, *Psycho*.

CHAPTER FOUR

Lana runs a brush through her wet hair. "So!" she says, plopping on the squeaky bed in her towel. "Who are we going to sweet talk into buying us beer?"

BAM! BAM! BAM!

Her face twists. "Who the hell is banging on the door?" she whispers. "I thought you said no one knows where we are?"

"No one does."

"Then who is it?"

"Beats the shit out of me! Go check the peephole."

BAM! BAM! BAM!

"Answer the damn door, Kate! I know y'all are in there!" A familiar voice growls through the door.

We stare at each other with dropped jaws. "How the hell did Wayne find you?"

"Not only is he a human lie detector, but he's also a human tracking device!" I whisper.

She peers through the peephole. "Holy Shit! It's the entire crew."

"Open the fucking door! We can hear you two whispering!" Wayne shouts as voices get louder and louder in the hall.

She lifts an eyebrow. "Well, at least we know who we can sweet talk into buying us beer!" Opening the door to my ex and his merry band of morons.

"Nice towel!" Wayne teases as Lana opens the door half-naked. He tumbles in clearly drunk, along with five other guys from our hometown.

I cross my arms. "How did you find me?"

"We saw you get out of the car," he answers smugly.

I pretend to fidget with my suitcase. "What do you mean you *saw* us get out of the car? Have you resorted to following me now?"

He crashes across the bed and grabs the remote. "No, smart-ass. We saw you guys from our room. Y'all pulled up, unloaded and walked in. I actually thought you were following me."

"Wait! What!?" I say, more confused than ever. "Are you staying at *this* hotel?

"Yep!" He laughs as he points toward the door. "Right across the hall."

"And Donny, Chris, and Toots have the room beside you." Wayne's best friend, AJ adds.

Lana and I stare at each other in disbelief. *Oh, God! This can't be happening!* I think.

I raise my voice so everyone in the room hears. "Let me make sure I have this straight. Out of hundreds of hotels in Panama City, we pick the *one* motel our entire hometown is staying in? And if that isn't enough, we get the room directly across from them?"

"Yep! Pretty Much!" AJ answers, laughing.

"Oh, don't even pretend like you're mad, Kate. It wasn't like we weren't going to run into each other at some point." Wayne says, rolling closer to me. "Especially, in *daddy's* car." He reaches over to rub my ass. "You two stick out like a fucking sore thumb in that thing."

I pop his hand. "Don't start, Wayne!"

"What!?" he snips, pretending he doesn't know what I'm talking about.

"You promised me we wouldn't have a repeat of Spring break."

"We won't," he interrupts. "You being across the hall isn't exactly ideal for me either."

"I guess you're right. Pretty hard to run women in and out, with your ex around to rain on your whore parade."

"Ok, you two!" Lana says, wrapping her arm around my neck, finally dressed.

"Awe, Lana," Wayne flirts. "I was enjoying you in your little white towel."

"Wayne? Be a dear and go buy Kate and me some beer, please?" she asks, ignoring the towel comment.

After wearing out his welcome, he finally stands to head out. He turns back. "Wait! You want me to buy y'all beer, so you can get drunk and cruise the Strip for other guys?"

"That about sums it up." She shoves a stack of twenties in his shirt pocket. "As many cases of Coors Lite a hundred will buy, please?"

"Oh and grab us a beer funnel while you're there!" she shouts as he heads down the hall.

It's the first night of our vacation and things are already off to a rocky start. Between the shitty room, a crappy dinner and Hotel Alpharetta, I'm beginning to worry this trip might not be the "do-over" I'm hoping for.

The traffic on the Strip is already bumper to bumper as far as the eye can see. It's a long-lived tradition for hordes of teenagers to pile in cars and the back of pickup trucks, with coolers loaded and music as loud as it will go; all to spend hours riding the "Strip."

The main parkway through Panama City Beach and a tradition I can't wait to commence.

"You look hot, Kate!" Lana says as we head out of the Seafood Shack. "Good call borrowing my shorts. Your ass looks better in them than mine does."

"Thanks!" I shake my butt at her. "But can you see my scar in this top? The straps keep falling."

"Nah. All the purple has finally faded, so it blends in more than it used to."

"It's about damn time. Nothing's worse than a constant reminder of my past stupidity."

"Did he ever apologize for what happened?"

"Only if you consider, 'Oops! My bad!' an apology."

"Don't give another thought on the loser. I'm so glad you finally got him out of your system. Focus on us and our beach full of possibilities!" She jumps into the passenger seat without using the door. "Have I mentioned how much I love this car?"

I laugh. "A time or two."

"Well, I think it's about time we go get into some trouble!"

"I love the car too. So maybe this is a good time for us to set some ground rules." I say as the annoying honks from a pack of rented scooters pass by. "Number one… Absolutely no drinking and driving. Number two… no fornicating."

"Party pooper!" she jokes.

"Number three… No smoking. This one's more for me. You know how I get cigarette happy when I drink. And number four," I say in my most authoritative voice. "The most important rule…no barfing in the car!"
She laughs.

"I'm serious Lana! I have to return my dad's car *exactly* how he gave it to me.

If I even get so much as bird shit on it, he'll disown me!"

"I knowwww," she moans. "Stop worrying! You're killing my buzz, Mom!"

I pull the BMW onto the slow-moving parkway, giving us time to unwind, find the perfect music, and people watch.

"I hate to bring up Wayne again, but I'm glad y'all were able to come to an understanding," Lana says, flipping the visor mirror to re-apply her lipstick.

"I guess. As long as he can hold up his end of the deal. Things are always fine until he gets to drinking. Then it's a whole new ballgame."

"Well, they're headed to Club La Vela tonight so I'm sure they'll be gone until morning. So at least we know we're in the clear tonight."

"Yep. We agreed he and his crew could go tonight and you and I will have it tomorrow."

She pops her cleavage up above her shirt line. "Do you think you'll be able to sneak me in?"

"All the bars here are nineteen and up. Wear a tight shirt and smile pretty. The bouncer will be too distracted to pay attention to your birthday," I tease as we creep down the Strip.

"I hate always being the youngest of the bunch."

"You complaining about it incessantly won't change anything. Besides, you look older than me. No one would ever guess you're only seventeen."

"You had an early birthday in school and I was cursed with a late one. It's so humiliating! July can't get here soon enough," she whines.

"Well, I guess you could always get a fake ID like my brother did."

"Speaking of James... what's he up to tonight?"

"Honestly, I have no clue. I figure we'll run into him at some point tonight. But if not, he's staying at The Sunspree. We can go by and visit tomorrow."

Her mouth falls. "Are you shitting me? Your brother is staying in the nicest hotel on the beach, while we're stuck in a vile roach motel?"

"Lana! Oh my God! For the hundredth time. It's not *that* bad!"

"It IS *that* bad, Kate! Earlier, I couldn't find an ice machine for the beer, so I went to the lobby to ask where one was. The guy at the front desk was watching porn! *Then* he proceeded to hand me an ice tray with twelve measly cubes. *And* then…" she shutters. "If it couldn't have gotten worse, he had the audacity to ask me what I was doing later!"

I laugh. "Well, don't be too jealous. There are seven of them all piled in one little room, all splitting the cost. James is stuck sleeping in the bathtub. So you may not have the nicest hotel on the beach. But at least you have a bed."

"Yeah, that's probably crawling with bed bugs!"

CHAPTER FIVE

Although it's been an hour, we've only made it a mile in the bumper to bumper traffic.

"Geez! I'm glad we didn't make plans with anyone tonight," Lana huffs, craning her neck to look down the long line of cars.

"Enjoy it! Two best friends on vacation, in a hot ride. The music cranked up without a care in the world. It doesn't get much better than this!"

"But I need to pee!"

I roll my eyes. "You *always* need to pee!"

I scan each side of the road for a place for her to use the restroom and notice a group of guys on my side of the road. They're tailgating in front of their hotel, drinking beer, and clearly having fun people watching as the traffic passes.

"Lana, look over here," I say, hitting her with my elbow.

She spots them instantly. "Whoa, Kate! Look at all of them."

We're stopped a few hundred feet from their hotel and as the traffic slowly inches closer, one of them begins to walk towards the road. Crossing the oncoming traffic, stopping dead in his tracks in front of the car. He lifts his arm to his forehead as the beam of the headlights blind him. His shirtless body illuminated as he walks closer and runs his hand across the hood.

"Damn!" He nods playfully as he rounds the corner of the car.

He bends down, propping an elbow on the driver's door. The top open allows him to be especially close.

"How's it goin'?" he asks, flashing a pearly white smile. His eyes scan the interior. "Nice car."

He's gorgeous, and he knows it. Guys who know they're hot, irritate me. His buzzed, blond hair, gives no protection to his shiny, sunburned forehead. His sharp, emerald green, eyes and a boyish smirk cause both us to shift nervously in our seats. A set of dog tags falls right above his smooth, chiseled chest.

"What are you beautiful ladies up to tonight?"

Before we have time to respond, he jumps in the backseat of the car in one quick swoop. "I'm Drew, by the way."

Lana and I blink in disbelief. "Um, I'm Kate, and the speechless one here is Lana."

"Well, hello Lana. It's a pleasure to meet you," he gazes. *Ut-oh! This has trouble written all over it.*

"You girls not drinking?"

Booming bass from a passing truck rattles Lana back to reality.

She bats her lashes. "Well, I have. But my uptight friend here hasn't had a drop because of the car." Finally finding her voice.

"Can't say I blame her," he chuckles. "This is a badass ride."

"My dad let me borrow it for the weekend, so I'm a tad paranoid," I say, chiming in as we inch closer to Drew's hotel.

"A couple of beers aren't going to render you inebriated. Why don't y'all stop at our place and drink a few?"

"We'd love to!" Lana says, immediately taking him up on the offer.

Leery, my nose scrunches. "Ehhh, I don't know. We're actually headed to hang out with some friends," I lie.

"Oh, come on. Please? I have lots of friends…" Hoping that'll entice me.

"I doooo need to pee," Lana says, looking at me with puppy dog eyes.

I cave a little too easily. "Fine, you win."

Once we finally make it to the front of Drew's hotel, I whip into a parking space in front of the yellow, glowing, Parker Motel sign. His friends surround the car, admiring it as Lana and Drew quickly pop out and bolt towards the rooms.

I take my time getting out. I close the top and grab our purses, choking down the awkwardness of being left alone. A honk startles me as I climb out. The keys falling to the pavement as *he* steps from the darkness, beautiful and stoic.

He bends down. The packed parkway goes silent as he stands. Butterflies dance as he places the keys in my hand. Trembling as his fingertips gently sweep across mine.

"Hi," is the only word I'm able to form.

He gestures with his chin. "They headed that way." His piercing blue eyes sparkle against the glow of the hotel sign.

My voice cracks. "Oh. Right. Thanks."

"Come on, I'll show you," he says politely, but with little emotion.

A few of his friends join in on the walk through the unkempt courtyard. They ask about the car and make jokes among themselves. No other words are spoken from the mystery guy as we arrive at their first-floor room.

"Thereeeee you are!" Lana shouts, beer already in hand. "What took you so long?"

She runs over and whispers in my ear. "If you tell them how old I am, I will kill you!"

"The guys were checking out her car," the mystery man answers.

"Oh! I see you met Max," Drew says, digging through a cheap, Styrofoam cooler.

"Sorda," I say a little embarrassed as I glance over at him.

Drew points and introduces a few more of the guys. "This is Santos, Jackson, and Palmer."

They all wave and welcome us with open arms. "Y'all must be pretty bored to want to come hang with this putz!" Santos teases, slinging an arm around Drew's neck.

Lana's eyes widen. "Oh my God! I'm in love with your accent!"

Santos chuckles. "Yeah, if the dark skin and hair didn't give away I'm Puerto Rican, the accent typically does."

"Cool! What part of Mexico is that?"

I close my eyes and cringe. The guys unable to contain their laughter.

"What?" she asks, completely clueless.

"Please forgive my geographically challenged, best friend. She's clearly having a blond moment."

He laughs. "No worries. Where are you ladies from?"

"We're from Atlanta," Lana pipes.

"A suburb of Atlanta actually," I correct. "About thirty miles north, in Alpharetta."

"Yep! And we're both twenty and students at The University of Georgia," Lana adds. Emphasizing the "both."

"Funny. There's a guy in our company from Alpharetta. He's a bit older than y'all, but you might know him? Last name Griggs," Santos says. His brow furrows as he tries to recall his first name.

"Hey, Max! What's Griggs' first name?"

"Kevin," he answers.

He snaps his fingers. "Yep! Kevin Griggs!"
Lana is intently focused on Drew and no longer paying attention to the conversation.

"The names not ringing a bell, but it's a pretty big town."

Santos hands me a Coor's Lite out of the cooler as the remainder of his friends settle into the room. There is a lot of different conversations and commotion going on, so I take the opportunity to survey the room. It's worse than ours if it's possible. *At least ours is beachside.*

It's a typical motel room with two double beds, vanity, and bathroom in the back. Cases of beer are stacked high in the corner and empty cans are littered across the dresser and table. Olive green rucksacks line the walls. Each one with a different last name on the outside. Between Drew's dog tags, their haircuts, and the bags, I quickly realize they're all soldiers. And it makes me even more intrigued than I already am.

The only light in the room is coming from the small lamp on the bedside table. Max flops on the bed near it, and I'm finally able to get a good look at how incredible he is. Short brown hair, square, clean-shaven, jawline and beautiful blue eyes. A striped navy and white shirt covers his broad shoulders and tan arms. He has a beer in his hand, but he's quieter than the rest. He's enjoying watching his friends be the life of the party. Only glancing over at me on occasion. I try not to stare as he rubs Carmex across his sunburned lips.

I clear out an empty spot on the dresser, near the small box TV and get the biggest kick out of watching the guys interact with each other. Their comradery is different from the guys back home. The partying is all the same, but with an unspoken respect level in the way they talk to each other. It's a true brotherhood and I'm blown away as I sit, taking it all in.

"Oh my God, Kate! Can you believe how hot these guys are?" Lana whispers in my ear as she slides in beside me, knocking over empty cans in her wake.

"I'm not sure I've ever seen so many gorgeous guys in one room in all my life," I admit.

"Especially Max!" she whispers a little too loudly. "He's a total babe. You should go talk to him."

I clench my jaw. "No, hush!" Cowering my head a little, in fear he might know we're talking about him.

"Yes!" she shouts.

"I appreciate your confidence in me, but there's absolutely no way a guy *that* hot would ever want to talk to me. Besides, what the hell would I say? I'd probably come across as a blubbering idiot. I'd like to keep my dignity intact tonight."

"Don't be such a chicken shit! Besides, you're being too hard on yourself." She tucks a stray curl behind my ear. "You're beautiful."

I glance at Max and lock eyes with him before nerves cause me to look away.

"Drew is being so sweet," she gushes. "He said they're all in the Army at Fort Benning, Georgia and off for the long holiday weekend."

"I kind of pieced it together. The matching haircuts kind of gave it away," I tease.

I finish the last swig of my beer and although cans are everywhere, I look around for a trash can to throw it in.

As I turn back, Max asks, "You want another?"

"Oh, um, yeah. Thank, thanks!" I stammer. *Dear God! Pull it together, Kate! I know he's out of my league, but there is no reason to act like a total fucking spaz!* I smile but curse in my head as he hands me the beer.

I take a deep breath to settle my nerves. "So I hear you guys are in the Army."

"Yep. The beach is only a few hours for us, so figured we'd take advantage of the break."

"How long have you been in the Army?"

"Say again?" he asks, furrowing his brow. "Sorry. Can't hear shit over all the yelling."

I spot Lana standing on top of the bed with a beer funnel in her mouth. The guys chanting, "Drink! Drink! Drink!"

I laugh and repeat the question louder. "How long have you been in the Army?"

Still struggling, Max points towards the door. "Hey, can we go outside so I can actually hear myself think?"

Butterflies rise in my stomach again. "Sure."

We walk outside and sit on the nearby stairwell. Music is coming from the cars on the Strip, but it's much quieter than the motel room.

"It was like being in the middle of Grand Central in there," he jokes as he sits.

"Why don't we start over?" he says. "Hello, I'm Chase Maxwell, known by most as Max." He stretches out his hand.

I grab it and laugh. "Hi, Max. I'm Katherine Carpenter. Known by most as Kate. It's very nice to meet you."

"*Now!* What were you saying?" he asks, popping the top of a fresh beer.

"Oh, I was only asking how long you've been in the Army."

"Third year of my four-year enlistment," he answers quickly. "The time has flown by!"

"So that would make you how old?"

"Twenty-two."

"And your friend. The one with Lana?" I ask.

"Oh, Drew? He just turned twenty-one."

"Interesting," I say. Trying to do the age difference math in my head.

"And you guys all work together?"

"Yep! We're in the same company, but we all have different jobs. Andrews and I are combat medics. The others are artillery, and Jackson, the stocky black guy, is a gunner. We have three more here, but they went to that Vela place."

"Well, it all sounds amazing. But I won't lie, I know absolutely nothing about the Army. It's like you're talking in a foreign language," I admit.

He laughs. "It can get confusing for sure. Don't get me started on ranks. You'll be utterly lost."

"I'll take your word for it," I say, joining in on the laughter. "Did y'all get down here today?"

"Yep. A few hours ago actually. Drew, Davis, and I rode all the way here in the back of Jackson's pickup truck. Packed the cooler and drank beer the whole way!"

"Which one's Davis?"

"Oh, he's not here right now. He ran off with a girl when we first got here and haven't seen him since. He's a nut! He and Andrews are crazy tight. He's six-four and a total ladies' man. Lays more pipe than the water company."

His joke catches me off guard, but I like hearing him cut up. "He sounds like a handful."

"That's putting it nicely," he says, chuckling to himself.

"Andrews?" I quiz.

"Drew, sorry. The joys of being in the military. You're forever known by your last name. His actual name is Joshua Andrews. I tried to come up with a cool, manly, nickname, but it didn't stick. So it's plain ole boring Max. The same name as forty-percent of the dog population."

Shouting from the Strip snags our attention. A girl in the back of a hatchback shows her boobs to the guys in the car behind her. We laugh as they and the next three cars, beg her to do it again.

"So Kate. Besides having an awesome Southern accent, what's your story?"

"There's not too much to tell if I'm being honest. I actually lead a pretty boring life, even though you wouldn't know it at the present moment." Pointing back to the room where Lana is.

"Oh, I don't believe that."

"Thankfully, I've got the summer off. It's the first time since I graduated high school, I didn't stay on campus and take summer classes. Lana and I have a few trips planned and we'll both be working part time until fall. Then life goes back to revolving around school."

"I heard you say you go to Georgia, right?"

I nod my head. "I'm starting my junior year there, studying Hotel Management. I hope to one day run some highfalutin Miami hotel or maybe a resort in Vegas. I went out there a couple of years ago and fell in love with it."

"Whoa! It sounds like a pretty cool plan," he says, impressed. "And family?"

"Yep! Two brothers. One younger, one older. Both of them are a big giant pain in my ass."

"So you're the only girl, huh? No wonder you were able to talk your dad into borrowing the car," he teases.

I laugh. "Damn straight! I've got him wrapped around my little finger." I tease, throwing my pinky in the air. "Actually, my little brother's down here somewhere. They came last night, started celebrating early."

"Is it his birthday?" he asks, as his hand accidentally grazes my arm and sends a shot of nerves rushing through my body.

Distracted from his touch, I say without thinking, "Oh no. He and Lana graduated high school last night."

"Ah! Awesome! Congrats to him!" He lifts his beer in the air to cheers.

Oh shit! I scream in my head. He pauses and I can tell he's piecing it together. I try to change the subject. "So where is…"

"I thought she said y'all were both in college?" he interrupts.

I look at him and grimace, knowing the jig is up. "I didn't lie. I swear."

"But your friend… she graduated high school *last night?*" he clarifies.

I grimace again. "Yeah…"

"Making her how old?"

"Uhhhh… seventeen," I confess with a guilty smile. "*But* she'll be eighteen next month." Hoping it will help ease the sting a little.

He rubs his hands down each cheek. "Hoooo - leeee shit! Drew is going to freak when he finds out."

"Well, Lana is going to freak when she finds out I spilled the beans."

"I say we have a little fun with it," he says, looking at me devilishly. "You in?"

Intrigued, I give a sly grin. "What did you have in mind?"

Lana is way further along on her drunk quest than I am as we join back up with the group. I shake my head when I see her on the end of the bed making out with Drew. *Well, that didn't take long.*

She yells as she spots me. "Katieeee! My dear…sweet…bestie. Where the hell have you been?" She grabs my hand to pull me on the bed. "Someone get this girl a beer!"

"I can't, Lana. I still have to get us home."

"Ugh! You and that damn car!"

"Home?" Max chimes in. "You girls can't head home yet. It's only ten. We should go out."

"Where were you thinking?" Understanding where he's going with this.

"Why don't we all head to Sharks? Y'all can ride in the truck with us so you won't have to worry about your car."

Sharks is a local dive bar with a large patio facing the beach. It's pretty run-down but is always packed with tourists, eager to consume their famous Bushwhackers. They have pool tables and a live band, but most importantly, it has a strict nineteen and over rule.

"Sounds good to me!" Drew says, jumping up from the end of the bed

"Ummm," Lana says, looking concerned. "That place sucks!"

"Oh really? I heard they had some awesome drink there," Max replies, watching her face as he speaks.

"Oh, those nasty things? Waste of money! And not to mention, it's a total shit hole. Y'all can go to La Vela with us tomorrow. You should come back to our hotel instead. We can chill on the beach, maybe go for a swim," she says quickly, hoping the change of venue will pique their interest.

"Are you *sure* you don't want to go because it's a dump?" Max quizzes. "Or maybe it's *another* reason?"

Lana snaps her neck, looking at me straight-faced. "You didn't!" she pleads, looking back and forth from Max to me.

"What's going on?" Drew asked, sensing he's missed something.

Max pokes his finger in Lana's side and says, "Why don't you ask little Miss. U.G.A. what she did last night?"

"YOU BITCH!" she shouts, throwing herself across me, trying to put her hand over my mouth. "I'm going to KILL y'all!"

Still confused Drew asks, "What happened last night?" Clueless, but still laughing at all the commotion.

"Oh, she and Kate's little brother graduated FROM. HIGH. SCHOOL last night!" Max says, being sure to emphasize the "*from high school.*"

Drew's mouth drops. "No way!"

"Yes, way!" Max confirms.

Speechless, Drew makes a quick grab for Lana's purse sitting on the floor, snatching her wallet before she can react.

"Nooooo!" she screams, jumping off me to tackle him.

Already pulling out the driver's license Drew begins to read aloud, as Lana makes a few poor attempts to snatch it out of his hand.

"Lana Michelle Mathews, 840 Arlington Drive, Alpharetta, GA. 98lbs. Blond hair. Blue eyes. Crazy hot," he adds with a grin. "Born….," he pauses. "July 17th, 1977! Making you?" Lana throws a pillow over her head as he says, "Dum, Dum, Dum, Dum…. Seven-teen!"

The room breaks out in uncontrollable laughter as Max and I high five each other over our brilliantly laid plan.

Lana's mortified but makes the best of it. "I'm glad I could give you all a good laugh tonight," she says, relenting. "I'll be eighteen in like three weeks!" she yells as most of the group heads back outside.

"It's all good," Drew whispers as he sits beside her. "It'll take more than a number to scare me off," burying his head into her neck.

After coming up for air, she asks, "Seriously, do you think everyone would be up for coming to our place?" she asks, looking over at me. "Kate isn't going to drink anymore because she knows she'll have to drive us back. I want her to be able to let her hair down."

"I can probably talk the guys into it," he says.

"I promise it'll be just as fun," she adds as he heads outside to round up the others.

It's almost midnight and I'm shocked at how well the night has turned out, after such a crappy start. The guys have been a blast to hang out with and at no point have made us feel uncomfortable or unwanted. They've been fun, but perfect gentlemen.

Conversations with Max are getting easier and the butterflies are starting to settle. So much so, we're flirting a little back and forth.

"We're moving this party to our place," Lana says, snapping me from my thoughts.

"We are?"

"Yep! So no more of this three beer limit bullshit!"

"Who all's coming?"

"Don't know yet. He's outside rounding everyone up."

Lana grabs her purse and both of us head towards the parking lot, giggling like schoolgirls, watching the guys in the distance.

"Isn't there always supposed to be at least one unfortunate one in every bunch? It's like we hit the hot guy jackpot," I say.

"I know. You could bounce quarters off Drew's ass," she whispers as we make it to the parking lot.

"You girls ready?" Drew asks as he and Max head towards the car.

"Your friends aren't coming?"

"Nope! It's only the four of us. They're all about to crash for the night. It's been a long day," he replies, throwing his arm around Lana and giving her a mischievous grin.

"I hope you don't mind?" Max asks quietly, directly to me.

"Of course we don't," Lana answering for me. "Do we, Kate?"

"No, no. Not at all," I stammer. My nerves getting the best of me again.

"Can you run us home later? It'll be a helluva long walk back you don't," Drew asked.

"Of course! Not a problem," I say as Lana and Drew quickly jump in the backseat together.

I'm in the driver's seat and Max has taken up residence beside me. Traffic's bad, but moving better than earlier. A group of girls we know from home honk and wave as they pass by. "Ain't Nothing But a G-Thang" spews from the speakers as the car cranks.

"Oh dear Lord!" Max shouts, turning the volume quickly down. "Not this shit!"

"Hey! Don't be hatin' on Dr. Dre!"

"Mind if I play DJ?" he asks, already flipping through the channels.

I pull onto the parkway. "Be my guest."

He hits about four stations, stopping as "Hotel California" by the Eagles begins to play. A band I know well thanks to my dad, but not one I typically rock out to on my own.

"I loveeeee this song! Turn it up!" Lana shouts from the backseat.

As we drive, the four of us belt the words to "Hotel California", "Feel Like Makin' Love," and "Back in Black" at the top of our lungs. We're laughing and dancing as we pull into the parking lot of our shitty motel. I choose a spot directly below our room so I can keep an eye on the car from our window.

It's late, but the motel is still buzzing with activity. We plan to sit on the beach, but yet again, Lana needs to pee. So against my better judgment, we make a pit stop in the room.

We round the top of the stairs on the third floor, as people dart in and out of the hallway around our door. My stomach drops, fearing it's Wayne and his friends.
Please don't be Wayne! Please don't be Wayne! Please don't be Wayne!
I chant to myself as we walk the long, musty, hall.

The door across the hall from ours is wide open and the girls who we had waved to earlier are inside. But thankfully there's no Wayne in sight.

"Hey, Kate! Hey Lana! Our friend from home, Joy shouts, running into the hall to greet us.

"Hey, Joy! What've you gals been up to tonight?" I ask as Lana, Drew, and Max head into the room.

"We were at the Sunspree with your brother. It was totally insane over there. They were tying bedsheets to the balcony railing and flinging themselves to other floors."

"Please God, tell me my brother wasn't in on it too?"

"Nah. You know your brother has more brains than most of the boys from home." She peers over my shoulder. "Clearly you girls were having more fun than we were. Where'd you find the hotties?" she asks, making a desperate attempt to slip past me.

"Oh, them?" I look back. "We picked them up wandering along the side of the road," I say with a smile, closing the door on her.

Lana flips off the lamp. Allowing the television to be the only light in the room and continues make-out session number six as Max refills the cooler.

"So much for a swim," I say, gesturing toward the lovebirds.

"Should we give them some privacy?"

"It definitely appears so," I say, a little uncomfortable by our voyeurism. "We're going to head to the beach, you two. Y'all come on when you're ready."

Lana gives a quick thumbs-up, never unlocking her lips from Drew's.

I check the room across the hall again before making the long trek to the beach. Where I take the time to give Max a quick backstory of Wayne and our unfortunate hotel debacle.

The moon is full, reflecting a bright path across the calm water. "What a perfect night," I say, spreading beach towels across the cool sand.

"So I have a confession," Max says as we settle into our spot.

"Do tell."

"The reason why the others didn't come along..." he nervously scratches the back of his head. "We didn't invite them."

Sensing confusion, he continues. "Drew's really into Lana. And well, I wanted some more time to talk to you and knew it would be a continuation of the craziness if the rest came. So we made it look like y'all only invited us."

Flattered, but shocked, I take a swig of beer to clear the lump in my throat. "Well, I'm glad you came." Trying desperately to keep my nerves in check. *God, he smells good!*

We're quiet for a moment, listening to the waves crash in. We watch a group of rowdy kids out crabbing pass by. Their flashlights snipping back and forth across the sand.

"So where's home?"

He smiles big. "I'm a proud Texan. Born and raised!"

"Oh really? What part?"

"Morgantown. It's about sixty miles west of Dallas. Blink and you'll miss it."

"And all your family is still there?"

"Yep, my parents, who've been married for twenty-five years, still live in the house I grew up in. I have an older sister who's a middle school teacher in town. She married her high school sweetheart and they have a baby girl who's nine months old." He reaches for his wallet and pulls out a small picture with tattered edges. "Adaline. I've only seen her once. When I was home for Christmas," he admits.

I lift the picture in the direction of the moonlight. "She's adorable Max. Look at all that hair!"

"They're going to have to batten the hatches of every door in town when she's a teenager," he chuckles.

"I bet you ruled the roost around there when you were younger."

He laughs. "Oh, yeah? What makes you think that?"

"Oh, come on, Max! Don't act like you don't know how good looking you are. I bet you had the girls lined up back in the day." I'm teasing, but serious at the same time.

He lifts his chin. "I may have dated the head cheerleader and prom queen back in the day."

"I'm not the least bit surprised," I tease, slinging a handful of sand across his feet.

"I guess spending the evening with the co-captain of the dance squad is small potatoes in comparison."

He gives a wink and taps the end of my nose. "I guess I can make the sacrifice."

"I was never the prom queen. That was always Lana's department. But I *was* voted 'prettiest smile' in high school."

"Well, I can definitely see why."

I chuckle. "I guess those two awkward middle school years in braces and hideous headgear were worth it after all."

He rubs his thumb across my jaw. "You're beautiful, Kate." His tone serious, causing a sudden shift in the mood.

His compliment catches me by surprise. "Thank you, Max." I look away. *Don't say something stupid and ruin the moment, Kate!* "Maybe it's my sweet Southern charm," I draw out in my best Georgia accent, hoping it lightens the air.

He places his hand on top of mine and our eyes meet. "I honestly haven't had this much fun in ages."

I don't know what to say as I pull my gaze from his. I run my fingers through the sand, to cover my shaking hands. Heat radiates from my cheeks. My heart pounds as he leans in. *Oh my God! This is actually happening!*

My breath quickens as our lips inch closer. My eyes close when his…

"Oops! Sorry, you guys. Didn't mean to interrupt." Drew says, looking off as not to be rude as we snap away from one another.

Max drops his head and huffs.

"It's ok," I say, a little embarrassed. I look over at Max who has frustration in his eyes. "What's up? Where's Lana?"

Drew's hands are on his thighs, breathless from the long trek across the sand. "Well, that's why I'm here. She walked out of the room twenty minutes ago and hasn't been back. I thought maybe she came down here with you guys."

I'm going to kill her! I think.

"She's pretty drunk. Lord only knows where she could have wandered off to," I say.

"The girl you were talking to earlier came back by. She and Lana talked for a few seconds, then she said she'd be right back. Haven't seen her since."

"Ok. Let's go find her," I growl, snatching up the beach towels.

When we make it back to the motel, I split us up. I'm pretty sure I know where she is and I don't want the guys to get mixed up in it. I send Drew towards the pool and Max to check the parking lot. Giving me enough time to check Wayne's room before they make their way back into the building.

The door to Wayne's room is shut, forcing me to knock. Voices are at the door and I can tell they're looking through the peephole. The door flies open and AJ lunges towards me and flips me over his shoulder.

Hanging upside-down I scream. "Put. Me. Down! Put. Me. The. Hell. Down!" Repeating it over and over, pounding my fists into his back. He slings the sliding glass door to the balcony open, setting me down to an already waiting Lana. He slams it closed and locks it before I have time to react.

The room clears instantly. "What the hell is going on?" I shout, banging on the glass. "Why did he lock us out here?"

"Wayne came back and Joy opened her big ass trap about Drew and Max being in our room."

My hands fly to my temples. "Oh no! Oh no! Oh no!"

"She came over and apologized. Asked me if I'd come help defuse the situation. I should have known it was all set up. Because the second I got in here they did the *exact* same thing to me. I've been stuck out here for a damn half hour, while they went on a wild goose chase looking for you. Too damn stupid to check the beach."

Shouts and commotion echo from the hall. "What are they doing to them?"

I already know the answer to my own question and realize how incredibly outnumbered they are. Rage begins to boil through my veins as Wayne and his crew pile back into the room, laughing and high fiving each other. Reenacting punches in the air, clearly proud of their conquest.

AJ shouts, "I hit that mother fucker square in the jaw," as Joy releases us from balcony purgatory. I'm happy to see he has a cut on his lower lip, indicating Max and Drew got a few good swings in.

"I popped the smaller one in the eye so hard my damn hands bleeding," Wayne yells from the bathroom.

I'm so angry I can barely speak. Wayne's pulled some pretty shitty tricks over the years, but nothing compares to this. "I hope you're all proud of yourselves!" I scream as the ruckus in the room silences.

Wayne storms out of the bathroom, a wet towel wrapped around his busted knuckles. "They were punk mother fuckers, Kate. Dumbass soldiers looking to get laid. They had no business being here!"

"Don't. You. Dare!" I slam my finger into his chest. "You had no right sticking your nose in my business. Who the hell do you think you are?" Lana's crying behind me as I continue my wrath. "I don't tell you who you can or can't screw. If I want to hump the entire U.S. Army, that's *MY* business. You stay the hell out of it!"

I grab Lana by the arm and head towards the door, turning back one last time. "Oh, and Joy…you're a fucking bitch!"

I fling the door to our room open and peer in. "They aren't here."

Lana throws on her shoes and wipes smeared mascara from under her eyes. "We've got to go look for them, Kate. They have to be around here somewhere," she chokes out between sobs. "We were their ride."

"We've got to explain what happened. They've got to know we didn't have anything to do with this," I say breathlessly, trying to calm the coursing adrenaline.

We head toward the stairwell we think all the madness happened. My hands fly to my mouth when we spot drops of blood on the concrete.

"Oh no, Kate! What if they're really hurt?" I'm unable to speak as my mind spins with worry.

"Let's split up. You check the parking lot and I'll head towards the beach," she says.

I say a silent prayer we find them as I scan the lot. There's no way we can let the night end like this.

After my search, I spot Lana as she's walking back up the boardwalk. "I see two people way down the beach, but I can't make out if it's them."

"They weren't in the parking lot either," I say, crashing on the concrete stairs. "I can only imagine what they must think of us right now."

She lays her head against the wall. "They probably wouldn't have believed us anyway."

"I know," I sigh. "It's just… Tonight I met the most amazing, sweet, drop-dead gorgeous man I've ever seen. And my stupid, redneck, sack of shit ex-boyfriend and his cohorts beat him up. I can't think of anything more horrible!"

"We could always go by their room tomorrow and explain."

"Maybe we should go tonight? They might still be walking," I say, hoping we may still have a chance to catch them.

"Kate, it's two in the morning. I'm mentally and physically exhausted and I have a terrible headache. Let's just call it a night." She moans as she drags up the motel stairs. "Besides, we're probably the last two people they want to see right now. We can check on them tomorrow after they've had a chance to cool off."

I blow out a heavy sigh. "I guess you're right. I'm pretty spent." Giving up, I drag my aching legs behind her.

Once we're back in the room, I notice a few things out of place we hadn't noticed earlier. It's not torn apart, just slightly disheveled. Lana's suitcase is open and a few of her clothes have been thrown out. And a bloody wet towel is flung across the bed.

Panic floods our faces when we both spot my purse open with my wallet pulled out.

"Oh God! Did they rob us?" Lana asks as I snatch up the wallet.

My face twist as I thumb through it. "No, all my money's here."

We both let out a huge sigh of relief. "I wonder what the hell they were doing in my purse?"

It hits us in unison. "THE CAR!"

"Oh shit! Oh shit! Oh shit!" I sprint to the window with Lana in tow. "Please tell me they didn't..." I shout, throwing the curtain back.

Speechless, I point at the empty parking spot.

"Are you sure that's where you parked?"

"Yes! I purposely parked it there so I could keep an eye on it!" I run back to my purse and dump its entire contents across the bed.

"Surely they wouldn't take the car," she says, trying to stay hopeful.

"The keys are gone, Lana! They stole the fucking car!"

She lifts her hands and takes a deep breath. "It's ok, Kate. Don't panic. We'll get it back, I promise."

My lip quivers as tears begin to pool. "My dad is going to kill me!"

"Let me go see if anyone's awake who can take us back to their hotel," she says calmly.

As she leaves my head spins in a panicked fury. I'm scared, confused, and pissed off all at the same time.

How could he do this? Especially knowing how freaked out I am about the car.

Noise rumbles through the hall as our hotel door flies open. "I told you those were some piece of shit mother fuckers. They think they got their ass whooped before. I'll kill those GI son's a bitches!" Wayne shouts.

I'm in a daze, too concerned about the car to worry about the crap coming from Wayne's mouth. Getting the car back is the absolute priority right now. If it means taking Wayne and his crew back to their hotel, so be it.

"Let's go, Kate. AJ's going to drive us," Lana says, sliding her flip-flops back on.

We make it to the parking lot when it hits me how stupid this plan is. "Wait! I can't take all you guys to their hotel. I may never get the damn car back. I've got to handle this on my own. Y'all will only make matters worse."

Lana shakes her head. "She's right."

"AJ, if you'll let me borrow your truck. Lana will drive it back and God willing, I'll drive mine."

"Bull shit! You're not going anywhere near those guys alone!" Wayne yells.

I clench my fist. "I can't do this right now, Wayne!"

"My truck's parked across the street on the last row," he says as I snatch the keys from him.

"Thank you, AJ. Now, for the love of all that's good and pure. *Please* get rid of him for me. You owe me this after the crap you guys pulled on us tonight."

Lana and I cross the street toward the directions we'd been given. It's past 3:00 a.m. and the Strip is finally quiet. No traffic. No partying. No music. As I hit the unlock button on the remote of AJ's truck, I glance over and spot dad's shiny, red BMW, perfectly parked under a street light in the far corner of the lot.

"Holy shit, Lana! There it is!"

We rush over, slowing as we get to it; making sure no one's around. "Thank you, Lord!" I shout as I run to the driver's side to check for damage.

"Do you see any damage on your side?"

"Nope! Not that I can tell."

For the first time in an hour, I can breathe again.

"Did they leave the keys?"

I open the door and there they are, dangling in the ignition. Dad's University of Georgia key-chain still swaying.

"Yep, they're here!" I reach in to grab them and spot a note written on a napkin, laying on the passenger seat.

"Phew! It looks like we dodged a bullet," she says.

I get out and lock it. Dazed, I walk to her side of the car. The napkin dangling from my fingertips.

"What? Do I have a booger?" she asks as I hand it over.

"No, dummy! Flip it over."

She reads it out loud…

"We thought long and hard about running the car into the ocean. But realized it wasn't worth going to jail over a couple of bitches!"

Her eyes widen. "Whoa! That was harsh." Clearly as hurt by the words as I am. "I guess that answers the '*I wonder if they blame us*' question."

My head falls in defeat. "Let's go to bed. I'm so over this night."

CHAPTER SIX

We sleep in, or at least Lana is. I've been up all night replaying everything that happened. It was like something out of a movie. Even though I'm sure they hate us, I have to try to make things right. I won't be able to forgive myself if they think we had anything to do with the fight.

Lana's snores sound like a lumberjack, making it virtually impossible to fall asleep. "I guess I'll go grab a shower," I say out loud as I fling a pillow at her head.

Waiting for the water to warm, voices begin to echo through the hall. Curious, I gaze through the peephole. My chin hits the floor when I spot Max, Drew, Jackson, and the rest of their friends, banging on the door across the hall. *Son of a…*

I jump back from the peephole. "Lana!" I whisper loudly, shaking her awake. "Lana! Wake up!"

"Whhaaatttt?" she moans as her eyes squint from the light.

I fling my arms in the air. "They're here! Get up!"

"Who's here?" She yawns as the bangs rattle the cheap framed art above the bed.

"Max, Drew, and the rest of those guys from last night! They're at Wayne's door. I guess they're here for payback." Finally understanding, she springs out of bed and runs to the peephole.

More banging. "Too scared to come out now that it's a fair fight, huh?" Drew yells.

"They glanced our way," she whispers as I plant my ear to the door. No one is answering the door, but I have no doubt they're in there. Too chicken to open the door. *What a bunch of wimps!*

They mumble something about us, but I can't make out what's said.

"Should we knock on their door?" Max asks.

"Hell no! I bet they're in there with those assholes anyway," Drew snips.

My head drops in shame and for a brief second, I consider opening the door but stop myself. *If they start chewing us out, Wayne will probably come out and all hell will break loose. I can't risk making things worse. Besides, they stole my car! Well, sort of stole my car* **and** *called us bitches!* I debate in my mind, hoping to justify the cowardliness.

After ten minutes of beating on the door, they give up. We watch them in the parking lot through a small crack in the curtains.

"There's so many of them."

"Those must be the ones who were out at the club last night," I say, hoping they don't spot us staring.

"Look at the tall one," she says, gawking through the crack below me.

"He must be Davis. The one Max was telling me about. He said he's the group playboy."

She smirks. "Damn! By the looks of him, I can see why."

"They're all even hotter in the light of day. I can't believe we screwed this up!"

She fans off my concern. "Don't worry. Let's get cleaned up. Go have a big breakfast, then we'll swing by their hotel and explain everything. I'm sure we can get all this sorted out."

Unsure, I collapse across the bed. "I sure hope so."

It's midday and our bellies are stuffed to the gills with The Pancake Palace. We make a pit stop to get gas and run into a souvenir shop. Procrastinating as long as possible, before finally mustering up the courage to head towards the Parker Motel.

My stomach churns. "I feel sick. I shouldn't have eaten so much," I choke out, sweat beading on my forehead.

Lana flips the mirror to check for food in her teeth as we pull into a parking space.

"Are you sure about this?"

She glides out without a care in the world. "Yes, silly! We've got this."

Traffic on the Strip whizzes by as I white knuckle the steering wheel, mustering up the courage to get out.

She taps her foot. "Would you hurry the hell up!"

It feels like a mile hike through the courtyard of the motel, second-guessing myself every few feet. "Maybe we should let this go?"

She pulls my arm. "We're already here. Let's get it over with."

I secretly hoped nobody would be here and begin to panic when I hear voices. I tap softly on the door, too softly. No one answers. Lana knocks again, louder this time. The voices grow silent. There's no peephole but someone moves the window curtain back. Muffled voices seep through the cracks, but still, no one answers.

Heat rises in my cheeks. "This is stupid," I say, embarrassed. "We shouldn't have come."

I turn to walk away as the door opens. Not much, only wide enough for a body to fit.

Towering over us is the gorgeous, tall drink of water, who we'd seen earlier. The sun glimmers off his hairy chest as he adjusts the top of his swim trunks.

"Hello, ladies. Here to get the rest of us jumped?" He gives a cocky smirk as coconut oil sweeps the air.

I let out a big breath, ignoring his comment. "We were looking for Max and Drew. Are they around?"

He crosses his massive arms, putting three Army tattoos on full display. "Nah. They're over at the beach."
Even though there's another hotel between us and the beach, my head instinctively turns toward the direction of the ocean.

"You probably don't want to go over there though. They were with some hot chicks from Birmingham when I left."

Disappointed and slightly intimidated by his presence, I find the courage to say, "We won't bother them. We wanted to come by and apologize for last night. Lana and I had absolutely nothing to do with the fight. Our so-called friends locked us on the balcony and by the time we were let out, they were gone. Then my car was gone." I'm rambling when he begins to laugh.

"Sweet ride by the way. I rode with them to take it back in case your boyfriend was still out. That thing is quite the bitch magnet," he chuckles.

I'm not amused. "He isn't my boyfriend and you better be glad the car came back in one piece!" I snip, finding my voice. Frustrated with how this is going. "Look, will you just tell them we came by and we're sorry?"

"Ok. Sure." Still laughing as he shuts the door.

My mind is all over the place when we get back to the car. I'm not happy about how the conversation went but relieved I got through it.

For a brief second, I contemplate walking to the beach but talk myself out of it. My only hope now is Davis will actually give him the message.

I smack Lana on arm, accidentally hitting her boob in the process.

"Ouch! What the hell was that for?"

"What happened to Little Miss 'We Got This'? You totally hung me out to dry back there!"

"Sorry! I choked."

"No shit!"

She looks towards the beach, rubbing the red splotch forming. "I guess it's officially over."

I lay my head against the steering wheel and let the reality of her words sink in. Not wanting to admit she's right.

"We came and apologized. That's what's most important. Let's not let this ruin the rest of our trip," she adds.

We watch four bikini-clad girls, swinging Subway bags, giggle past the front of the car. "How about we go get shit-faced?"

"Now *there's* the Kate I know and love!" Her mood lifting in an instant.

She reaches for the volume dial, turning it up as far as it will go. I drive away, mentally saying goodbye to the two soldiers who'd stolen a piece of our hearts.

We spend the day on the beach with friends from home. Although I'm pissed at most of them, beer is numbing the anger. Wayne's here but we aren't speaking. It's a beautiful, hot summer day, and the beach is packed with party-goers. Coolers used as chairs, beer cans, and hot pink funnels checkerboard the sand.

My stomach flutters each time someone new pops down the boardwalk stairs.

I'd hoped Max would magically show up today, especially after hearing about our apology visit. But as the clock strikes five, it appears I'm out of luck.

Lana's passed out on a towel in the sand. I position the umbrella over her so she doesn't burn any more than she already is. We're going out tonight and getting as far from this shitty hotel as possible. Thankfully, James is coming to get us so I don't have to worry about driving.

"Wake your drunk ass up." I jostle her with my foot. She swats at me, never opening her eyes. "You're baked. Did you put any sunscreen on today?"

"Not unless you consider baby oil sunscreen," she mumbles.

"You dumbass!"

"The sun's setting, so you need to start getting dressed. James will be here soon," I say, still shaking her.

She finally stirs from her spot and makes it to our room and in the shower. Hoping it will give her a chance to sober up a little, me too for that matter. I got more sun than I thought, so I choose a loose-fitting dress and desperately try to cover my raccoon eyes with makeup.

AJ stops by the room for a visit. We have idle chit-chat while I wait for Lana. He's been drinking all day and can barely make a coherent word.

Without warning, he lunges across the bed. His crusty lips inches from my face. I push him off. "What the hell are you doing?"

He reeks of booze, cigarettes, and body odor. I jump off the end of the bed, fighting the urge to vomit. My muscles tense as I lunge for the door. "I think it's about time for you to go!"

He stumbles toward me. "Come on, Kate. Wayne doesn't have to know," slurring his words.

"Wanting you to leave has *nothing* to do with Wayne. But if he catches you in here, he's going to lose his shit!"

I think he's heading out, but he blocks the door instead. He throws his arms around me and buries his face in my neck. "I saw you looking at me today."

"*What?* No. I. Wasn't!" My eyes narrow as I push him off, disgusted. He stumbles towards me as I reach for the door. "GET OFF ME, AJ!"

From the shower, Lana hears the struggle and asks if I'm ok. "No, AJ's in here, crawling all over me! I can't get him to go!"

She flings the shower curtain back and is out of the bathroom in the blink of an eye; stark naked, soaking wet, with shampoo caked in her hair. "Get the hell off of her!" she screams, jumping on his back. Clinched on like a spider monkey as I swing the door open.

"Ok, ok. I'm goin'! Damn!" he slurs.

Guests file into the hall as Lana continues to scream every obscenity in the dictionary. AJ scurries away in shame as jaw dropped onlookers stare at the sight of her.

She throws her hands on her wet hips. "*What?* Like you've never seen a naked person before?"
It was quite possibly the funniest thing I've ever witnessed.

It's Saturday night and we've made our way to Club La Vela. The most popular dance club in Panama City. And as planned, Lana's easily able to get through security with a low cut top and a few bats of her eyelashes.

"I can't get over how big this place is!" Lana shouts over the music.

"I know! I think it's the largest nightclub in the U.S." I turn to survey the room. "It has ten different bars, each one with its own theme and music."

"Which one should we pick?" she asks as we wind our way through the sea of people.

James and his friends head toward the live band area, while Lana and I opt for a small two-story section playing eighties music. It's a bit of an older crowd but we couldn't resist it when we heard Prince bellowing out the door. It's busy but not as packed as the other areas.
Lana spots an open table on the second floor and makes a mad dash to grab it.

"I still can't believe you ran out in the hall naked," I say, laughing as we settle into our seats.

"Well, duh! I had to protect my best friend's honor. But had I'd been sober, I probably would have grabbed a towel on my way out."

"Well, I appreciate what you did. Even if I did see more of you than I would have liked."

"Sorry! I can't help AJ tried to molest you before I had a chance to shave the vag."

"Sick, Lana! You're just plain sick!"

We have the perfect view of the downstairs bar and dance floor. We gaze over the railing and chuckle as a wasted, older lady, shimmies her saggy boobs in a short, skin-tight dress. Her flowery granny panties glow against the blacklights as she dances off beat to Michael Jackson. She makes quite the scene as everyone gawks and points amongst themselves.

I scan the small, laughing, crowd sitting at the bar in front of her. My eyes narrow on a familiar face standing out from the rest. *Fuck! It's Max.*

He's watching the same woman. I crouch but he glances up and spots me. Our eyes lock and the entire place seems to go into slow motion. My heart pounds so loud I can feel it over the beating music; those familiar butterflies rising in my stomach. Lana says something, but it doesn't compute.

"Kate? Did you hear me?" she repeats as I blink out of my fog.

"They're here." I'm finally able to mutter, shrinking into the stool, out of his sightline.

"Who? Wayne?"

"No!" I snip and point. "Max and Drew!"

Her chin drops as she cranes her neck to peer over. "Shit! They're all looking up here."

"Do they look mad?"

Her brow furrows. "I can't tell."

I try my best to act natural but nerves get the best of me. "I have to get out of here."

I fly to my feet and dart for the stairs. Max must do the same because as I crest the top he's at the bottom looking up. I'm paralyzed. My knees weaken and for a split second, I worry I might pass out. His blue eyes never leave mine as he climbs his way up.

He cracks a small smile as he reaches the last step. "Hi." I'm at a loss for words as I scan his face. A scab has formed over a small cut on his right brow and a purple bruise shines on his left cheek. He's hurt, and it's all my fault.

"Oh God, Max! I'm so sorry!"

"It's ok. I promise I'm fine."

"We had nothing to do with the fight, I swear. One minute I'm searching for Lana and the next minute I'm locked on a balcony." I bow my head. "I'm so humiliated."

"I know it wasn't your fault."

"I'm so sorry. You guys did not deserve any of it." I repeat, too embarrassed to look up.

He pulls my chin. "It should be me apologizing to you."

Confused, I shake my head. "Apologizing to me?"

"For the note. The whole bitch comment."

"No. We deserved it."

He shakes his head. "No, you didn't. No matter what the situation, there was no cause for that. It was a dick move. Davis actually wrote it, but I should have stopped him. I've felt like shit about it all day."

"Davis wrote it?"

"Well, I wrote the part about driving the car into the ocean. Which we did consider," he chuckles. "But he added the rest."

His joke lightens the moment and my nerves relax a little. "We came by your hotel today."

"I know. I was there," he admits.

"You were?"

Guilt floods his voice. "Yeah, we both were but asked Davis to cover for us."

I look away. Embarrassed to know he heard me rambling and didn't come out.

"It was terrible, I know. I had convinced myself you two had sent those guys to get rid of us. Even though deep down, I knew you didn't. By the time I came to my senses you were gone."

I smile, thankful to know the rest of the story. I say "I'm sorry," one last time, hoping he fully understands how much I mean it.

He steps close and wraps his arms around my waist. "I'm sorry too."

When we pull out of our embrace, it's as if someone pressed the play button and the world began to spin again. I'd been so focused on Max, I hadn't noticed Drew and Lana talking and all appeared to be forgiven on their end too.

The night's young and I don't want to assume Max and Drew want to spend another night hanging out with us. Especially in a place with beautiful, half-dressed, women. All breaking their necks to look at these gorgeous men, who definitely stand out in a crowd.

I climb into my chair. "You know I'll understand if you guys want to go back downstairs."

"You don't want to hang out with us?"

"No. It's not that, I promise. Nothing would make me happier. It's just… I know you all were having a guy's night out and I don't want to interrupt."

Without speaking, he walks off. I watch as he grabs an empty stool from another table and drags it over. He pops up on it. "The only reason I'm here is because I was looking for you."

I smile as my heart melts like butter. "It was?"

"Yes, silly woman! Lana mentioned you might be coming here last night, so I took a chance."
I'm blushing and I'm sure he can tell.

Over his shoulder, I spot Davis walking up. His presence captivating the ladies' around us. They stop mid-sentence to turn and stare.

He smirks. "So I guess you four kissed and made up."
I arch my neck. "It appears so."

Max jumps up to grab another chair. Davis takes a swig of beer as his chestnut eyes scan the room.

"You know you kind of remind me of Lurch from the Addams Family."

"That's a new one. I typically get Goliath." He wipes his hand with his shirt and holds it out. "I guess I should officially introduce myself. I'm Davis."

I grab it. "It's nice to meet you. I'm Bitch 1 and this is Bitch 2," pointing to Lana with a smug grin.

He laughs. "Heard about my extra little line I guess."

I snatch my hand back. "I did."

He eyes a group of girls a few tables over. "I got a date with a pair of gymnasts from Jacksonville while we were out joyriding in your car. So I guess I should thank you."

"Is that them?" I dare ask.

He flashes his smirky grin again and it makes my skin crawl.

"Nope! Those are sorority sisters from Ole Miss."

"Well, maybe you should take the Hotty Toddy sisters for a spin on the dance floor."

Although he's ridiculously hot, I'm not in the least bit amused by his charm.

I hoped he'd get the hint and leave. But instead, he keeps lurking around, making dumb jokes and interjecting his arrogance into the conversations. Girls ask him to dance every few minutes, giving Max and me a small reprieve. But it's never quite long enough. My patience is wearing thin. Between the loud, silly girls vying for his attention and his vain ego, I could hardly stand to be around him a second longer. My focus is on Max and relishing every precious moment we have. Not playing who has the biggest dick with Davis.

"Your friend's a douche," I tell Max as Davis heads to the dance floor with yet another drunk girl.

Max laughs. "He can be. But he's actually a decent guy when he wants to be."

"Well, he needs to follow one of these silly ass girls back to their hotel because he's getting on my last nerve."

"I don't think he knows quite how to take you. He's more used to girls throwing themselves at him."

"Ick!" I shudder. "He's a vain, pompous, smart-ass. And frankly, I'm a little disappointed in my fellow sisterhood for not picking up on it."

He laughs, taking the last swig of his beer. "You want to get out of here?"

My shoulders relax. "Yes! Music to my ears."

As I search for James to tell him we've found our own way home, Max rounds up Lana and Drew. We're starving and decide to make a late-night Waffle House run. While Max brings the truck around, the three of us shoot the shit while we wait.

"Oh my God, Drew. You're going to die when I tell you what Lana did today." I crack up thinking about it. "She got in a huge fight and came running out of our hotel room completely…"

"Hey! Where you guys goin'?"
I cringe as Davis's voice bellows behind me.

Drew waves him over. "We're headed to Waffle House? You in?"

Please don't want to come! Please don't want to come! I scream in my head.

"Hell yeah! Scattered, smothered, covered, baby!" He high fives Drew as he approaches.

"Wonderful," I mumble, straight-faced.

"Oh, come on… I said I was sorry about the bitch thing," Davis slurs, throwing an arm around me. Too drunk to notice my disdain for him.

I crawl out from under his arm. "No. Actually, you didn't."

Max pulls up to the club entrance in Jackson's mustard yellow, hooptie. I screw on a forced smile. "Look, Max. Davis is here. He's joining us. Isn't that fantastic news?"

"I could see you doing cartwheels as I pulled up." he teases.

The Waffle House is packed with drunks on the hunt for a good meal and a chance to sober up. We're stuffed in a tiny booth with Davis's gigantic ass in a chair at the end. Although we're packed in tight, we make the best of it. Enjoying the food, laughter, and antics of all the different characters throughout the little diner. We even get quite a hoot watching our server hit on Davis.

Max reaches over and grabs my hand, sending those electric tingles through my body again. He's gorgeous, but it's his kind heart and his undeniable charm I find myself more and more attracted to. I'm so thankful I've been given the chance to make things right. Even though our time together will soon be coming to an end, I'm going to cherish every second of this.

I'm outside with Drew and Davis, while Max pays the check and Lana uses the restroom for the hundredth time. I overhear them mention something about heading back early. I try to piece the conversation together, but I can't make out if he meant to head back to the room early or back to Fort Benning.

"You guys aren't leaving tomorrow are you?"

Disappoint fills his eyes. "Yeah, it looks like we're going to have to."

"All of you?"

"Yep."

My stomach drops. "I thought y'all were here until Monday?"

"We were supposed to be, but Jackson's our ride. His girlfriend's in a tizzy about our guy's trip, so he wants to go home early to calm her down."

Davis snickers. "Which is exactly why you should never have girlfriends."
My eyes narrow and bite my lower lip to keep from saying something rude.

"I mean…after the first night they should be rendered useless," he adds.

I'm unable to hold my tongue any longer. "Your asshole must get jealous of all the shit that comes out of your mouth."

Drew laughs. "Damn Davis! I believe that was code for shut the fuck up!"

"What'd we miss?" Max asks as he and Lana walk up on the tense conversation.

"They were telling me you guys were leaving tomorrow." Dismissing the whole Davis part.

Lana grabs her chest and gasps. "WHAT!? Y'all can't leave early!"

"We won't have a way home if we don't,"

"What about Santo's car?"

Drew gives a frustrated kick. "It's a four-seater Mustang and there's seven of us. There's no way we'll all fit."

I let out a disappointed sigh. "I knew the sand would eventually run out of the hourglass. I just thought we had one more day before it did."

Max grabs my hand. "I know. I'm sorry. I didn't mention it earlier because I've been wracking my brain to figure out a way to stay. I thought maybe we could rent a car."

"Dude!" Davis says behind a toothpick. "It's a holiday weekend. There's no way in hell you're going to find a rental." It irks me to have to admit he's right.

"You would do that to stay a little longer?" I ask.

"Of course I would," he replies as we pile in the truck to head home.

Davis is meeting the Jacksonville gymnast, so he has us drop him off at their hotel on our way back. It helps calm the added irritation his overall presence adds. Although we're all trying to make the best of our last few minutes together, there's a sense of sadness amongst the four of us.

"You know what? If this is our last night together, I say we go out with a bang!" I blurt.

Max nods. "Hell yeah!"

"What did you have in mind?" Drew asks.

I laugh. "I have absolutely no idea."

Lana's voice explodes from the small backseat. "Skinny Dipping!"

There is an old abandoned house on the bayside of Panama City. Lana's dad would take us there to fish when we were kids. It has a long pier and a perfect view of the bay bridge. Not too many people know about it and we were glad to see the driveway empty as we pull up.

Lana and I have been out here several times over the years when we needed a break from the madness. I love the idea of spending more time with Max, but the idea of getting naked in front of him terrifies me.

"You just *had* to suggest skinny dipping, didn't you," I whisper as we walk the overgrown path to the water.
She knows my anxiety about my body and knows *exactly* what I'm referring to.

"Relax, Kate. You're beautiful! Besides, it's too dark to see your baby boobies anyway," she teases.

I kick her in the butt. "You're such a bitch."

We make our way to the water, where I only have the courage to strip to my panties and bra and thankful to see Max has kept his boxers on.

"Cannonnnn Balllll!" Drew shouts, running across the pier buck naked; his Johnson flapping in the wind.

"You need to put that thing away before you poke someone's eye out!" Max shouts.

"Impressive!" Lana adds with a devilish grin.

The four of us goof off like a bunch of school kids. After a cannonball competition, a game of chicken and a race to see who could swim to the shoreline the quickest. We relax and watch the traffic cross the long suspension bridge. The lights from the cars twinkling like Christmas. The moon peeks from behind a heavy cloud, casting a stormy gray across the water.

"I can't believe this is almost over," Lana pouts.

"Yep," I sigh. "The sun will be up soon."

"It doesn't have to be," Max says, pulling himself from the water.

I shrug. "I know, I know. It's only a month. But the Fourth of July feels like an eternity away."

"No. I mean this weekend. Y'all could come back to Post with us tomorrow. Stay the night…see our world."

Lana's face beams. Immediately jumping on board with the idea. "Holy shit! Yes! That would be so cool!"

He can't be serious? I'm still processing why this wonderful, perfect, sweet man is spending his entire vacation with me. *Now he wants me to go home with him? We haven't even kissed yet!*

Something's weird about this. "I don't know, Max," I say, hesitantly.

He reads my face. "If you're uncomfortable with it, I'll completely understand. I thought it might be nice to spend a little more time together."

"It would be, I just…"

Lana waves off my concern. "Pay her no mind. She's being a nervous Nelly. As long as Drew's good with it, count us in!"

"Hell yeah, I'm good with it!" Drew says, swimming over to plant a wet kiss on her cheek.

"Lana, we need to think this through first."

She flips her hands up. "What's to think through? We aren't supposed to be home until Tuesday, so it's not like anyone will be looking for us. And our first shift at work isn't until Wednesday. Besides, it's not like we're driving across the country. Fort Benning is practically on the way home."

I process what she's saying and must admit, she does have valid points. "Ok, for argument's sake…say we do this. I thought you guys lived in a barracks? Where the heck will Lana and I sleep?"

Drew and Max both chuckle. "It's not like the movies, where everyone is piled in a room packed with bunks. We all have our own rooms," Drew says.

"Less barracks, more college dorm," Max adds.
I chew on a nail as I let the idea roll around in my head.
They all glare, waiting for an answer.

"Errrr! Fine! Ok. You win!" I reluctantly cave.

"Are you sure?" Max asks.

"Yes, I'm sure. As long as you promise to keep Lurch as far away as feasibly possible."

He laughs. "Oh, I was thinking you two could bunk together."

I nudge him in the side playfully and as I do, he pulls me in close. The laughter shifting to desire.

He places his hands on my cheeks and whispers, "Thank you." I close my eyes as he slowly leans in. The tip of his nose grazing mine.

Lana gasps, startling us apart. "What the hell!?" We follow her pointed finger as floodlights pop on behind us.

Max huffs an exhausted breath. "You've **got** to be kidding me."

Shadows appear on the rickety porch, followed by the sound of faint sirens in the distance.

"FUCK! Someone called the cops!"

"Runnnnn!" Drew screams, springing his naked body from the water.

In a frenzied panic, we gather our clothes and shoes strewn throughout the pier and make a run for it. The sirens are getting closer as flashing blue lights reflect off the trees.

Max races through the front lawn. "I thought you said the house was abandoned?" he yells over his shoulder.

"Clearly someone bought it!" Lana yells back, trying to hold her clothes over her boobs.

"Go, go, go!" Drew shouts, coming up behind us.

We make it to the truck in record time. Lana's the last one in, flinging across me in all her birthday suit glory. We speed away seconds before the cops arrive.

We're speechless. Only the sounds of huffs and puffs as we look back to make sure we've made a clean getaway. It's only after we know the coast is clear, the four of us break out in side-splitting, uncontrollable, laughter.

Drew grabs his heart and collapses into his seat. "Oh my God, I think I shit my pants!"

"Well, I guess it's a good thing you aren't wearing any then," Max teases.

"Yeah, I've had Lana's lady bits in my face twice in one day. This has to be a record," I say as tears stream down my cheeks.

"At least I had *her* all groomed up this time!"

Drew raises an eyebrow. "I can vouch for that!"

"Well, I must admit ladies… There's never a dull moment with you two around," Max says.

We make the short drive back into the city just as rain moves in. We're still laughing about our near brush with the law and know we've all made a memory that'll stay with us forever.

"I can't remember the last time I've had this much fun," I admit.

"Me either." Max grabs my hand kisses it. "Maybe one of these days I'll be able to kiss you without the entire world interrupting us."

I look at him, looking at me. "Stop the car."

"What? Here?" he questions.

"Yep! Pull over. Right over there."

I point to a small beachside pull off and as soon as the truck's in park, I jump out. Max is already out as I make it to his side of the truck. He reads my mind and knows why we've stopped. He grabs my hand and pulls me gently through the dunes and across the sand, not stopping until we've made it to the shoreline. With the rain falling and flashes of lightning electrifying the night sky, he pulls me into his arms and presses his soft lips to mine. There's no time to be gentle, as two days of pent-up desire is finally released. Passion erupts, sending us into a fiery charge. His tongue and mine in perfect sync. He moves his lips to my neck, causing my body to go weak in his arms. I'm unable to tell if the pounding I hear is the sound of thunder or my heart.

We finally find the strength to pull our lips apart. With his chest rising and falling, both of us drenched to the bone, he whispers in my ear, "*That* was worth the wait."

He wraps his arms tightly around me as my head falls into his chest. We stay there holding each other as the sun begins to rise. We watch as the orange sliver peaks across the water, bringing an official end to the most amazing night of my life.

A sleeping Lana and Drew don't flinch when we start the truck and make our way back to the hotel. "So do you still want us to go home with y'all tomorrow?"

He grabs my hand. "Of course I do."

"What time were you wanting to get on the road?"

He senses my concern. "I know you're a little freaked out about this whole thing, so if you want to back out."

"No, Max. Please don't think that. My hesitation was never about not wanting to go."

"Then what is it?"

"I just…"

"Look! Let's make a deal with each other, ok?"

"Ok?" I say, hesitantly.

"The rest of the guys are planning to pull out around ten-thirty in the morning. If you're there, we can all caravan back. If you're not, we'll know you've changed your mind and we'll ride home with them. We can let this be the amazing weekend it was, no strings attached. No hurt feelings. Go home with lifelong memories and hope we run into each other on the Fourth. Deal?" He sticks out his hand.

I smile and take it. "Deal!"

As we make it back to our hotel, I stir sleeping beauty and send her to the room. Max gives me one last hug and kiss goodbye. "Try to get a few hours of sleep."

"You too."

"And if you don't come, I'll understand. But I pray you do."

I don't respond, because I genuinely don't know if I will go yet. I don't have a peace about it. I stare into his eyes, hoping to find some clarity. I kiss him softly on the lips and walk away. Turning back to look at him one last time. Just in case.

CHAPTER SEVEN

I feel my way around the nightstand for my glasses. I push them on and read 9:30 a.m. across the alarm clock. Yet, another night I haven't slept a wink. Two days with no sleep is officially kicking my ass. I can't shut my mind off as it replays the entire weekend. *How could two nights with someone make me feel this way? And those lips… oh dear Lord… those lips! What on earth is he thinking? He could have any girl he wants. Why me?*

"Lana!" I jostle her. "Lana! Wake up!"
It's like waking the dead.

"What? Geez… I'm up… I'm up," she growls.

I sit on the bed, Indian style and light the end of a cigarette. "We need to talk about this whole going to Fort Benning thing."

"What's to talk about? We've already told them we'd go."

"I know. But I talked to Max later and told him I was having some second thoughts about it."

She scrunches her face and fans the smoke. "Why would you have doubts? He *clearly* likes you."

I stand and pace the room. "See, that's the thing. Don't you think it's a little odd he's into me? I'm not trying to be hard on myself. But let's be honest here…he's a ten. Actually, he's more than a ten. He's like an eighteen because he's hot, sweet, *and* a good kisser."

She crawls from the bed and heads for the bathroom. "It's about time you two kissed."

"Don't make jokes, Lana! I'm freaking out here."

"Why are you freaking out? It'll be us hanging out. But instead of being at the beach we'll be in an Army barracks."

"Exactly! And what if we get there and this is all some big ruse so his female soldier friends can whip the shit out of us as payback?"

She stomps back into the room with her hands up. "Please God, tell me you're joking?"

"It could happen."

"Yes, Kate. You're right. They're going to spend the entire night with us. Stay out till dawn, buy us drinks, take us to dinner, and nearly get arrested for indecent exposure. All with the ulterior motive of revenge."

"Well, when you put it *that* way."

"He likes you and wants to spend more time with you. Plain and simple."

"I like him too. But why do I have a gut feeling I'll be nursing a broken heart at the end of all this," I finally admit.

"I guess it's a risk you're going to have to take. Besides, we *have* to go. Drew told me he's getting out of the Army in a few weeks and will be heading back home to Michigan. This trip was his last hoorah. If we don't go, I'll never see him again."

"Oh, gee thanks, Lana! No pressure or anything."

She sits on the end of the bed and pulls her hair in a ponytail. "It's still ultimately your decision. If you don't think it's a good idea, then so be it. I may want to kill you later, but I'll support it."

I fall back into the pillow. "I guess I was hoping for some clarity that this is the right move."

Ten seconds later, there's a tap on the door. In my sleepless brain fog, I open it without checking the peephole.

"Please tell me you weren't out all night with those fucking GI's again?"

I slam the door in Wayne's face without a word. "Lana! Pack your shit. We're going to Fort Benning."

Once the decision to go was made, we got dressed, packed our things, and checked out of Hotel Alpharetta in record time. And although I haven't had any sleep, I'm wide awake with excitement. We pull into The Parker Motel without a minute to spare.

Jackson's truck and Santos's car are gone and Max and Drew are nowhere to be seen.

"I'm sure they're waiting for us in the room," Lana says, jumping from the car.

"I hate being late."

She rolls her eyes. "It's 10:31 for crying out loud!"

I look around as we make the long walk across the motel courtyard. The coolers sitting outside the door are gone. We knock, but no one answers. Lana checks the other room, but no one answers there either.

"Maybe they all went for breakfast," she says, hopeful.

"Maybe," I shrug.

"Are you sure he said ten-thirty?"

"I'm positive, Lana!" I shout, louder than I should of.

We head back to the car, disappointment sinking in. "I knew this was all too good to be true."

I pull the keys from my pocket as the door of the lobby dings open behind us. I turn and out walks Max and Drew. A huge smile crosses his face when he spots me, causing a wave of relief in my chest.

He sweeps me up for a much-needed hug. "You're here!"

My cheeks flush. "I'm here."

"We were checking out of the rooms."

"You scared me a little when we couldn't find anyone."

"Oh, yeah. They all left about an hour ago."

My head tilts. "I thought you said ten-thirty?"

"I did. But they were all up and packed, so they went ahead and got on the road."

"Well, ok. But what were you going to do if we didn't show?"

He laughs. "I guess we would have been hitchhiking it back to Post."

"I'm serious, Max. That was one hell of a gamble, don't you think?"

"It was a risk I was willing to take. Besides, I knew you couldn't resist spending more time with this handsome face," he says, easing close for a kiss.

You got that right! Is what I think. "Cocky much?" is what I actually say out loud.

He smirks. "Oh, I've been known to be a time or two."

"Well, as long as you don't hit on Waffle House waitresses, I think we're all safe."

Lana and Drew are already in the back seat with a cooler full of ice-cold, Coors Light between them. The top's down, letting in the warm May morning air. Max is up front with me and is busy thumbing through my CD case.

He holds up my Vanilla Ice CD. "We really need to work on your choice of music, Kate."

"Come on now! You have to admit, 'Ice Ice Baby' is pretty damn catchy."

He shakes his head. "I have so much to teach you."

Drew pulls off his T-shirt, soaking up every last ray of sunshine. "Kate, have I mentioned how much I love this freaking car?" He runs his hand across the tan leather seat.

"Me too!" I roll out my lip. "It's going to be hard to hand it back over to dear ole dad. My Honda doesn't have quite the pizzazz as this one."

"No kidding! If it hadn't been for the car, I may not have noticed the hot ladies piled inside of it."

"Thank the Lord for Kate's shitty stick shift driving!" Lana teases as she strips to her bathing suit top.

Max leans over and whispers, "I noticed you way before I noticed the car." Giving a wink as he leans back.

I shake my head and laugh. "You're so full of shit, Chase Maxwell. But I like it!"

"It's true! Scout's honor," he says, holding up Boy Scout fingers.

"It's a three and a half-hour drive, Lana. You're burned bad enough as is. You better put some sunscreen on."

"Ok, Mom! Want me to wash behind my ears too?"

"Nobody likes a smart-ass," I say, pulling out of the parking lot.

Max chuckles. "You two crack me up."

We sit quietly and enjoy the ride, taking in our last glimpses of the Gulf before we make the turn north. Poetically, "Life in the Fast Lane," by the Eagles plays as we wave goodbye to the city that brought us all together.

"So what's on the agenda for us tonight?" I ask.

Drew slings his arm around Lana. "You gals are going to have so much fun with us tonight. We're going to show you around, introduce you to some of our friends. Then I thought we'd hang out in my room, drink a little, throw some Chemlights around. Drink a little more, then who knows."

"Sounds great!" Lana beams. "But what the hell is a Chemlight?"

They laugh. "It's too hard to explain. We'll have to show you tonight," Max says.

"I'll take your word for it," I say. Clueless on what it is either.

The drive is going by in a flash thanks to the constant chatter of the group. There hasn't been a lull in the conversation and I've laughed so much my side hurts. Drew and Max are both drinking, but Lana's one beer away from being cut off. Cops are out in full force, so I've been extra cautious knowing there's a car full of open beer. Max doesn't want me to feel left out and offers the occasional sip. But I know I have to get us *and* Dad's car back in one piece, so it's only Dr. Pepper's for me.

Max slips his arm on the headrest and rubs the back of my neck, causing goosebumps to rise. "You better stop or I might have to pull the car over and ravish you right here on the side of the road," I tease.

He inches closer. "Well, in that case, let me use both hands."

Fort Benning is situated between Columbus, Georgia and Phenix City, Alabama and the minute we cross into the town, it's clear the Military Post is the town's core infrastructure. Army surplus stores, tattoo parlors, bars, strip clubs, and pawn shops are on every corner. Each one advertising their own *"Special Rate with Military ID."*

A large monument greets us as we pull through the entrance. *Welcome to Fort Benning—Home of the Infantry.* A guard shack with two large, intimidating MP's monitoring the gate, step out to check Max and Drew's ID's, and it causes an uneasy feeling again.

"Is it ok to be here?" I ask.

"Of course! Don't worry. We're allowed to have guests," Drew assures.

"But is it ok we're staying the night, right?"

"It's all good. I promise," Max says, trying to calm my visible nerves.

"She's only freaking out because she thinks this was all a ploy to get us here," Lana says, spilling the beans.

Max's brow furrows. "A ploy?"

I give her evil eyes through the rearview mirror. "Shut up, Lana!"

"She thinks you guys only invited us here so you could have your badass Army bitches whip the shit out of us for payback."

Max's head snaps in my direction and his mouth falls open. "Is that true? Do you think this is all some ploy?"

I grimace. "Maybe a little."

"Oh my God! It's all water under the bridge, Kate! I swear! Is this why you were so hesitant to bring us home?" he asks, laughing.

"If I'm being a hundred percent truthful… *yes*. But I always overthink things. I know you wouldn't do that to me."

As we wind our way through the Post I read off the names of beige and white buildings. Post Headquarters, Legal Services, and Infirmary. Max tells us about each one as we pass. We learn a PX is the military's version of Walmart, and the grocery store is called a Commissary. He chuckles and says they spend a lot of their time in the Class Six, which is the liquor store. The only thing I recognize from the outside world is the Burger King.

I'm certain we've traveled at least four miles before finally coming to the housing area.

Rows of three-story, long, beige block buildings with entrances at the end and middle. Max points to Jackson's truck and I pull alongside it and park.

I climb out and stretch as the others collect their things. Two girls jog down the stairs of the building and my stomach drops. *I knew it! Here we go!* Bracing myself for the inevitable payback. They wave and shout a quick, "hey guys" to Max and Drew and head towards the other side of the lot. While I say a quick prayer of thanks and wipe the invisible shit from my pants.

Max was right. The building's more dormitory than a summer camp bunkhouse. Long stark white hallways with fluorescent lights glare against the white tile floors. Doors about every fifteen feet, line both sides of the hall. Some doors are propped open and Max and Drew introduce us as we pass each one.

We make our way to the end where Drew's room is. It's small, with a twin bed and a small couch. He has a mini-fridge with an assortment of liquor bottles stacked on the top. Army gear is piled high in the corner. His camouflage uniform is hooked on the front of a small wardrobe. I take a seat and study the large black flag hanging over his bed. The outline of a parachute and the word Airborne written across it.

"So does this mean you've jumped out of airplanes?" I ask.

"Yep! More times than we can count." Drew says proudly.

"Fort Benning is where jump school is for the entire country. So at some point, most everyone will make their way through here," Max adds.

Lana throws herself across Drew's bed like she's lived here all her life. "No way, Jose! I'd be scared to death!"

"Ah, it's not so bad. After you get past the nerves, it's one hell of a rush," Drew says, sliding in beside her.

"Well! You both scored some major cool points in my book," I admit.

It's obvious there's no bathroom in Drew's room and I would love the opportunity to get cleaned up. The grit and grime of the two-hour convertible ride has me in desperate need of a shower.

"Soooo is there a bathroom close by? I'd love to grab a quick shower?"

"I could use one too," Lana adds.

"The female latrine is three doors past the stairwell we came in at."

Lana lifts up on her elbows. "Um. I'm sorry, what?"

"A female latrine, huh? This should be interesting."

"Oh, I have no doubt it will be," Max chuckles. He walks into the hall and waits as I gather up my stuff.

"Let me show y'all where it's at. While you're getting dressed, I'll go unpack."

I tug the door to close it behind us, but it won't latch. "Drew, did you know your door's messed up?"

"Yeah, we have auto locks on the door. They'll open from the inside, even if they're locked on the outside. I got drunk and forgot about it. Locked myself out and had to disassemble the whole damn thing to get in. It's been broken ever since."

"So you just leave it cracked open all the time?"

"Yeah," he chuckles. "There isn't anything in here anybody would want. Other than the booze, maybe."

Max walks us to the latrine door. "I'll meet you back in Drew's room in a little bit."

He gives me a quick kiss goodbye. The gesture meaning more to me knowing I'm in his *real* world.

We walk through a large restroom full of typical bathroom stalls and open sinks, eventually coming to the "Latrine Showers" sign. We round the corner of a large open shower room where the ladies shower together.

"Communal showers? You've *got* to be kidding," I say, loud enough my voice echoes through the room.

"Enjoy your shower ladies!" The guys shout as they laugh through the door.

"Thanks for the heads up, ya shitheads!" Lana yells.

"There's no one in here right now. Let's hurry and get this over with."

Her bag slips from her shoulder as she stares into the empty room. "I can't do it, Kate! I'm sorry." She walks backward, her bag dragging across the tile. "I'll get stage fright if some big, butchy ass, Army chick walks in."

She's gone before I can protest. "I'm going to kill you!" I shout as the door slams shut.

I feel disgusting. There's no way I can bail-out too. I take my chances, hoping I can get in and out before anyone else walks in. But just in case, I shower in my bathing suit.

I jump in, monitoring the door every few seconds, shaving in record time. As I rub shampoo in, the sound of feet sliding across the tile stops me in my tracks. With one eye open, I slowly turn; praying its Lana. *No. Such. Luck!* Standing before me is a 230+ pound, naked, Sasquatch, sporting a skull and bones tatt on her boob and a bush big enough to catch fish with. I snap my head back toward the water, trying desperately to rinse the shampoo out.

Although the room is full of empty showerheads, she picks the one *right* next to me.

"How's it going?" she asks, roughly.

I'm speechless for a few seconds.

"Uh. I. I'm ok. Thanks," I finally mutter.

It's fine, Kate! Calm down! I keep repeating in my head. *Finish up and get the hell out of here!*

I frantically plop a handful of conditioner on my head, when in walks another lady you wouldn't want to meet in a dark alley. *Oh dear God, help me! This is the payback! They're going to beat the shit out of me in the shower with no witnesses! Less mess!* She strips and slides into the shower directly on the other side of me. My hands shake as I scrub my hair. The seconds feel like hours, causing the most awkward two minutes of my life.

As soon as the last of the conditioner is out, I bolt. Sopping wet, water pouring from my suit. I snatch my bag and swing open the latrine door. I fly into the hall where Lana, Max, and Drew are buckled over in laughter.

Lana points. "Oh, we got you so good!" she says, barely able to speak through her laughter.

Tears roll down Drew's cheeks as Max grips his side.

I cross my arms putting two and two together. "You assholes set me up didn't you?"

Drew clutches his side. "Well, Lana told us how much you liked seeing her lady parts yesterday, so we thought we'd give you a few more to look at."

"Drew promised he'd do their laundry for a week if they'd do it," Lana says.

Max throws up his hands in surrender. "It wasn't my idea, I swear!"

I nod. "Alright, I'll admit it. Y'all got me! But you better believe payback's a bitch!"

It's late evening. Two pepperoni pizzas and a half case of beer later, we're sitting in Drew's room reminiscing about all the crazy excitement we've had this weekend. As the holiday comes to a close more and more people trickle back in from the break. Santos and several other friends stop by to say hello, including one of my new shower friends. Who came by to make sure there were no hard feelings.

As the sun finally sets, full-bellied and rested, Drew claps his hands. "Alright! It's time!"

Max and Drew have mentioned this Chemlight thing at least a half a dozen times, but we still aren't computing what exactly it is.

"Time to see what all the fuss is about," I say, still confused.

"Lana, you might want to change your T-shirt. White tends to stain," Drew explains.

She does as instructed as Max and Drew open the wrappers of large glow sticks. They're like the ones used for Halloween, only bigger. Purple, green, orange, blue, and yellow illuminate the room as they crack each one. I watch mesmerized as Max punches a small hole at the ends of each one with a safety pin. Passing them over one by one.

Drew flips off the overhead light, allowing only the glow from the sticks to shine. "Are you girls ready?"

He cranks up his stereo. "Now watch this!"

It's like something out of a dream as they begin to fling the contents of the sticks across the walls. We join in as a 3-D rainbow of neon colors splatters every inch of the room, and us. An acid trip on steroids as the room glows like a circus funhouse.

"Won't this ruin his stuff?" I ask Max, slightly concerned.

"Nope! Watch this." He flips the light switch on and the colors instantly vanish. He flips it back off and they reappear.

I'm in awe. "How long will it stay like this?"

"It wears off in a few hours," he says, slinging green and purple colors on me. I squeal and sling mine back.

"This is *in-sane*!" Lana yells, joining in on our game.

In less than ten minutes we'd drained all the liquid out of the sticks. Painted in it, we sit in silence, gazing at the masterpiece we've created. Lana and Drew use the opportunity to have an under the lights make-out session, while I snuggle on the couch with Max.

I look around the room. "This may be one of the coolest things I've ever seen."

"I'm glad you like it," he says with pride.

"Thank you for this."

"You're welcome."

It doesn't take long before it's clear, four's a crowd. So Max and I make our way to his room. It's different from Drew's. Simple and clean. Bunk beds made up with a small pile of folded laundry on the top. A few moving boxes are stacked up near the door and work gear is neatly organized on the shelves of a bookcase. Other than an American Flag, nothing else is on the walls.

"As you can tell, I don't spend a lot of time in here," he says, picking up a pair of work boots from the middle of the floor.

I nod toward the boxes. "Coming or going?"

"Coming," he says. "I've only been in here about a month. I haven't taken the time to unpack yet."

"Where were you before?"

He sighs. "Well, it's kind of a long story."

"We've got all night," I remind him.

"Yes we do," he says. "And I tell you what… why don't you get comfy while I go get out of these clothes? When I get back, I'll tell you all about it."

It's late and the halls have grown quiet. Max is back and has changed into a T-shirt and gym shorts, looking hot as ever. He turns on the radio, barely loud enough to hear. The lights are off, but the streetlight outside lights the room through a crack in the blinds.

I'm on the bottom bunk, my back propped against the wall. He climbs in beside me and pulls me to him until we're face to face. He swipes a stray curl from my face. "Thank you for coming up here."

I smile. "Thank you for *letting* me come up here."

"I know we have plans to meet on the Fourth, I just wasn't ready to let you go yet."

I shake my head. "I still don't get any of this. You. Me. It's like a dream. It honestly doesn't make any sense."

"I'm crazy about you. I hope you know that?"

"No, that's not what I meant," I say, frustrated with myself. "You've been amazing this entire time and I find myself liking you more every minute we're together. What I don't know or understand is *why* you do. I mean, don't think I…"

He grabs my hand. "That ex of yours did a number on you, didn't he?"

I don't answer right away. The brutal truth, hard to admit. "Yes, he did. And as you saw Friday night, I still battle it every day."

"He's an asshole, Kate. You're way too good for him."

"I know," I say with a heavy sigh. "I don't love him anymore. Honestly, I'm not sure I ever did. It's more about history than anything else.

When you've worked so hard to make something work, it's difficult to let go. Even if it was never reciprocated. Or appreciated for that matter."

"Well, for what it's worth, I think you're one of the most genuine, down to earth girls I've ever met. I honestly couldn't tell you the last time I've had this much fun. Or Laughed this much. The fact you're beautiful is just icing on the cake."

"Thank you. You're not so bad yourself," I tease, reaching over for a small kiss. "So you want to tell me about the moving boxes?" I ask, not letting him off the hook.

"Eh, it was a complicated, dysfunctional, relationship that left me on a bit of a roller coaster of my own."

"I had a feeling it had something to do with a girl."

"She's enlisted here. We met about a year ago through mutual friends. Things started off great. We had an amazing first few months. I was spending all my free time with her. I was at her place more than I was here, so eventually moved in. But as time went by, other than work, I realized we had absolutely nothing in common. She was needy and had a wicked jealous streak. She couldn't stand for me to do anything away from her. I tried bringing her around the guys. Well, you've seen how they are. They're crazy as hell, but all genuinely good guys. Even Davis."

"I will take your word for it," I chuckle.

"Jody wouldn't give them a chance. Her personality and theirs didn't mesh at all. They couldn't stand her and she couldn't stand them. So I tried to focus on the two of us for a while. But we could never get on the same page. I'm all for fighting for love, but it was a never-ending cycle of turmoil."

"When did all this happen? When did you guys break up?"

"I guess we've been on and off since Christmas. But it was about six weeks ago when I cut the cord for good."

"Whoa! Six weeks? Not too long ago then."

"It was over way before, though. I kept hanging on hoping it might get better."

"Did you love her?"

He thinks for a second. "I did. I really did. But it wasn't meant to be. Thankfully, her time's up in August. She'll be heading back to Idaho, which will be a blessing for all of us."

"I'm sorry, Max. I'm sure it's been a tough few months for you."

"Well, I was serious when I said I couldn't think of the last time I had this much fun. The beach was great, but meeting you and getting to spend time with you and Lana, made it a weekend I'll never forget."

"I'm glad I could be of service!"

We talk until the wee hours of the morning. To the point of sounding delirious. "We need to get some sleep. You have to work in the morning," I say between yawns.

"Yep. Back to reality."

"Boooooo," I whine.

"So here's what's going to happen in the morning… We all have to be up at five and head to First Formation. We'll have PT, then come back and have about an hour before we have to report to work.

"PT? As in physical training, right?"

"Yep! See. You'll have this Army stuff down pat in no time."

"Doubtful," I admit.

"You can sleep in and when I get back, we can exchange numbers and say all our dreaded goodbyes."

"Not good-byes. Say our see you laters."

He smiles. "Absolutely," he says, kissing me goodnight. A soft, loving, kiss that slowly releases the chains around my heart.

As we close our eyes, Bob Seger's, "We've Got Tonight," softly plays on the radio. It's as if the universe is confirming how much we truly needed this time.

We barely close our eyes when the alarm clock begins to scream.

"Oh Max, I feel terrible I kept you up all night."

"Worth every minute," he says as he slowly rolls out of bed.

He runs to the latrine to get dressed as the hall grows louder and louder as everyone begins to stir; like the halls of high schools between bells. Davis walks by the open door on his way back from the latrine wearing nothing but a white towel. His tall frame making it look the size of a washcloth.

"Morinin', Skeeter Bites!" he shouts, clearly proud of himself for coming up with a small boobs joke.

"Like I've never heard that one before, Lurch!" I shout back as he passes.

My jaw hits the floor as Max walks back in. He's wearing a gray T-shirt with ARMY written across it, camo pants, and black boots.

"Damn, Max! You look…"

He smirks. "You like?"

I wipe the invisible drool from my mouth. "There are no words."

"I'll be back in about an hour, so get some sleep while I'm gone. I'll wake you when I get back."
He finishes tying his boots and gives me a quick hug. A hint of Carmex on his burned lips trails as he leans in for a kiss.

"Just a baby kiss! I have some serious morning breath."

He laughs. "See you in a bit."

With a quick smile from his beautiful face, he's gone.

The halls are silent again as I cozy back under the covers. The door flies open. "I had *the most* amazing night!" Lana shouts, clearly on cloud nine.

I know *exactly* what she was busy doing. "I'm glad you had a good time."

She plops on the bed beside me. "We did it so much I'm sore."

I cringe. "I'm starting to worry about the closeness of our friendship."

"Ha! The best part, he gave me his number last night and asked if we could come back in a couple of weeks, so I can see him one last time before he heads home."

"That's encouraging news."

"Nah, we're just having fun. It won't go any further. But I'm sure as hell going to enjoy it while it lasts."

"What about you and Max? Any under the sheet action?"

"Nope. We kissed and talked," I say, proudly.

"*Talked?*" What is this? Middle school?"

"Things are different with him. Our time is important. I can't explain it."

"Well, it sounds B. O. R. I. N. G. if ya ask me!"

I raise up and fluff my pillow. "I'll tell you all about it on the way home. But he and I were up all night, I could use some more sleep before we head out."

"Me too, but I don't want to be in Drew's room alone. The door not shutting all the way freaks me out. Please come in there with me? Pleaseeeeeee," she begs.

"It didn't freak you out last night when you were doing the horizontal hokey pokey."

"I'm serious, Kate!"

"Why don't you lay down here?"

"Pleaseeeee?"

"Ugh!" I fling the covers back. "Fine! If it'll shut you up!"

I drag to Drew's room and Lana and I settle into his bed. To save space, she lies at the head of the bed and I lay at the foot. The lights are off and I fall asleep as soon as my head hits the pillow.

I'm not sure if it's been thirty seconds or thirty minutes when voices grow at the door. My brain's not awake enough to determine real-life and dream world. The bright fluorescent light flips on, instantly pulling me from my sleep.

A male voice booms across the tiny room. "WHAT. THE. HELL. IS. THIS!?"

I freeze, too scared to move from the end of the bed. Lana pops up. "WHO THE HELL ARE YOU?" he growls.

I watch through a crack in the sheet, but he doesn't notice me. The huge, angry, black man, with lots of stripes on his uniform, stands over the bed quizzing Lana. While another one stands at the door.

I startle him when I pop up. "THERE ARE **TWO** OF YOU? WHO SAID YOU COULD BE IN HERE?"

"They, he, brought, home, beach, Max said, ok, here." We try to explain ourselves, but it comes out as a bunch of rambling gibberish.

"Go get Andrews *RIGHT* now!" The angry man shouts to the other. "*Somebody* better have an explanation for this!"

He continues to scream like it's our first day in boot camp, "You two stay here! I'm going to get the bottom of this!"

He finally leaves, but we hear him yell down the hall for someone to call the MP's. We stare at each other in shock.

"Holy shit! What have we done?"

Tears pool in her panicked eyes. "I thought it was ok for us to be here?"

"We have to get the hell out of here, Lana! Get your shit together! We have to go NOW!"

We spring out of bed, gathering our things in hurried chaos. My legs shake as I race to Max's room. I snatch my purse and not even stopping to put on shoes. Lana meets me at the door as I fly out of his room. Juggling a handful of clothes, her purse, and trying to slide her flip-flops on and run at the same time.

"Hurry! Hurry! Hurry!" I shout over my back. "You grabbed the number right?" I ask as we jump the stairs two at a time.

"Yes! It's in my purse!" she yells as we make it to the door.

The guys are lined up in rows doing jumping jacks as we clear the building. I'm so scared, I don't dare look over. We sprint across the lawn to the parking lot. Lana is a pace slower with her hands full. I'm in the car and cranking it as she flies in. I throw it in drive before the door is shut and speed off as fast as I feasibly can.

We don't speak until Fort Benning is safely in our rearview mirror. We don't even take a breath until we're back on civilian land.

"I have to stop," I say, my hands still shaking. "I need to calm down before I can drive us home."

We pull into a Hardee's and go in. We sit in silence, letting our nerves settle as we replay what happened.

Lana finally musters up words. "Um, did *that* just happen?"

"I think it did," I say, straight-faced. "I don't think I've ever been more scared in my whole life."

The corner of her mouth turns up. "Did you see the look on his face when he saw *both* of us in Drew's bed?"

And just like that, we bust out in hysterical laughter.

Exhausted, it's a quiet ride home. The radio's tuned to seventies music, allowing us to be a little closer to Max and Drew in spirit. We didn't need to talk. We already knew how the other felt and how much our lives had been affected by this amazing weekend.

I pull up to Lana's house and ask again, "You got the number, right?"

She pats her purse. "Yep! Right here in my purse. I triple checked."

"Ok, good."

"Since they don't have phones in their rooms, it's the number to the hall phone they share."

"I hate I didn't get a chance to tell him goodbye," I say for the hundredth time.

She grabs her pillow from the backseat. "You'll still be able to. We can call them later." She swings the door closed and leans into the window. "You don't think they sent their boss in there to kick us out, do you?"

I climb out to hug her goodbye. "Surely, not. It wouldn't make any sense if they did. We were leaving in less than an hour."

She hugs me. "Go home and get some sleep. I'll come over later so we can call them."

I climb back in the car and yell through the open window. "Well! We wanted a 'do-over' weekend and dammit if we didn't have one hell of one!"

92

CHAPTER EIGHT
Father's Day Weekend

"How many times do I have to say I'm sorry, Kate? I was drunk and clearly transposed a number."

It turns out, in Lana's inebriated state the night of the Chemlights, she jotted the last two digits of Max and Drew's phone number wrong. So when we call, we get Fort Benning, only it's *not* the building we need. We've been trying for weeks to reach them with no luck.

I sit on Lana's bed, flipping through TV channels while she finishes up last-minute college forms. "It's been three weeks and we've tried every possible number sequence there is and we still haven't gotten them," I say, irritated.

"I thought the guy we talked to at the mess hall sounded hot."

I lean back and bury myself into her mound of throw pillows. "It's not funny. I can't get him out of my head, Lana. There was something there. I felt it. Not to mention, I'm sure Drew told Max he gave you the number and now thinks I'm purposely not calling him."

"You're going to see him in a few weeks at the beach. We can explain what happened then."

I lean up on my elbows. "But don't you want to say goodbye to Drew?"

She drops her pen. "Of course I do, but what am I supposed to do about it?"

I grin with pleading eyes. "We could always take a quick road trip."

Her head cocks. "When?"

"Right now?" I ask, using her signature puppy dog eyes.

"It's nine at night, Kate. It'll be almost midnight before we get there."

"Please? You owe me this for screwing up the number in the first place."

"That's a cheap shot!"

"Yeah. Well. I'm sorry. This is important to me."

She huffs. "You couldn't mention this *before* I took my make-up off and got in my pajamas?"

We didn't pack bags, we just left. Making it to Columbus faster than we thought we would. Relieved the guard at the gate allowed us through, after checking our ID's and giving Max's name.

Butterflies dance in my stomach the closer we get. Second-guessing my decision to come. *What will I say? What if he isn't happy to see me?*

"Kate, haven't we already passed the rec center four times?"

"Yeah, I think I missed a turn."

"None of this looks familiar. Are you sure you know where you're going?"

"I think so. But the first time through I was going where Max pointed and the second time we were being chased out by the jackass Drill Sergeant."

We drive in circles until the clock on the dash strikes midnight. "I think we're lost."

"No shit! We've wasted an hour crisscrossing this damn place.

We're never going to find it in the dark. I think we need to throw in the towel. We can get a room and try again in the morning."

As much as I hate to admit it, she's right. Driving around aimlessly is getting us nowhere. I reluctantly wave a white flag as we make our way past the gate and back into Columbus.

"What the hell is going on? That's the fifth hotel we've passed with their no vacancy sign on."

"Maybe we should stop and see what's going on."
I pull under the awning of a crappy Red Roof Inn and let Lana out. I put the car in park and stretch my arms and legs. Reveling in the much-needed break from driving.

She scowls as she walks through the sliding lobby door. "We have the shittiest luck sometimes!"

"What?"

"Well, between Father's Day weekend and some big Army graduation ceremony, there isn't a single room available in the entire city."

"You're joking?"

"I wish I was," she huffs. "I swear, we have the shittiest luck sometimes."

It's after one and we're both too tired to try to make it home. Crashing in the car is our only option. I take the two-mile drive over the Alabama state line and find the most lit parking lot I can, praying we make it through the night in one piece. We lay the seats back and within minutes are both passed out cold.

TAP, TAP, TAP…TAP, TAP, TAP. *What is that?* I think as I start to rouse.

"Ladies, you need to wake up!" TAP, TAP, TAP.

My eyes pop open. Completely forgetting we're in the car, I jump and bang my knees against the steering wheel. "Lana, wake up! The cops are here."

It's daylight out as I swing the car door open. My eyes squint, adjusting to the light. People pass by and stare as shopping carts clatter across the lot.

"You know you can't overnight park here, right?" the pudgy officer asks.

"I'm so sorry, sir. We came to visit friends and tried to find a room, but everything was booked and…," I'm rambling again.

"It's ok," he chuckles. "Y'all need to move along now, ok?"

"Yes! Absolutely, sir! No problem. We're leaving right now. Thank you!"

I jump back in the car and breathe a sigh of relief. "That scared the living shit out of me! What is it with us and the law in this town?"

"Thank God he wasn't an asshole about it."

"No kidding!"

She looks around at all the cars. "What time is it, anyway?"

"It's ten. I can't believe we slept this late. No wonder they called the cops on us."

She stretches and rubs at a kink. "My neck is killing me."

Customers are still staring when I start the car and make our way out of the busy Walmart parking lot. "We get ourselves in the damndest messes sometimes, don't we?"

She laughs. "No shit! We could write a book and title it, The Best Friend Guide of What *NOT* To Do."

We make our way back to Fort Benning for one last-ditch effort to find the housing area. And as luck would have it, I drive straight to it.

"How the hell couldn't we find this last night?" I say looking up at the white building in disbelief.

Lana grabs her stomach. "Whoa! I'm nervous all of the sudden."

"Me too. It's going to be pretty damn embarrassing if they were the ones who had us ran off and we go knocking on their doors like a couple of clueless dumbasses," I admit, pulling the keys from the ignition.

"Kate, look! Isn't that Max?"

I focus my eyes on a guy across the parking lot. He has Max's build but his back is turned to us.

"I can't tell. He's too far away."

He slides on a helmet and climbs on a black Harley Davidson.

"It's probably him. You better yell at him before he leaves."

My face twist as I grab the handle. "When did he get a motorcycle?"

"Who fucking cares! Just yell! Jesus!"

I roll down the window and wave. "Max!"

His engine is cranked and can't hear me.

"Maxxxxx!" I jump out of the car and try again. "Dammit!" I throw my head back as he speeds off. "He doesn't know this car, and it's too far for him to tell it's us."

Lana climbs from the passenger's seat. "Don't worry, I'm sure he'll be back soon," She smiles, hoping to reassure me. "Let's go in and visit Drew for now."

It's Saturday afternoon and the halls are eerily quiet. We tiptoe our way to the end of the hall and immediately see Drew's things are gone through the crack in the broken door.

Her shoulders fall. "Damn, I thought he had another week."

"I'm so sorry, Lana. I know how much you wanted to tell him goodbye."

She lays her head against the wall. "It looks like this was an entirely wasted trip."

I sigh. "It definitely looks that way."

Her feet drag as we walk the dark, glum hallway. Sunlight peers through an open room door as we pass. We glance inside but continue on without speaking.

"Hey! I know y'all!" he shouts.

We stop and turn in unison. "Ya do?" Lana asks.

"Yeah. You're those girls from up around Atlanta, right?

She eyes him cautiously. "Uhhhh, maybe…"

He chuckles. "Oh, you two are infamous around here!"

"Why? Because we got ran out of here by your boss?"

"Well, *that* and the fact Andrews had two women in his bed."

"Literally scared us half to death." Lana laughs and invites herself in.

"Max told us about all the crazy stuff that happened in Panama City. We cracked up for days over it."

"Is he here, by chance?" I ask, taking a seat on his worn out, beige loveseat.

"Nah, you just missed him. Left about five minutes ago."

"Yeah, we thought we saw him. He was on a motorcycle, right?"

"Yep! That was him. I'm Sam by the way." He reaches out his hand. "But everyone around here calls me Artie."

"So let me guess. Your last name is Artsfield?" Lana asks.

He smiles. "Close. It's Armstrong, actually."

Lana twirls a sprig of hair as she sashays next to me. "I hate you missed out on all the Memorial Day weekend fun."

Artie looks different from the rest of the guys we've met. He's shorter than the others and has a runner's build. There's a gentle spirit about him and a kind, soft, tone to his voice. He's good-looking but doesn't seem to realize it. I see a small spark between him and Lana, but I'm too focused on Max to pay it much mind.

Someone's coming up the hall and it makes my stomach flip.

"Well, well, well. Look what the cat drug in." An unfortunate familiar voice says as he walks into Artie's room.

"Good to see you too, Davis," Lana says, jumping up to hug him.

I give a quick wave but I don't speak.

"You know Drew was discharged two days ago, right?"

"No, but figured it out when we saw his room cleared out."

He sits on the arm of the loveseat and sighs. "I'm going to miss that little bastard. He was one hell of a guy."

For the first time since we met, he actually sounds genuine.

I glance at my watch and tap Lana's arm. "As much as I would love to stay, we need to get on the road."

She turns her hands up. "I thought you wanted to wait for Max?"

"You'll be waiting a while. He's on a date," Davis says, back in his usual cocky tone.

"Oh. Okay," I manage to mutter. Hoping to sound cavalier.

Heartache stabs me in the chest but I refuse to let it show. I want to know every single detail of who he's with, what he's doing, and what's been going on since we left, but I don't ask.

It would hurt too much to know. And I refuse to look pathetic in front of Davis.

Lana's lip snarls. "Um, who the hell is he on a date with?"

"It's fine. That's his business." Interrupting her interrogation. "But we *really* need to get on the road." I glare at her hoping she gets the hint.

She reads my face and crawls from the small loveseat. "Are you guys going to the beach for the Fourth?"

"Yeah, I'm pretty sure we all are," Artie says.

She raises an eyebrow. "Good! We're staying at the Sunspree this time. Hopefully, we'll run into you."

Artie gives a bashful smile. "I sure hope so."

It's all I can do to choke out a goodbye as I fight back tears. "Thanks for letting us hang out, Artie." My eyes fall to his feet. "Maybe it's best you don't tell Max we were here."

Tears flood my eyes before I hit the door and I pray I make it to the car before breaking down. I don't want anyone to see me hurt. All I want to do is get the hell out of here as fast as I can.

Lana grabs my shoulder as I scurry to the car. "You ok?"

"This was a mistake. We shouldn't have come here," I say, between gritted teeth.

"*KATE?*"

"Keep walking, Lana!" I demand, recognizing Max's voice across the lot.

"Kate! Wait!" he yells, running towards us as I unlock the car door.

I quickly try to dry up tears and pat the splotches from on my face.

"Kate? Holy shit! You're here!" he says, grabbing my arm.

I slap on a smile. "Max. Hey..."

"I can't believe you're standing here! It's so good to see you." He wraps an arm around my neck and pulls me close. His woodsy cologne envelops me and it's all I can do to not break down in his arms. "I was so worried about you after that morning. The way things went down."

"We're ok. Lana wrote the phone number wrong and wanted to say a proper goodbye to Drew, so we rode down. But it appears we missed him."

He's sensing something wrong. I can see it on his face.

"I've thought about you constantly. It drove me nuts I had no way of getting a hold of you. I tried calling every listed Carpenter number in Alpharetta."

"You did?"

"Yes. Of course, I did. I knew I'd see you in a few weeks at the beach, but I didn't want to wait that long. I wanted to make sure you were ok."

I toe at a rock under my foot. *Was Davis lying to me about the date thing?*

"We saw you leaving. I yelled out to you." I say, hoping it will prompt him to say where he's been.

He glances at the car. "I thought I was hearing things. You're in a different car."

"This is my car." I thumb towards the aging, silver Prelude. "Unfortunately, no more Beamer."

He laughs. "You finally got driving a stick shift down, huh?"

"Pretty much," I say, realizing he deflected his whereabouts.

"Well, why don't you come back in so we can catch up on everything?"

"We can't, Max. I'm sorry. We've already been here longer than we should have. We were supposed to be home hours ago."

He looks at me with those eyes, the ones that make me melt. "For a few. Please?"

My heart wants to say ok so badly, but my head is saying no. I know who he was with. He loves her and I can't compete. Nor do I have any desire to be mixed up in some twisted love triangle. "We've been here since yesterday and it's Father's Day weekend. We're taking my dad out for dinner tonight."

His head cocks. "Since yesterday?"

"It's a long story. A long, crazy, typical Lana and Kate story."

"Ok," he says, reluctantly. "But I'll get to see you in a few weeks, right?"

"Yeah, of course. We will be down Thursday through Sunday."

He takes a deep breath of relief. "Good! Y'all staying at the same place?"

"I'm so sorry, Max. But we've got to get on the road. I'll see you in a couple of weeks though, ok?" I say, avoiding his question.

"Ok, Kate. I understand." His eyes fall as he pulls me in for another hug. He knows I know and he knows exactly who told me. But as he holds me, my guard falters enough to fall into his embrace.

Lana takes a swig of Dr. Pepper as we pass through the gate, headed home. "Maybe Davis was lying?"

"He wasn't. I'm sure of it. I read it on Max's face."

"But he sure seemed happy to see you."

"Do you mind if we don't talk about Max? I need some time to process all this," I ask, hoping she'll leave it be.

"Of course," she says, quietly.

I feel bad and try to lighten up the mood. "You sure did look like a smitten kitten with Artie."

"He was a sweetheart, wasn't he?"

"Very! Pretty damn cute too," I add.

"I know! It's like the hot guy capital of the world wrapped up in one damn building."

Lana falls asleep twenty minutes into the drive and I'm thankful for the silence. My mind's in a million places and I'm not sure what to make of any of it. I can smell Max on my clothes and it triggers flashbacks of us kissing in the rain. I can't be mad at him for going on a date. Hell, we aren't together. We have no commitments to each other. *But why does it hurt so much that he did?* He appeared genuinely happy to see me, even though there was confliction in his eyes. *Maybe I was the rebound?* Or maybe our time together showed him how much he missed her?

Ugh! I can't do this to myself. *Snap out of it, Kate!*

CHAPTER NINE
Fourth of July Weekend

"If I see one more fat, ugly, bleach blond, redneck degrading the American Flag with one of those bathing suits, I may lose my shit," Lana says, peering over the balcony railing of our big, beautiful, *clean*, hotel.

I pop open a Coors Light. "Awe, come on! I think they're cute."

"They are! But not on ninety-nine percent of the girls wearing them," she snarls.

I take a big swig of beer. "Oh, don't be such a snob!"

"So this makes how many for you today?"

"No clue. Lost count! HA!"

"You know, just because Max didn't come, doesn't mean you have to drown your sorrows in booze the whole weekend."

"No! It's *exactly* what it means!" Irritated she said his name. "I knew it was all too good to be true."

"Are you going to be able to handle Artie and them coming up here?"

"I'm fine, I promise. You two hit it off last night. I'm not going to let all this Max bullshit stand in the way of you two."

She slides her sunglasses up her nose. "There's a chance Davis might be with them."

"Oh, joy!" I groan. "Because I was hoping we could see just how miserable this trip could be."

Lana and I, along with our two closest friends Jenn and Ashley, arrived in town yesterday afternoon. Within an hour, Artie had made his way to our hotel. We met Davis later on, who enjoyed telling me all about Max and Jody getting back together and how he stayed in Columbus to spend the holiday with her.

We went to La Vela as a group and I tried my best to make the best of it. Trying to not let the news of Max ruin my trip. Lana and Artie hit it off right away and Davis and Jenn flirted all night. Which helped as a buffer since I wasn't in the mood for his antics.

"If he does grace us with his presence, it's only to see Jenn. Those two were all over each other last night."

"Actually, that's something I wanted to talk to y'all about," Jenn says, joining in on the conversation. "Last night, after everyone went to bed, Davis and I went for a little stroll on the beach." She lifts an eyebrow and grins.

"I *thought* I heard screams coming from the beach last night!" I shout.

"Well, that's the thing. We got there. One thing leads to another and next thing I know Davis has my jeans and underwear pulled down…"

Lana throws up her hand. "Ok, ok! We have the visual. Just get to the point."

I lean back in my chair. "Sounded like things were just getting interesting if ya ask me."

"Well, I had borrowed Ashley's cute combat boots last night, remember? But her feet are bigger than mine, so I had to double-knot them to keep them on. Davis was having a hell of a time trying to untie them, so I told him to pull hard. Well, when he did, I bounced across the sand like a skipping rock, straight over a big ass blue crab! Who proceeded to pinch me straight in the taint!"

Five seconds go by. Jaw dropped, we sit blinking.

"Ummm. Did you say a crab pinched you on your taint?"

"Yes! So now I have an entire beach coming out of my crotch and a cut straight across my no-man's-land and *still* didn't get laid!"

My chair slams on the balcony floor. "So it *was* you I heard! It just wasn't screams of pleasure!"

"Don't you know you're not supposed to have sex on the beach? It's literally *the* worst place imaginable!" Lana says, finally able to form words through the laughter.

Ashley was in the shower when Jenn told her story, so we got the pleasure of re-telling it. Laughing even harder the second time around.

"Dang, Jenn! You have the worst luck when it comes to crabs at the beach," Ash teases, reminding us of her Spring Break debacle.

After finally catching our composure, all three of them begin primping for the male visitors, who are due any minute. A cloud of perfume floats across our ransacked room. The idea of being stuck here in hook up heaven makes my skin crawl.

Ash slides on a pair of white jean shorts and pulls a t-shirt over her black bikini. I lean in to read the front of it. "Who's the Dave Matthews Band?"

"Duh! Only the most awesome band on the planet."

I shrug. "Never heard of em'."

She flips open a half-eaten pizza box. "I didn't see you when I got in last night. Did you sleep on the balcony?"

"Yep! Between Jenn's snoring and Lana and Artie yip yapping all night, it's the only place I could get some actual peace and quiet."

Lana grabs her heart. "He was so sweet, y'all! We stayed up talking until sunrise." Her hand flies to her mouth. "Oh, Kate! I'm so sorry! I didn't mean…"

Physical pain explodes through me, but I'd rather cut a limb off than let it show. "Pfff! Don't be sorry! I'm fine," I lie, waving her apology off.

I'm not in the mood for the added company, so I grab a fresh beer and walk out on the balcony when the guys knock. The room growing louder and louder as they file in. I wish I could slap on a happy smile and join them, but I can't seem to muster up the energy. I roll my eyes as Davis's boisterous voice carries over everyone. For some reason, I think he gets genuine pleasure from this whole Max thing.

They're talking about me like I'm deaf. "She's outside. She keeps saying she's fine, but I know it's bullshit."

I shake my head. *Lana knows me far too well,* I mumble to myself.

"I'll go talk to her," Davis says.

Oh please don't! I think as the balcony door flies open. I stare out at the ocean, not acknowledging him.

"How's it going, Skeeter?"

"Fine, until you got here, Lurch."

He laughs and steals the chair I'm using to prop my feet on. "You girls moved up a few stars on the hotel choice."

"Lana refused to stay anywhere else after she found a roach in her suitcase," I say flatly, still not looking over.

"Can't say I blame her," he chuckles.

I take a swig of beer. Already over the stupid small talk. "I'm ok, Davis. You don't have to babysit me."

"Oh yeah. You certainly seem it."

I roll my eyes, annoyed. Refusing to comment.

"Look! I get you think I'm the Tin Man and believe women fall at my feet…"

"…And you go through them like Tic Tacs? Yes. It's *exactly* what I think!" I say it harsher than I intend. He doesn't say anything and I can tell I've hit a nerve. "I'm sorry. I'm not trying to be rude." I say, dropping the attitude. "I'm pissed off and been drinking."

"I could tell you had fallen for him."

"It was stupid, I know. I actually thought there was something there." I say it to him, but speaking more to myself. I look at him for the first time. "I mean, am I wrong? Did I completely misread our time together?"

I can tell there's something he wants to say but is holding it back. "What?" I stare. "What aren't you telling me?"

He shifts in his seat. "I didn't want to be the one to tell you this…"

"Tell me what?" I demand.

The side of his mouth curls as he hesitates. "It might have been Drew… but I'm pretty positive Max is the one who had the Platoon Sergeant run y'all off."

Speechless, my hand covers my jaw dropped mouth. Memories of Lana and me darting across the front lawn as they all watched, flash in my head.

"But why? He knew we were about to leave on our own? Why would he go to the trouble?"

"I honestly have no idea, Kate."

"Well, if he was trying to humiliate us, it sure as hell worked!" I say as anger begins to boil.

"Look! I only told you because I thought you should know he isn't the saint you think he is."

My jaw clenches. "He most certainly is not." I unglue my body from the patio chair and make my way back into the room.

I don't want to spoil Lana's time, so it's best to keep this news to myself for now. I need to rally enough words to get out of the room without her suspecting something is wrong.

She looks up from the bed as I pass. "Where ya going?"

"James is down at the beach. I'm going to go hang with him for a bit." I force a smile while grabbing my ID and cash.

"Ok, Love!" she says, buying it.

Ashley jumps up from the other bed. "I'll go with you!"

Fuck!

James and Ashley are good friends, so it will look suspicious if I tell her not to come. "Sure. Grab your ID, just in case."

When we're finally in the breezeway, I explain what's going on. "If you don't want to go, you better turn back now."

"Where are you wanting to go?"

I look out at the city below and give an evil grin. "I feel like getting into a little bit of trouble."

It's late. I have no idea how late. I'm not only drunk...I'm one of those loud, obnoxious, stumbling, drunk girls I hate. Ashley and I are at Spinnaker's nightclub and I've somehow managed to win a hot body competition.

I slide off my barstool and give a pageant wave. "I would like to say a special thank you to whoever invented the padded bathing suit top." I give a big, beauty queen smile as I finish my pretend acceptance speech.

Ash glances at her watch. "Kate, I'm glad you're having a good time. But don't you think it's about time we head back?"

I ignore her. "Isn't my crown and sash beautiful?" I mumble to the guys who've taken up residence the table next to us.

"It's almost as hot as you are," one says, walking over and putting his arm around my neck.

"We *really* need to get out of here," she pleads.

"But I was just getting to know my new friends here," I stammer.

She gives them a cringy smile and grabs my arm. "You've had *way* too much to drink tonight. I've *got* to get you home."

I snatch my arm away. "Don't be such a buzzkill, Mom!"

She doesn't respond. Her lips tighten as she glowers at me. Her long auburn hair hits me in the face as she turns to walk away. The room begins to spin; my brain officially mush. I lay my head on the hard, sticky table.

I'm not sure how much time has passed when I feel myself being lifted. I squint enough to see I'm on upside-down on a shoulder, caveman style.

"Heyyyy! You made me drop my beautiful crown!" I yell, having no clue who has me.

"I've got your crown, Kate."

I lift my head to see who's following us. "Lanaaaaa! My best friend in the whole world!" I'm able to make her out even upside-down.

We make our way through the club. "I don't know who you are, but you've got a great ass." Getting an up-close and personal view. "I can walk ya know!" I yell as we make it out the door.

"You wouldn't know it by the way you were passed out on the table," the mystery carrier says.

I know the voice but my beer fog isn't letting it compute. They're all talking as the car pulls up. He sets me in the passenger seat. "Oh, great. It's *you*." Disappointment and nausea churning in my belly.

"What? Were you hoping it was Max?" Davis snarks sarcastically.

"Why are you here? Don't you have some sluts you should be screwing in some seedy motel somewhere?" I mutter.

"I know you're not my biggest fan, but I know what I said upset you. So when Ashley called and told us where you were. I had to come."

I give Ashley the evil eye and point. "Traitor!"

We slowly make it out of the parking lot and back on the Strip, but traffic is a nightmare. The hotel is in sight, but the lanes aren't budging.

Sweat beads on my forehead. "What's taking so long, Lana?" I whine.

"There must have been a wreck or something because this is worse than usual."

I try to get, "I'm not feeling so good" out when I feel it come. I tear at the handle and hurdle from the car. Stumbling to the side of the road before a day's worth of beer, six shots, a hot body contest, and one upside-down carry-out, catches up with me.

"We've got a pukin' rally, here!" spews from the car behind us. I shoot him the bird between retches.

Davis jumps out. "Don't make me come back there, asshole!"

His nose scrunches. "Feel any better?"

I get out, "a little" just before round two begins. He grabs my hair to hold it back and oddly enough…I appreciate it.

I finally feel more myself, but traffic still isn't moving. The thought of sitting in the car for the next hour isn't on my list of things to do tonight.

"Hey guys, I'm going to walk back, ok? I'm sure I'm going to get sick again and would rather not do it on the side of the road."

Ashley jumps from the backseat. "I'll go with you, Kate." Volunteering for more babysitting duties.

"Two drunk girls do not need to be walking the Strip alone," Davis says. "Hang with your friends, Ash. I'll take her back."

It's pointless to debate, so I start walking. Not giving a damn who follows.

"I don't need a babysitter. I'm fine by myself," I say as Davis jogs up behind me.

"And miss another chance of watching you barf your guts up? Not in a million."

I roll my eyes and keep walking.

"Honestly, I was worried about you."

My eyes grow suspicious, but I manage to get out a quick, "thank you" with some shred of sincerity.

"Besides…Jenn wouldn't stop getting in my face and her breath smells like a cat shit in her mouth."

"And *there's* the Davis we all know and love."

"I'm kidding. I'm kidding!" he chuckles as I get several steps in front of him. "You know you don't have to play the tough act with me, Kate. I know you're upset and you have every right to be."

I kick a crushed beer can across the road. "I'm not upset."

"You're a terrible liar."

"It was a one-time, crazy weekend; with plans to maybe do it again. I didn't ask for anything else from him. I have no right to be upset. He loves her. They have a history. He's a smart enough guy to not let some girl he met at the beach stand in the way of a potential future."

I search his face, hoping to convince myself as much as him.

"For what it's worth, I think he really did like you."

"Then why have us ran out of there? I keep replaying that morning over and over in my head and it doesn't make sense. We were leaving an hour later."

He shrugs. "I wish I had an answer,"

I stop dead in my tracks. "Unless…"

"Unless, what?"

"Oh my God! That's it!" I smack my forehead. "I've figured it out." Talking more to myself.

A group of girls scream out and it causes him to look away. They ask him if he needs a ride. They flirt back and forth, but I'm too in my head to wait on him.

He catches up. "Well, are you going to clue me in?"

"Jody must have been coming up there. He must have seen her on his way to PT and given him some indication she was going to meet him afterward."

"I didn't see her, but it doesn't mean anything."

"That has to be it! There's no other explanation on why he couldn't wait. He knew all hell would break loose if Jody saw me in his room."

"Sounds plausible for sure."

"It was still a dirty ass thing to do, regardless of the reason why. More like something straight out of the Davis playbook."

He grabs his heart. "Ouch, Kate! Harsh!"

"I know. I'm sorry. Well, sort of sorry," I tease, but with some truth to it.

I'm in desperate need of food as we make our way back to the hotel. I ask Davis if he would grab me a bottled water and a few snacks from the lobby vending machine, while I call the elevator.

A drunk guy with fraternity letters on his shirt, walks up and waits for alongside me.

"Heyyyy, I know youuuu," he slurs and points.

"Uh, sorry. I think you have the wrong person."

"No, I saw you. Earlier. You're that girl. The one from the contest."

"Ah… Yes. Not one of my prouder moments now that I'm sobering up."

He steps forward, his stale beer breath inches from my face. "You definitely deserved to win."

Uncomfortable, I take a couple of steps back. Not responding to his comment.

He stumbles towards me again. "What room are you staying in?" he asks, tugging at the sash I'm still wearing.

I'm pinned. "Please, don't touch me!"

Chips, cookies, and soda scatter across the lobby. "Get the hell away from her, asshole! Before I spill your blood all over this pearly white floor!" Davis yells, pushing him away.

The drunk bows his chest. "Damn. We were only talking, dude! You don't have to be a douche!"

"Come on, Davis! He's not worth it. Let's go!" I plead for him to get in the elevator, trying desperately to end this.

He does as asked, but as the doors begin to close, he gets in one last dig. "You better hope I don't see you again, Dickless!"

The drunk yells, "Fuck you, Asshole!" But thankfully, the doors have closed.

"Oh no, that son of a bitch didn't!" Davis says through gritted teeth, punching the lobby button. "I'm going to rip him to pieces!"

"Let it go, Davis." I grab his forearm, hoping to calm him. "You getting in a fight and ending up in jail won't go over too well with the Army."

He huffs, knowing I'm right. His attention turning to me. "You, ok?"

"I'm fine. Thanks for stepping in."
It's a quiet ride until the doors slide open to our floor.

"Thank you for walking me back. I guess I needed a babysitter after all."

After changing clothes, popping three ibuprofen, and getting some food on my stomach, I'm slowly feeling more myself. I make my pallet on the balcony and relish in the peace and quiet. Davis sits on a patio chair as I settle into my makeshift bed.

He leans on the back two legs and chuckles. "I still can't believe you're sleeping out here."

"Well, it's either out here or in there with Ms. Cat Shit Mouth."

"Ah-ha! Enough said."

"You don't have to sit up here with me. I'm sure you're ready to get back out there."

"Nah, I'm done for the night. I'd rather chill with you until Artie gets back, if it's ok?"

I bury my head in the lumpy pillow and yawn. "I'm ok with it. But I can't promise I won't pass out on ya."

We don't speak for a while as we both revel in the sound of the ocean. A warm breeze sweeps across the cool concrete. "So you're from Chicago, right?" I ask, breaking the silence.

"Yep! But it's been ages since I've been home."

"How come?"

"I haven't needed to. My parents and sister have driven down a few times, and we met in Nashville for Christmas last year. So it's been over two years."

"No long lost love you need to go back and see?"

"Hell no!" he says quickly. "I'm too much of an asshole to keep a girl around long enough to travel thirteen hours for."

"Well, you're a good-looking guy. Maybe if you drop the whole cocky asshole thing, you'd find one that's worth the drive."

"Most girls get on my nerves. I mean, it's fine for a quick flirt in a bar, but when I try to have an actual conversation, they're all so damn silly. I can't help but be an asshole. Besides, you're one to talk. From what I hear, that ex of yours is a real piece of work."

"Touché, Davis. Touché."
He laughs.

"You're right though. He's a tried-and-true douchebag," I admit. "But we run in the same circle, so he's always around. It got better after I left for college, but he always manages a way to rear his ugly head any time I'm home. Thankfully, I haven't seen him since Memorial Day. He found out we're still hanging with you guys. So I think he's a little intimidated."

"He should be. What he did was a bitch move."

"Yes, it was. And if I'm being completely honest, I think that's why I was so attracted to Max. He was the polar opposite of Wayne and I appreciated that about him."

The hotel room door creaks opens and voices grow. "Sounds like the Cavalry has arrived."

"I have some Tic Tacs in my purse if you want to casually pass some out as Jenn walks by."

"Oh look who's a comedian now," he says as the group makes their way onto the balcony.

After some late-night chit-chat and giving Jenn and Davis hell over the crab incident, we call an end to my night of heartbreak rebellion.

I lay alone, looking up at the stars. Hoping to convince myself to end this ridiculous notion of me and Max ever being more. I fall asleep trying to not focus on the disappointing outcome, but instead, grateful for the time we had.

CHAPTER TEN

The next morning, with a stiff back and an enormous hangover, I'm stirred from my makeshift bedroom by the voice of my annoying little brother.

"Wake your ass up," James says, nudging me in the side with his foot.

"Go away," I mumble.

He slips my plastic crown on top of his head. "I heard you were crowned Belle of the Ball last night."

"Please don't remind me of any of the stupid shenanigans I got myself into last night," I groan as Lana walks out to join the conversation.

"I also heard the tall, cocky one went and got you. Helped get you home."

"Oddly enough, as much as it pains me to admit it. Davis was actually pretty great last night. Don't get me wrong, he's still an asshole who gets on every nerve in my body. But he kept it in check last night."

"Did y'all? Ya know…" Lana smirks.

"Ew, Lana! No! Of course not."

"I wouldn't blame you if you did. He's a total babe," she says, fanning her face.

"He is. But he's way too vain. That's a deal-breaker."

He cringes. "Do y'all have to talk about this now? I'd rather not be a part of the *who my sister's banging* conversation."

"Oh my God! We didn't hook up!"

Today is the 4th of July and after a slow-moving morning, we spend our last full day relaxing on the beach. It's a glorious, hot summer day, and the beach is packed. A perfect breeze blows across the calm, crystal blue ocean. The thirty dollars we spent on the hotel beach loungers and umbrella has been worth every penny. I try to read the National Enquirer someone left in our hotel room, but I can't seem to focus.

"Hello? Earth to Kate."

"Huh?"

"I asked if you wanted a beer," Lana repeats as she digs around the cooler.

"Yuck! No thanks. The mere thought of beer makes my stomach churn."

"*Please* tell me you aren't going to be a drag on our last day. We have the fireworks show tonight and Artie's going to make a bonfire."

"I won't be, promise," I say, trying desperately to perk up. "Are we allowed to have fires on the beach here?"

"I doubt it. But when have I ever been a rule follower?"

"This is true."

"We've hardly had a minute to ourselves since we got here. This whole Max thing... I know you're disappointed he didn't come."

"I'm trying to not let it bother me, but I'm so confused by it all. Did Artie mention anything about it?"

She squirts sunscreen in her palm. "The only thing he said was Max had to CQ duty this weekend. And he highly doubted he was the one who had us ran off. Said he heard it was a big joke to mess with us. So who knows?"

"I guess it doesn't matter either way. He didn't come. That speaks volumes."

She doesn't respond as she rubs the last trace of white SPF 15 into her shoulder.

I slam the magazine in my lap. "What is CQ duty, anyway?"

"Hell, I don't know. I think it's a 'barracks bitch' rotation or something. Artie said he had it last weekend, and it was twenty-four hours of clock-watching, torture."

The sun has set on our last day. After feasting on bar-b-que, the entire group has settled in for a low key night on the beach. I make a weak vodka cran, but it's only to keep Lana off my back. Everyone gathers around the small fire to play "never have I ever."

"Ugh! I hate this game!" Ashley chuckles. "It always reminds me of how inexperienced I actually am."

"Never have I ever… had sex on the beach," Artie asks as the entire group erupts in laughter.

We all turn and eye Davis and Jenn. "Well, we know two people who certainly gave it the ole college try!" Lana yells as Jenn, Davis, Artie, and I all drink.

"It's not all it's cracked up to be," I admit.

Jenn grabs between her legs. "No shit! I'm still picking sand out of every orifice of my body."

"I've drank a bunch of sex on the beach cocktails. Does that count?" Ash adds, making everyone laugh.

"Never have I ever… had a threesome," Jenn asks.

Davis is the only one who drinks. "I'll be more than happy to knock that one off the list for any of you bi-curious ladies."

"Yes, volunteering your services is a true sacrifice," Artie teases.

"It's your turn, Kate," Lana says as she snuggles in between Artie's legs.

It takes me a few seconds to think of a good one. The group quiets in anticipation. A voice bellows in the darkness behind us. Our heads snap toward the top of the dunes.

"Never have I ever… driven three hours to spend one night with an amazing girl."

My mouth falls as butterflies explode. "Max!" Lana shouts.

He walks over and gently takes the vodka cran from my hand and takes a sip. The light from the fire flickers off his blue eyes as he leans over, dropping his helmet on the cooler.

I'm speechless as the shocked group welcomes him with hellos and hugs. "Holy shit, Max! I can't believe you're here! Artie says as he raises his hand for a high five.

Ashley stands and introduces herself. "So you're the Max I've heard so much about?"

"Did you really drive down here just for the night?" Lana asks in dismay.

"Yep! Had too. I felt terrible I wasn't able to get out of CQ Duty. No one was willing to give up their holiday to watch the desk. So as soon as I got off, I made a mad dash here." He eyes me as he finishes answering. "Thankfully, Artie had mentioned which hotel you were staying in or I might never have found you."

"I'm so sorry I wasn't able to be here sooner," he says quietly, loud enough for only me to hear.

I glance at Davis, who appears as shocked as I am at the sight of Max.

"I thought you…" I can't find the words. I'm so happy to see him it feels as if my heart might stop. But my head is spinning. All I do is stare. Those beautiful eyes of his looking straight into my soul.

"We missed you so much, Max. It wasn't the same without you here." Lana pipes, breaking the intense gaze between us. "I mean, don't get me wrong. We managed to stir up some trouble on our own."

He laughs. "Do I dare ask?"

"Kate won a…"

I interrupt her. "It was nothing!" Finally finding my voice, I jump to my feet. "Up for a walk?"

"I'd love to," he replies, but I can tell he senses something is wrong.

"Don't be gone too long. The fireworks start at nine!" Lana yells as we head toward the shoreline.

The beach is packed as everyone awaits the fireworks show. The moon is hidden behind clouds and it makes the beach feel ominous. The only light comes from random snips of flashlights, as a clatter of music from different radios pollutes the air.

"You're upset with me, aren't you?" Max asks as we make it to the water. "I'm so sorry I'm late getting here, I promise I did everything I could to get out of work."

I shake my head. "I can't put into words how it felt to look up and see you. But I won't lie… I'm super confused right now."

"Confused?"

I sit in the sand and settle myself, hoping to find the right words. "They told me you weren't coming." Forcing myself not to look at him.

He sits next to me. "I didn't think I was going to be able to when they left. The guy who was scheduled, conveniently 'got sick.' I was the back-up."

I process what he's saying before I speak. "Listen, Max. You driving here to spend a few hours with me might possibly be the sweetest thing anyone has ever done for me.

But why are you here? Why come all the way down here knowing you've started things back up with Jody?"

"Wait. What? Who told you I was back with Jody?"

I'm embarrassed but answer him. "Well, the guys told me you two were seeing each other again."

A vein on his forehead slowly protrudes as he shakes his head. "Let me guess. Davis?"
I don't respond, but he knows without me saying.

He rubs the nape of his neck. "I'm so sorry I wasn't able to get here sooner and even sorrier you had to hear it from anyone but me. But I promise you, the things he knows are entirely misguided."

I shrug one shoulder as I stare at the sand. "Well, it sounds to me like maybe there's some truth to it."

He looks out at the night sea and I can tell he's trying to find the right words to say. "Kate, from the moment I met you, my heart has been pulled in a hundred different directions…"

I interrupt. "Hold on now. I didn't ask for anything from…"

"Wait," he says, putting his hand on my arm. "Please, let me finish."

He moves in front of me. Forcing me to look at him. I'm holding back tears and growing more uncomfortable by the minute. *Don't cry, Kate! Don't you dare let him see you cry!*

He throws his hands up, frustrated with himself. "I've had a hole in my heart for months that I didn't think would ever heal. Bound and determined, I was either going to be alone or in a completely dysfunctional relationship for the rest of my life. I was in an absolute funk for months. Hell, the guys had to physically drag me here for Memorial Day.
I honestly wanted no part of it. But once I got here, I figured, dammit! I should at least attempt to have a good time.

So when the first night, this funny, Southern beauty comes walking into my life. It was like fate." He grabs my hands and my heart flutters. "Do you realize the second you stepped out of your dad's car that night and said 'hi', with your sweet accent and infectious smile of yours, I've been hooked. It's like you put a spell on me or something." He laughs.

I smile. Appreciative of his kind words. "But they said you were back with...," I pull my hands from his as I trail off.

"I know what they said. And for about five minutes I thought we were too." He rolls up on his knees. "See, when you and Lana took off that morning, I was a total mess. I had no idea how I was going to get a hold of you. Then I found out you had the number but hadn't called. I thought maybe the connection we felt was only in my head. So I tried to force you out of my mind. Next thing I know, Jody's standing in my doorway, filling my head with the *we're meant to be* bullshit. I went through the motions for about a week, knowing deep down it wasn't going to work. Then I saw you again. The second I laid eyes on you I knew I had made a huge mistake."
My lips purse as Father's Day weekend flashes in my mind.

"I also know Davis told you where I was. I saw it in your eyes and it about killed me."

I fidget with a stray thread on the bottom of my shirt. "So you didn't stay home because of her?"

"Of course not, ya goof! I ended things the same night. I promise there is nowhere else more I wanted to be. But I got stuck working last minute and made the dumb mistake of asking Davis to tell you."

I drum my fingers against my lip. Confusion rattling my brain. "So he lied?"

"It appears so because he knew I broke things off a couple of weeks ago."

"But it doesn't make any sense."

He flips his hands up. "I know. Unless maybe he's got a thing for you."

I shake my head hard. "Oh, that's absolutely not it. He knows I can't fucking stand him."

I turn towards the group. Davis is watching us but glances off when he sees us both looking. "It makes sense, come to think of it. You don't put up with his bullshit. It probably drives him nuts."

I close my eyes and dig deep for the courage to ask the question that's tormented me for weeks. "So you weren't the one who called your boss on us that morning?"

Max throws his head back and puffs out an exhausted breath. "Oh my God! Did he tell you *that* too?"

I grimace, feeling bad for believing it so easily. "He told me he heard it was you or Drew."

Max jumps to his feet, pulling me up with him. He places his hands on both my cheeks and looks straight into my eyes. "Listen to me. I would never and I mean *never* do that to you."

The tears I was fighting begin to fall. He wipes one away. "I know it sounds crazy because it was only one weekend. But I'm completely head over heels for you, Kate."

He pulls me into his arms and I cry. Between the lack of sleep, our talk, and his admission. I could no longer hold back. "I'm crazy about you too, Max."

He kisses me as the first round of fireworks light up the night sky. The clatter of the radio stations shifting to synchronized music.

Not wanting to waste a single minute of the few short hours we have left. We sit in silence, holding each other and kissing through the show.

Under the fire-lit sky, he pulls me close and whispers in my ear, "I'm going to marry you one day, Kate Carpenter. Standing right here, on this very beach."

And just like that, he held my heart in the palm of his hand.

Max scowls as we join back up with the group. "Where's Davis?"

Artie's smile fades when sees the scowl on Max's face. "He said he was meeting up with some girl he met on the last trip."

"It's probably the waitress from the Waffle House," clueless Lana says, trying to get a laugh out of us.

Hoping to diffuse their impending argument, I slide my arms around his waist. "It's not worth worrying about, Max. You know how he is."

He takes a deep breath. "Ya know what? You're right. Tonight is about you and me. I can deal with him later."

"Well! You two officially have twelve hours to catch up on five weeks. Better make the most of it!" Lana says.

I slip out of Max's arms and take a sip of my watered down vodka cran. "It wouldn't be the first time we've pulled an all-nighter. Maybe this time we can make it through the night without getting run off by the police."

"Or get into a fight and forced to steal a car!" Max adds. Everyone laughs, but we can both see Artie doesn't find it quite as funny as we do. So Max sits and tries to quickly pull the subject off of our previous adventure weekend and on to the current one.

"So Lana, what were you saying Kate won?"
I stare in desperation for her not to spill the beans.

"Please don't...." I beg with pleading eyes.

"Oh, she got her drunk ass on stage at Spinnaker's and danced her way into winning a hot body contest."

"… And she does." I cringe, completely mortified.

Max turns to me in dramatic animation. "Ohhhhh, Really?"

"Yes," I admit. "*But!* In my defense, I was dared to do it and you know me…it's hard to turn down a challenge."

"It was hilarious, Max. She ran off with Ash and by the time we found her, she was so inebriated Davis had to throw her over his shoulder and tote her out."

Unfortunately, the mere mention of Davis's name brings immediate irritation back to his face. "So he played Prince Charming this weekend, I see," he groans, quietly.

"Oh, it was nothing. He happened to be around during his downtime between conquests," I whisper back, trying desperately to downplay the night.

"Well, if we're telling on each other. How about this one… Lana farted in her sleep this morning and Artie was AWAKE!" I shout.

Lana gasps, turning ten shades of red. "*Please* tell me you're lying!"

"Nope!" I fan my nose. "It stunk up the room too!" It didn't, but I add it for theatrics.

She buries her head in her hands, too embarrassed to look at Artie as everyone breaks into hysterics. Even Max's furrowed brow falters in laughter. *Nothing like a good ole fart joke to help ease the tension!* I think. And quickly take advantage of the mood shift to get the hell out of dodge, before anything more can be said.

Looking for any excuse to leave, I ask Max if he's hungry. "Have you had dinner yet?"

He rubs his perfectly toned stomach. "Now that you mention it, I am pretty hungry. Want to go grab something?"

"There's a Taco Bell across the street. We could make a Run for the Border." I say, grabbing his hand to pull him up from the sand.

He raises his voice loud enough for the group. "I gotta go get filled up on bean burritos, so Lana and I can have a farting contest later."

Lana shouts, "Oh my God! I hate y'all!" as laughter explodes through the group again.

It's going on eleven and The Strip is as wild as ever. Max and I take our time walking to the restaurant. Enjoying all the craziness that makes Panama City Beach so infamous. But with the celebration of the holiday added in, it appears everyone's in particularly rare form. There's a comradery tonight. American flags wave as people shoot off bottle rockets, sporting their patriotic red, white and blue attire.

Max takes my hand as we jog across the busy parkway. "I guess the Fourth has everyone in the mood for country music, because 'Family Tradition,' was playing from almost every car that passed by."

"I'm never going to get that damn song out of my head now," I groan as we make it inside the packed Taco Bell.

I pull sweaty hair off my neck as we file into the ridiculously long order line. Max belts out the lyrics to the famous Hank Williams Jr. song and sounds surprisingly good.

"I'm impressed, Max! If this whole Army thing doesn't work out, maybe you should try singing as your next career."

He rolls his eyes. "Yeah, right!"

I give a sly grin. "You're certainly hot enough to be a singer."

He cocks his head and smiles. "You think I'm hot, huh?" Poking his finger into my side.

"Take a look around." I throw my gaze across the dining

room. "Every one of these girls has been staring at you since we walked in the building. You'd think I was splitting tacos with the President."

He nudges me with his hip. "Oh, come on now. That's not true."

We step up to the register. "Whatever you say, Mr. President."
The lady taking our order is frazzled by Max's presence and makes a terrible attempt at hiding it. She throws in an order of cinnamon twist to make up for the long wait, although no one else is given the same freebie.

"Case in point." I smirk as he struts away from the counter.

He laughs. "Maybe she could tell how hungry I am."

I raise a knowing brow and chuckle. "Right. That's it."

After catching Max up about mine and Lana's crazy night sleeping in the Walmart parking lot and him telling me how he called every Carpenter in the phone book the week after Memorial Day, it was time to head back to the hotel.

"So do we count this as our first official date?" I shout as dodge cars across the Strip again.

"Absolutely not!" he yells back. "Watching some guy pull down his pants to pee in a trashcan cannot count as our first date!"

I chuckle. "But I thought the drunk girl who smashed her boobs against the glass was the highlight of the dinner."

Everyone's crashed out when we get back to the room, so we quietly make our escape to my room under the stars.

"Sleeping on concrete feels like I'm back in boot camp! My back's going to feel like a ninety-year-old's by the morning."

Max teases, trying to find a comfortable position on the balcony floor.

I slide in beside him. "We'll be fine as long as a thunderstorm doesn't pop up."

He pulls me close. "Oh, I remember us handling the rain quite well in the past."

"Very true," I admit.

He wraps his arms around me and gives me a kiss on my forehead. I close my eyes and breath in his amazing scent. Still shocked at this wonderful turn of events.

"Max?"

"Yes?"

"Thank you for coming. I can't put into words how much you coming here means to me."
With my heart full and passion pulled from my core, I kiss him. A long, slow, intense kiss, leaving me breathless and yearning for more.

We're nothing but lips and hands for a good twenty minutes. But force ourselves to stop. Both agreeing our first time together shouldn't be on the dirty concrete of a hotel balcony. Instead, we stay up the entire night talking, laughing, kissing and holding each other. His Army Company will be out of touch for a few weeks for field training, but we make plans for me to come to Fort Benning as soon as they're back home. We also make one hundred percent sure we both have each other's "correct" phone numbers this time.

We lay entwined in each other as we watch the sun slowly rise in the horizon, bringing a silent sadness between both of us. With the beginning of the new day, comes the end of our whirlwind night together.

CHAPTER ELEVEN
Lana's 18th Birthday Weekend

Lana's uncle Jack owns a small, but popular, pizza restaurant in Alpharetta, called DiMaggio's. It's been our summer job for several years and it works out perfectly since he gives us time off pretty much whenever we need.

With Max and Artie in training, Lana and I keep busy with extra shifts and the occasional night out with Jennifer and Ashley. But no matter how hard we try, nothing compares to our Fort Benning life. We talk about them incessantly, reminiscing about our crazy adventures. They've changed us, or at least brought out a part of us neither one of us knew existed. We're passionate about things far greater than the little bubble we've always known. In our eyes, nothing compares to them or the happiness we feel when we're with them.

Lana wipes pizza sauce off the prep line. "Is it me or has the last two weeks felt like an eternity?"

"Yes! And thank God there's light at the end of the tunnel!"

"What do you think Artie has planned for my birthday?" she quizzes again, for the millionth time.

"Even if I knew, I wouldn't tell you, Lana. He clearly wants it to be a surprise."

"Errrr! The anticipation is killing me!"

I adjust the tie on my apron and chuckle. "Good things come to those who wait."

Unbeknownst to Lana, Max has already spilled all the details of Artie's birthday plans. He made reservations for the four of us at a steakhouse in Columbus and bought tickets to see Journey in concert at the civic center. Since Lana has an amazing talent for getting things out of me, pretending I don't know anything is the best option to ensure it remains a secret.

"Well, at least tell me what time you're wanting to get on the road?"

"Jack doesn't have anyone to fill my shift Friday night, so it'll be nine or later before we can head out."

Her nose crinkles. "Nine? Why can't Carlos stay over?"

"I tried, but his brother's getting married on Saturday and he has to be at the rehearsal dinner, and Rob can't do it because he's already covering Saturday's shift for me."

Her shoulders fall. "Well, shit! That sucks."

"Don't worry. If we're on the road by nine-fifteen, we should be there by ten-thirty. The night will just be getting cranked up there." I sling pizza dough in the air. "Let's hope the damn hurricane brewing in the Gulf doesn't screw up any of our plans."

She throws her hands on her hips. "Oh, we're going! Come hell or high water, we're going!"

The remainder of the week inched by as slow as the last two. But a late-night call from Max letting me know they'd made it back to Post and how excited he is to see me, helps to relieve the heartache I've had bottled up since our time apart.

After a quick chat about our travel plans, my curiosity gets the best of me. "So are things still awkward with you and Davis?"

"Eh, a little, but he apologized. Said it was a misunderstanding. Blamed the rest of it on booze."

I pull the cordless off my shoulder as I climb into bed. "That's good, I guess."

"Yeah, it's better than it was when we first got back. We have to work and live together, so we had to call some kind of truce. I love the guy, but I'm still leery about him being around you. Which is why I'm glad we have plans *far* away from Post this weekend."

I kick my leg in the air. "Finally! This has been the slowest four weeks of my life!"

"You better rest up tonight because we have a month of catching up to do this weekend."

I roll into my stuffed panda bear and smile. "And I can hardly wait!"

"Do me one favor though…" His tone grows serious. "Keep an eye on the weather, ok? Hurricane Alexander is headed toward Alabama, but it's supposed to cause some pretty shitty weather for Georgia tomorrow."

My heart melts from his concern. "I've been keeping an eye on it. They think it'll just be some heavy rain. I'm sure it will be fine."

"I'm serious, Kate. If it gets bad, promise me you won't chance it."

There isn't a snowball's chance in hell I'm missing an opportunity to see Max over some rain. But I don't want him to worry so say a quick, "We won't, I promise." Before saying goodnight.

"Beep. Beeeep. Beeeeeeep. The National Weather Service has issued a tropical storm warning for all counties in Georgia beginning at 6:00 p.m. Eastern standard time." The message scrolls across the top of the local ABC channel as I and the other few employees at DiMaggio's, sit in the empty dining room, playing cards.

"It doesn't look too terribly bad," I say, gazing out the restaurant window.

Jack looks at me like I'm nuts. "You're kidding, right? Kate, the trees are literally doubled over."

I sigh. "Wishful thinking I guess. I'm praying it eases up in the next little bit."

"There's no way you and Lana are still planning on going to Fort Benning tonight, are you?"

I worry he'll rat us out to Lana's parents if I say yes, so quickly play it off. "No. No, not at all. We canceled it yesterday. I was only hoping it might fizzle out in time for us to still make it."

Relief floods Jack's eyes as the power flickers off and back on again. "Well, it clearly looks like we aren't going to get any business tonight, so we might as well close up early; get you three home before it gets any worse."

My heart begins to race the second he has the words out of his mouth. Hurricane Alexander is *not* going to screw up our weekend. I make a quick call to Lana to tell her we're going to be able to get on the road sooner than planned.

By the time I pick her up, the weather has died down to a slight drizzle and I feel confident we can make it to Fort Benning before the next band moves through.

"See! It's not as bad as they're saying. We'll be fine," I say as she climbs in.

Water flings across the dashboard as she fumbles her umbrella closed. "I sure hope your stick shift driving has gotten better because this might be one hell of a drive."

We've made it thirty minutes down 1-85 when another weather advisory breaks over the radio. This time warning us of potential flash flooding. Within minutes, the rain begins to fall again.

Heavier and heavier each mile we travel until the cars in front of us are no longer visible.

"Kate," Lana says flatly. "Maybe this wasn't such a good idea."

Other than the light illuminated by the harsh lighting, the road is pitch black. We slow to fifteen as the blinding rain falls in sheets. The windshield wipers are no match for the intensity of the storm. We join a slow caravan of cars, all with our flashers on. Some fleeing to the sides of roads and under bridges. Trees whip violently back and forth, many snapped from their roots. Limbs, trash, and debris fly through the air and sweeps the road. The power of the vicious wind jostles the car. It's all I can do to keep it on the road. I don't dare speak, forcing myself to stay calm. I grip the steering wheel tight, knowing even the slightest of distractions could cause devastating results.

Hickory Creek is about to crest the top of the road as we cross the bridge outside Newnan. It won't be long before the interstate is completely impassable. The car shimmies, then fishtails into a full hydroplane. I release the clenched grip on the wheel and lift off the gas.

Lana grabs at my shoulder in desperation. "Oh, God. Please help us!"

The car straightens, but this was a sign. The sinking in my gut screams at me to turn around and head home. No words are spoken as I get off at the next exit and turn back on the northbound side. Heartbroken and disappointed, both of us know this is our only option.

To avoid any more time in the madness, Lana agrees to wait out the storm at my house. It's late by the time we finally make it back, both mentally shot. The power's out, adding to the ominous mood of the night. By the light of a candle, we try to call the guys to break the unfortunate news.

After a long night of intense rain, destructive winds, and tornado warnings, we finally make it to morning. The power is still out but the worst of the storm is over. Leaving the great state of Georgia flooded, dark, and somber.

"Dammit! The line's still busy," Lana scoffs, slamming the phone down for the fiftieth time. "How can it *still* be busy?"

I use a flashlight to guide my way through the house. "The storm must have knocked their phones out. If it got this bad up here, imagine how it must be down there," I shout from the kitchen.

"We were supposed to be there last night. They must be worried sick," she says as I walk into the room.

"The storm was the last thing Max and I talked about. I promised him we wouldn't chance it if it got bad. I'm sure they've figured it out and will call as soon as they can. In the meantime..." I pull a honey bun with a single lit candle from my behind my back. "We have some birthday celebrating to do!"

Her face brightens as James, his buddies, and I break out in a terrible rendition of "Happy Birthday."

"Sorry, I don't have a cake. Thanks to Hurricane Alexander I had to improvise." She blows out the candle and smiles for what feels like the first time in days. And with heartfelt sincerity, thanks me for bringing a little joy to this crappy weekend.

"Remind me to kick Alexander's ass for screwing up my birthday," she says, licking honey bun frosting from her fingertips.

Besides trying to get through to Max and Artie, we spend the remainder of the weekend trapped inside playing Uno and Scrabble with James and his friends.

Slowly things begin to improve and power is restored throughout the city.

With a serious case of cabin fever, Lana and I agree to pick up the Sunday night shift for Jack. Which turns out to be a blessing, because the restaurant is slammed. Busier than a Saturday night during college football season.

The bell on the door jingles as the last customer leaves. "Tonight was *complete* insanity!" I shout as clear off their table. "I guess everyone was sick of being cooped up."

Lana flings her dirty apron across the counter. "I'm pooped! *But* I made $212.00 in tips, so totally worth it!"

I flip the door sign to closed. "I haven't counted mine yet, but I'm sure it's somewhere in the ballpark."

"Are we going to try to call the guys tonight? Surely the phones are back up by now," she asks.

"It's midnight, Lana. Even if the phones are back on, they have to work in the morning. I doubt they're still up."

She sighs. "You're probably right. As much as I'm dying to talk to Artie, I guess I'll wait until tomorrow."

After scrubbing the ransacked restaurant, I drag myself home, making it to bed around one in the morning. I'm dog tired, but unable to unwind. Restless, I toss and turn. Too curious to know if the phone lines on Post are back up. I give it a shot and squeal with happiness as the glorious sound of ringing comes from the other end. *No more busy tone!*

I hang up and fall asleep contently, knowing I'll finally be able to talk to Max tomorrow.

Exhausted and taking advantage of every minute of my day off, I sleep until noon. Spending the rest of the day in PJ's, catching up on the latest scandal on Days of Our Lives.

Mom's made my favorite dinner tonight. Her famous chicken and rice with fried okra and cornbread. I devour the amazing meal, monitoring the clock, counting the minutes to six.

I convince myself it's best if I let Max call me. As dad always says, 'No one likes a girl who's too needy.' So when eight rolls around and no word from him, I start to get a little antsy. Not wanting to cave, I occupy the time by calling Lana instead.

"Have you heard from Artie yet?" I ask as she answers.

"No," she whines. "I was hoping you were him."

I chuckle. "Sorry to disappoint."

"I wonder what could be taking them so long. You don't think we should be worried, do you?"

"I sure as hell hope not. But won't lie, I've had a weird uneasy feeling in my gut all day. I felt it when we were on the road Friday night too. I don't know why, but I can't seem to shake it."

The line goes quiet. "I'm sure we're just being paranoid," she says.

I change the subject to ease our minds. "Did you hear about what happened at Carlos's brother's wedding?"

"I did! He said they were literally saying their vows in a foot of water."

"I know. Bless their hearts. Looks like we weren't the only ones Alexander screwed this weekend."

"That bastard!" she growls.

"By the way, you should have come for din…"

She stops me mid-sentence. "Hang on, Kate. Someone's beeping in." Quickly switching the line over.

Within seconds, she's back. "Eeeeee! It's Artie!" she squeals. "I'm sure Max is going to call as soon as we get off, so call me back as soon as y'all are done, ok?"

I hang up beaming with anticipation over the impending call. I haven't been this excited over a guy in...well, *ever*.

Unfortunately, because there are only two phones in the building, it will take a while before it's Max's turn. So I nervously clean my room, hoping it will help the time go by faster.

I'm arranging shoes in the closet when to my surprise, the phone rings minutes later. A big stupid grin stretches across from ear to ear. *Chill out! It's just a phone call!* I say to no one, taking a deep breath as I lift the phone.

"Hello?" I beam from ear to ear.

"Kate…"

My smile drops. Lana's tone is flat and whittled with concern, causing that gut feeling to rush through me again.

"What's wrong?"

She doesn't answer right away. She sniffles. "I have something to tell you."

I swallow the lump in my throat. "Did someone die?"

"No. No. It's nothing like that," she quickly says. "But it's still not good."

I don't speak, waiting for her to continue.

She repeats, "I have something to tell you." But this time adds, "And I'm going to need you to sit down."

I'm becoming irritated at her stalling but I do as she says. Taking a seat on the corner of my bed. "Ok. I'm sitting."

She is silent for a few seconds and I can tell she's having a difficult time saying whatever she needs to say.

"Kate,…Max…Max got married."

Frozen. I'm completely frozen as her words swirl in my head. My hand slowly lifts to my mouth, unable to speak. The receiver slipping from my shoulder as my body begins to tremble.

"Wha…I…how?"

"There's more," she says, reluctantly. "Evidently, Jody showed up at Max's door Friday night with a positive pregnancy test in her hand."
Speechless, I slide off the end of the bed and onto the floor as every nerve in my body numbs.

"Artie said she spent half the night begging him to marry her. Said he could hear her crying and pleading through the walls. And by morning she'd convinced him marrying her was the honorable thing to do."

"Lana, please tell me this is some sick, twisted, joke and this isn't really happening right now?" I plead, gasping for breath.

"Kate, you know I would never joke about something like this."

"But how? I don't understand!" I shout.

"I guess fearing he might change his mind, she pulled together a quick shotgun wedding at the chapel on Post Saturday night. Artie told me he was the best man."

I'm taking an emotional bullet with each wave of new information. I physically can't stomach any more.

"I have to go," slamming the phone down. Vomit rises as I race to the bathroom to throw up Mom's dinner.

I lay on the bathroom floor in a crumpled ball and cry until sunlight seeps through the blinds. Forcing me to admit it wasn't all a dream. I was living this nightmare. In one short five-minute phone call, it's over. Just like that.

CHAPTER TWELVE
Labor Day Weekend

The pain I've experienced over the last four weeks is indescribable. Those three little words, *"Max got married,"* still haunt me to my core. Every ounce of my heart, body, and soul is broken. Every moment spent together destroyed. Every thought of a possible future, shattered. I'm hurt, humiliated, and angry all rolled into one. And even though I know without a shadow of a doubt, Max marrying her *was* the right thing to do, I want to hate him. I want him to feel pain like I do. I want him to know the rage that courses through my veins.

How could he do this to me? How could he allow me to hear it from anyone other than him? Call me selfish, I don't care. Say I'm living in a fantasy world to believe I deserved an explanation. He never even made an attempt. Not a single one. It was as if I had never existed. Max said he was going to marry me on the beach one day. I guess the jokes on me.

Lana stayed with me every night the first week. Although I was inconsolable at times, she was the perfect best friend. She was my rock. She let me cry when I needed to cry. Scream when I needed to scream and left me alone when she knew I needed to be alone. She filled my shifts at work and forced me to get out of bed each day. I bought cigarettes, got drunk for four days straight and even had hate sex with Wayne. All without a single word or shred of judgment from her.

School started last week. Lana and I moved into our apartment together in Athens, not far from campus. The pain is still there, but I'm coping better. Or at least I'm doing a better job at hiding it. I've buried it deep in my soul, along with any ridiculous fantasies of Max showing up at my door to tell me it was all some huge mistake.

The bags under my eyes from lack of sleep are finally fading and I'm able to eat a full meal without feeling sick. I remind myself daily, I can count on one hand the number of times Max and I were together. *One. damn. hand!* I tell myself being torn up over someone I barely know is completely ridiculous. It was a silly summer crush and just like summer, it's over.

Lana and Artie are still together and going strong. The Journey concert was rescheduled for mid-August, so she spent the weekend in Fort Benning having a birthday do-over. I was invited and wanted to be supportive of the two of them, but I couldn't go. I opted for a much more exciting weekend of staying home, reading Pride and Prejudice; while assuring myself my own Mr. Darcy is out there somewhere.

I'm not sure when or if I'll ever be able to go back to Columbus. The wound is still too fresh, too deep. Lana doesn't talk about Artie much out of respect for me, but I can see how happy she is. She deserves it and I tell her every day.

I told her I didn't want to know any more about Max. I made her promise me, even if I get sloppy drunk and beg her for the latest details, she would keep them to herself. As far as I'm concerned, I never want to hear the name Chase Maxwell ever again. My heart can't take it.

It's Thursday, the beginning of the long Labor Day weekend. Typically we would be beach-bound, but the mere thought of going back to Panama City makes me physically sick to my stomach.

My brother and a few of his friends made plans to head north for the holiday. They rented a cabin in Gatlinburg and are going white water rafting down the Nantahala River. Lana had never been and thought it would be the perfect alternative to the beach. And since I'm doing good to actually shower these days, she took over the reins of planning. She rented us our own cabin and invited Artie and whoever else wanted to go. I'm not sure if I'm ready to be around Max's friends yet, but since Lana and Artie are still together, I guess it's something I'll have to get used to.

I sit on the hood of Lana's car and light the end of a cigarette. "So did he tell you who all was coming?"

"When are you going to quit smoking those disgusting things?"

"Please don't bitch. It's a coping mechanism," I say, blowing a big puff of smoke in her face.

She fans the air and coughs. "Well, you smell like an ashtray."

I repeat, more annoyed this time. "Are you going to answer the question?"

"What question?" she snips, flipping open a Tennessee road map.

As I start to ask again, Santos's blue Mustang creeps into the gas station meeting spot. Even though I know Max isn't with them, I'm nervous. Before it's in park Artie leaps from the passenger's seat. He swoops Lana in his arms and causes a pang of envy in my chest. Slowly, Jackson and Santos make their way out. I see the large outline of the fourth person in the back seat and know immediately it's Davis.

I should be furious he's with them but for some reason, I can't find the strength. Our eyes meet as he climbs from the car and although we don't speak, he mouths, "I'm sorry."

"It's great to see ya Jackson, but I'm a little surprised. I figured you'd be spending the holiday with Gigi," Lana says.

"Eh, we're on a bit of a break. Long-distance is proving to be harder than we thought. The jealousy monster is a true and evil thing and anytime we're apart, it rears its ugly damn head. We both turn into terrible versions of ourselves."

I guess I'm not the only one licking the wounds of a broken heart this weekend.

After everyone says their hellos, Artie looks my way. "So what's the plan?"

I shake my head. "Don't ask me. Lana's the travel coordinator for this trip."

Lana claps her hands. "Well, first we need to go by and pick up Jenn and Ashley. I figure Jenn can ride in Santos's car with Davis, and you can ride with us. I was just checking the map. It looks like we'll have time for two pee breaks and still make it to the rental office before it closes."

I chuckle when Davis grimaces at the plan. Four hours trapped in the car with Jenn is the payback he deserves.

The drive to Gatlinburg is going by fast. I can tell Artie is making a wholehearted effort to avoid any subjects related to Max. And I'm proud of him for putting up with the antics of three cackling gals, as we take the "What is Your Sex Position IQ," quiz from my Cosmo.

Once we arrive and unload the ridiculous amount of luggage Lana packed. We take the grand tour of our huge mountaintop chalet. It has an incredible view of Mount LeConte and a partial view of downtown Gatlinburg. The leaves are beginning to turn, creating a beautiful light orange and red hue across the skyline.

The main room of the four-bedroom cabin has tall open windows, soaring to the top of the beamed ceiling. Upstairs is a loft overlooking the living room, with a pool table, dartboard, and an air-hockey machine. The best part, a gorgeous wrap-around porch with a swing and an eight-person hot tub.

"Damn, Lana!" Santos shouts. "This house is off the chain!"

"Yep! My parents hooked us up!" she says, giving him a high five. "Granted, they think it's only us girls and have no idea we are housing half the US Army," she adds, pinching Artie on the ass.

"Should we go ahead and assign beds?" Jenn asks.

Davis rubs his hands together. "I'm sure I will make my way through them all before the weekends over. I bet this town's crawling with hot, single ladies in desperate need of a good hair pulling, ass smacking, bang fest."

Lana rolls her eyes as she grabs her bag up. "You're not bringing any of your slutty pickups back to our nice cabin, Davis."

He cocks his famous smirky grin. "Who needs to go out when I have a house full of single women right here?"

As hot as some hair-pullin', ass smackin' sex sounds…I'm positive I will *not* be hooking up with anyone this weekend. *Especially* Davis, so I quickly volunteer to take the sleeper sofa. I make a drink and unpack our groceries while the others disappear to the bedrooms to divvy out sleeping arrangements.

"So what's on the agenda for tonight?" I ask Lana as she makes her way back into the kitchen. Thankful she took care of all the planning.

"Well, I thought it would be fun to hang here tonight." She pops the top of a Coors Light.

"Artie's going to throw burgers on the grill and Ashley is dying to try out the hot tub."

"I think James and his bunch want to come over later," I add.

Lana lifts her beer in the air. "Sounds like one hell of a night if ya ask me!"

It's early evening and the sun is setting. A slight chill is in the air, but not cold enough to need coats yet. My feet scuff across the porch as I sway back and forth in the swing. Cigarette in hand, taking advantage of a few minutes of quiet time. The porch door creaks open behind me.

I don't speak as Davis comes and sits in the swing beside me. "Since when do you smoke?"

"You know this thing probably has a weight limit," I say, ignoring his question.

"You calling me fat?"

"No, but with your six-five, two hundred-forty pound Lurchy ass, it's definitely questionable," I snip, straight-faced.

"Are you going to be mad at me all weekend?"

"Probably." I look at him and crack a smile, breaking the tension. He playfully throws an arm around my neck, giving me a noogie on the top of the head.

I nudge him in the side with my elbow. "If you mess up my hair I'm going to kill you!"

As I straighten up his smile falls. "I'm sorry about everything. I know Max…"

I throw my hand up. "Davis! Stop! Please don't. There's absolutely no reason to discuss *him* or any of what happened. It's all water under the bridge."

He turns his body towards me. "But I feel like I owe you an explanation."

I stand to leave. "There's no reason. I'm over it. *Completely* over it." I'm lying and he knows it.

James and his friends have joined us and the night is in full swing. Lana, Artie, Ashley, Santos, and I are in the hot tub, while everyone else is upstairs in an intense game of pool. Music and laughter echoes through the house, bringing a much-needed smile to my face.

Artie's made friends with a raccoon whose made camp under our porch and he's throwing Cheez-It's down to it.

Lana grabs a handful and throws a few. "It's so stinking cute!"

I sit on the side of the hot tub and watch. "You know if y'all keep feeding the damn thing, it's never going to go away."

"Yuck!" Ashley shutters. "It probably has rabies."

"It doesn't have rabies, ya dumbass! But Kate's right. It'll probably be back tomorrow with all his friends," Lana says, swatting a handful of water at her.

"What are y'all looking at?" Davis asks as he rounds the side of the porch with Jenn in tow.

"Ooh la la! It's hot tub time!" she squeals.

Lana's the first to answer. "Artie made friends with a raccoon. Come look!"

I've kept some distance from Davis tonight and having Jenn around has helped. He's actually tolerating her better than he did at the beach. Perhaps it's due to his lack of options. Either way, I'm thankful.

Ashley and Santos hit it off right away, and before long it's clear everyone is pairing up. Even my brother brought a girl from home to occupy him for the weekend.

I'm in couple hell!

"Damn, Ashley! Those are some nice floaties ya got there! Who knew you had those hid under all those good girl shirts of yours." Everyone laughs. "Maybe you can let Skeeter Bites over there borrow some."

I flip him off and I give him an eat shit and die look. "I'm actually pretty tired, y'all. I think I'm going to crash for the night."

Ashley whines. "Oh, Katie! Don't be a party pooper! Davis was only joking around."

"She's right. I'm just cuttin' up. You don't have to run off," Davis chides.

Thankfully, Lana can read my mind and knows I've had enough of Davis and all the coupling up.

"What time are we supposed to be on the bus in the morning?" I ask.

She speaks loudly for the whole group. "We have to be out of here at seven. It's a two-hour bus ride to the river. We'll have a short safety briefing and should be putting rafts in the water by nine-thirty."

"What time is it now?" Artie asks.

"It's after one, I think."

"Damn! If we have to be up and gone that early, maybe we all need to call it a night," he says.

Jenn gives Davis a sly grin. "Mmmmm, sounds good to me."

I throw my hand up for a quick wave. "And on that note…Goodnight all! Except you, Davis. I hope you get mauled by a bear in your sleep."

By the time I change clothes and ready for bed, James and his bunch are gone and everyone else in the house had headed toward their arranged bedrooms. Which is good, since I am the one sleeping in the middle of Grand Central Station.

Tipsy, I fumble around the couch in the dark, talking to myself. "How the hell do you fold this fucking bed out?"

"Need some help?"

"Jesus Christ! You scared me half to death, Davis!"

He laughs. "Sorry. I was trying to give Jenn some time to pass out."

I pull the cushions off the couch. "Finished already? Maybe you don't live up to all the hype after all."

"Oh, look who has all the jokes tonight." He throws a side-eye as he joins me. "She's sweet and all, I'm just not feeling it." He pulls the handle, exposing the thin, lumpy mattress.

I grab a sheet and spread it out over the bed. "It looked like you two were hitting it off pretty good tonight."

He grabs the blanket and pillow and helps me finish. "Ehhh, she doesn't blow my skirt up."

"I guess as long as she's blowing *something*, that's all that matters."

He shakes his head. "And they call *me* the perv."

Davis pulls the covers over me as I settle in, practically tucking me in. This rare act of kindness catches me off guard and I'm not sure what to think. *Is he actually being nice or is this some weird twisted way of hitting on me?* Uncomfortable, I say a quick "thanks." He must sense my recoil because he immediately heads towards the hall without another word.

Morning came quickly as the house slowly comes to life. An extremely hungover Jenn slugs her way into the kitchen.

"Ugh!" she moans. "Please tell me the coffee's ready?"

Lana buries her hand into the soapy sink of dirty dishes. "Yep! Cups are in the cabinet by the microwave."

I'm awake but haven't found the energy to get out of bed yet. "How are you this perky already?" I moan across the room.

She turns and gives *the look*.

"Never mind. Forget I asked."
I throw the blanket over my head as Artie walks in.

"And how is the most beautiful girl on Earth doing this morning?" He kisses the back of her neck as she towel dries the last glass.

"Well, I'm glad to know at least *one* of us got laid last night," Jenn snickers under her breath, but loud enough for everyone to catch.

Lana kicks the sofa. "Kate! You only have twenty minutes. Get your lazy ass up!"

"In what warped universe have we teleported to, that Lana is the responsible one of the two?" Jenn asks.

"Kate's not been quite herself lately, so I'm helping pull a little bit of the momma bear duties," Lana tells her. "So again, I repeat! Get the hell up!"

I flip the covers off. "I'm up. I'm up!
I stretch and I slowly make it to my feet. Out of the corner of my eye, something moves.

Three little raccoons are at the porch door, staring in. They've tipped over the garbage can and rummaged through last night's trash.

"I told you that little bastard would be back with his buddies!" I shout to Artie.

We all rush toward the windows. "Aww, look! Their faces are like little bandits!"

"Yeah, little bandits who destroyed our back porch," Jenn sneers.

I grab my bag to get dressed, passing Davis as he heads into the living room.

"Good Morning, Skeeter."
"Morning, Lurch."

As Lana planned, it was nine-thirty on the dot when we arrive at the drop-in point with our big yellow, rubber rafts. Our long-haired, hippy guide gives us a quick history lesson on the river as we wait our turn.

"Located in a valley along the Appalachian Mountains, the Nantahala River is forty miles of winding, fast, white-capped rapids. The water is lined with rock and low-hanging trees that form a natural canopy over the river. The section we're taking is eight miles long and considered the novice of river rafting."

My parents have taken my brothers and me white water rafting for years, so James and I both know what to expect. A few others have done it, but this will be a first for the majority of the group.

It's busy with holiday travelers today. Groups from all over the country, crowd the drop in the area, taking pictures of themselves in their wetsuits, life jackets, and paddles. We ask our guide to take a group picture with the waterproof camera we picked up on the way.

"Holy shit! It's freezing!" Lana screams across the gorge as she steps into the water.

"*Very* cold," our guide concurs. "The river maintains an average forty-five-degree temperature year-round."

"My nuts are going to be the size of raisins by the time this is over!" Davis yells.

One by one, we make our way into our rafts. Davis takes the front, Jenn and I are behind him. The others fill the remaining rows, with the guide in the back.

The trip starts off fairly slow and calm, giving everyone an opportunity to get acclimated to the raft and to learn how to paddle as a group. With everyone smiling with excitement, I snap a few pictures before we head into faster water. I brace my feet under the row in front, as adrenaline begins to pump. Screams, cheers, and laughter explodes through the raft as we make it through our first big drop.

"Wooooo Hooooo! That was in-fucking-credible!" Jackson yells, pumping his paddle in the air.

I look over to see Jenn straight-faced and pale white. "You ok?"

"I don't know how you all are laughing. That was scary as hell!" she shouts over the noise of the river.

I pat her leg. "You'll get used to it pretty quick. I promise."

Mile after mile, the rapids get faster and the drops get bigger. Only slowing long enough for us to take quick breathers. The group has found their sea legs and finally paddling in unison.

As we make our way to the end of the three-hour journey, Santos yells from the back, "I won't lie. I wasn't too sure about this when Artie first mentioned it. But gotta admit, this has been an absolute blast!"

"Damn right! This is freaking awesome!" Artie says. "Max is going to be so bummed he missed out on this!"

My stomach sinks at the mention of his name. I spot Lana nudge his knee and he grimaces when he realizes what he's said.

"It's ok guys. You don't have to tiptoe around me." I smile, hoping to sound as unnerved by the comment as possible.

My arm and leg muscles are beginning to cramp. So I'm glad to see the end in sight. One final fall that's optional to go down, is all that's left.

"*The Beast* isn't for the weak at heart," our guide says as we drift to the drop-off point. "Who's with me?"

Lana, Jenn, and Ashley quickly bail as we make it to the water's edge. Which is the same thing I've done on past trips; always too chicken to make the last run. But even though I'm exhausted, there's something inside of me determined to conquer this final "Beast" of a fall.

"Oh my God, Kate! You're not actually thinking about going on, are you?" Ashley yells as I contemplate.

I grin. "Yes, ma'am. I do believe I am."
Her mouth falls open and all I can do is laugh.

Lana shakes her head, not believing what she's about to do. "I'm going to kill you for this!" she yells as she jumps back into the raft.

Artie gives her a high five. "That's my girl!"

I throw Jenn the waterproof camera. "Take some good shots of us as we make this beast our bitch!"

Jenn and Ash take off to the falls observation deck, as me, Lana and the guys get ourselves rearranged in the raft. Davis takes the empty seat on my row, Artie and Lana are right behind us. Jackson and Santos fill the remaining spots. Our guide sits on the back edge and gives us a quick run-through of instructions on what we need to do, to successfully get down the drop.

We push off from the river bank and for a brief second, I consider jumping out but force myself to stay put. The roar of the water gets louder and louder as we paddle our way towards the top of the fall. Hundreds of people are watching from the sides, cheering as each raft plummets.

James's group is ahead of us, disappearing from sight as they take their turn. My heart pounds faster and faster as we crest the top. My eyes widen as I take in the overwhelming site. The water is foamy white as it churns violent, raging, rapids down the thirty-foot incline. The raft bounces vigorously from side to side as we begin our descent. I vaguely hear the guide shout "paddle, paddle, paddle," as the motion of the river bounces me up and down the seat like a rag doll. Weightless, I close my eyes and the river grows silent. And if like magic, the pain of the last month blissfully escapes my body, allowing complete freedom for the first time in weeks.

I open my eyes and we're at the bottom. We've made it through. Cheers, high fives, and hugs erupt through the raft. The guys yell, "Holy shit! That was awesome! Let's do it again!"

As we make it to the river bank, Lana jumps out and pumps her fist in the air. "We came! We Saw! We kicked its ass!"

Artie swoops her in his arms. "You two never cease to amaze me!"

Davis reaches out his hand to help me from the raft. "Gotta agree with you, Artie. They're a couple of fearless badasses!" He pulls me in for a congratulatory hug.

Pumped full of adrenaline and excitement, I embrace the moment without hesitation. Surprised how well my head fits perfectly in the nook of his chest as I breathe in his sweet sweat and deodorant.

Jenn shouts as she and Ashley catch up to us. "I think we got some *amazing* pictures!"
I pull away from Davis, dismissing how comfortable it felt in his arms.

After a good long rest, we grab lunch at a small restaurant overlooking the river. It has the perfect vantage point to watch others conquer The Beast. We visit the souvenir shop before dragging our aching bones back to the bus. The ride back to Gatlinburg is quiet as we all bask in the much-needed rest.

It's late afternoon when we arrive back at the cabin. Everyone's relaxing in the living room as we decide what we should do tonight. Santos tries to rouse a napping Davis for his vote. But he's out cold.

Lana's first to chime in. "My vote is a trip into downtown. We can eat at the seafood place I was telling you about. Then maybe head to the dance club we passed on the way in."

"Sounds good to me," Artie says, reaching to give her a kiss on the cheek. "I would love nothing more than to take my baby out on a date."

Jenn yawns. "Y'all, I'm beat. I think I may have to sit this one out."

"Me too. I hate to miss out on the fun, but every muscle in my body is screaming at me right now," Jackson says.

"By the looks of it, I'm guessing Davis is out too," Jenn says on his behalf.

After Ashley and Santos agree to go, Lana makes her way to me. "Kate? What about you? You up for getting out?"

I think for a second before answering.

"You know what? I think I will. I'm actually in the mood to get a little crazy tonight."

Davis peaks his eyes open and I know instantly he will not be staying behind

CHAPTER THIRTEEN

It's a beautiful, starry night, as we stroll the streets of downtown Gatlinburg. Rows of little shops flank both sides of the narrow two-lane road. Restaurants, candy shops, and novelty stores wind through the quaint little valley town. We're dressed to the nines and already buzzed from the two bottles of wine we devoured during dinner.

Artie rubs his belly. "The meal was incredible, Lana!" Giving her props for her restaurant choice.

"This whole trip has been incredible!" I add, grabbing her around the neck. "You did us good, girl!"

She beams with pride. "I have to admit, it has been a pretty awesome trip if I do say so myself."

The bass bumps off the buildings as we walk toward the entrance of the club.

"Let the games begin!" Davis yells as he holds the door open for us. "Let's show this place how to party!"

Thankfully, the lady attending the door was the perfect victim for Davis's irresistible charm, because we're able to slip Lana through unnoticed. The club is packed, the music is loud, and the drinks are flowing. The distinct smell of chocolate mixed with cigarette smoke wafts through the air.

We manage to score two high top tables close to the dimly lit dance floor, as Santos buys us all a round of shots. He returns with six blue, flashing, souvenir shot glasses that read, "Everything's Better in the Smokies."

I take a sniff. "Oh, Lord! What are these?"

He laughs. "They're Red Headed Sluts."

I cock my head, leery.

"They're good. I promise."

"Before we drink, I'd like to make a toast." Artie raises his shot in the air. "To my incredibly sweet, incredibly beautiful, girlfriend Lana, for planning this amazing weekend for us."

He gives her a quick kiss as Ashley yells, "Hell Yeah!"

"And to my hard-working comrades, who I am proud to call friends for life!"

Everyone raises their glasses in the air. "Wait! I'd like to add one more," Lana pipes. "To Kate! My amazing best friend and partner in crime. We may not be sisters by blood, but we certainly are at heart. Here's to many more crazy adventures together!"

"Cheers, everyone!" There's a tug in my heart as the six of us clink our glasses and drink.

I shiver from the taste of the shot and grimace as I choke it down. "Oh my God! There was Jager in that!"

"Yep!" Santos laughs, enjoying my torment.

"Disgusting!" Ashley coughs out.

Davis surveys the crowd as he slams his shot glass on the table. "I have dibs on the next round!"

By all appearances, with three girls and three guys, it looks as though our group is all paired up. So to avoid raining on Davis's chick parade, I purposely plant myself between Lana and Ashley.

Sure enough, it only takes a few minutes before the ladies begin their gravitational pull towards him.

"Scouring the room for your next victim?" I yell across the table, over the music.

"Yep! I've got my eyes set on the big tit duo sitting at the bar."

"Well. Happy hunting!" I say sarcastically, as one of the girls heads our way.

The beautiful, "big tit" brunette in a hot pink tank top and jean short shorts, saunters to our table. "Hey, my friend over there was wondering if you're here with someone?" she asks, eyeing Ashley and me.

He's turned away from me and the music is so loud, I'm unable to make out what he says to her. Whatever it is, she flashes a smile and flags her friend over.

She flips her stringy hair off her shoulder. "Well, we think you're hot!"

I roll my eyes. *That was fucking original.*

Our server, April, brings us another round of drinks. Long Island Ice Teas are the drink of choice for the night and even though I'm only one in, they're definitely living up to their reputation.

"Am I losing my mind or does it smell like chocolate in here?"

April laughs. "Yeah, we get asked that a lot. The club backs up to Griffin's Candy Shop. They make their candy in-house. Every night I go home smelling like a chocolate-covered ashtray."

After she leaves, I dance in my chair and people watch. I eye Davis and give him kudos for his impeccable talents with the opposite sex. It's entertaining to watch him work. Between his exceptional good looks and bad-boy façade, he has them both eating out of the palm of his hand. Eventually, they pull him on the dance floor. One dances in front of him, the other is at his back, as they grind on him to Coolio's, "Fantastic Voyage."

"I'm so sick of this song!" I moan to Lana, who's wrapped in Artie's arms.

"Oh, I like this one!" She sings a few lyrics. "It's the damn Ace of Base song I'm sick of hearing."
There's a tap on my shoulder as the music changes.

"Hey, Beautiful. Up for a dance?"
I'm caught off guard by the handsome blond who's popped up behind me. "Oh! Hey," I say, a little lost for words.

Artie gestures towards the dancefloor. "You should get out there!"

"Yeah! Go show those bitches how to shake some ass!" Lana adds.

Hesitantly, I agree. "I'm Kyle, by the way," he says as we make our way to the middle of the dance floor.

"Kate!" I shout in his ear.

The effects of my drinks are catching up to me now that I'm up and moving. The wonderful numb feeling, lifting away every care and worry. I let the rhythm of the music take over, as my new friend pulls me close.

"You smell good!" I yell.

"Thanks! It's CK One. I got it from…" He keeps talking, but I have no idea what he's saying. The music's too loud.

The room sparkles from the prism of the crystal ball spinning above the packed dance floor. I'm in a tipsy fog, but continue dancing as the next song begins. I lift my hair off the sticky sweat pouring from my neck. I spot Davis dancing on the other side of the floor, towering over everyone. He may be hot, but he's got *zero* rhythm.

Davis looks over and our eyes lock. The room slides into slow motion and we become the only two people in the room. Tunnel vision I can't seem to pull myself out of.

"Where are you from?" Kyle asks, tearing me from the moment.

I shake off the unexpected intensity. "I'm sorry, what?" Needing him to repeat his question.

He moves closer to my ear. "No worries. I was only asking where you're from."

"Oh, yeah. I'm from Georgia. You?"

I don't catch what he's saying or care enough to have him repeat it. The song ends and I'm not interested in dancing to another one.

"I'm going to go take a break. But thanks, Kyle. This was awesome." I say quickly, before sprinting back to our table.

Confusion is slapped across Lana's face as I sit. "Um, did I see you and Davis have a weird moment?"

I play it off. "What? No! I wasn't even paying him any attention."

"Well, he sure as hell was paying you attention. He couldn't keep his eyes off you."

I shake my head. "Nah. You're seeing things. Must be all these adult beverages you've consumed."

"No. Seriously! Even Artie noticed it." She elbows him to grab his attention.

"Yeah, he looked over at you every time you and that guy started talking," Artie adds.

Davis is walking back to the table, so I give Artie a quick nod to let him know he's coming up behind him and quickly change the subject.

I point towards the dance floor. "It looks like Ash and Santos are hitting it off."

Davis glances over as he sits, but he doesn't speak. He wipes the sweat from his forehead. "It's fucking hot out there!" Downing the rest of his beer.

He flags April over, flirting with her for a few minutes before ordering another round of shots.

Lana props her elbow on his shoulder. "What are you poisoning us with this time, Davis?"

"I got us some good ole, classic, tequila shots coming!"

She throws her arms in the air. "Oh, hell yeah!"

It's been ages since I've had tequila and honestly, I don't think I have it in me to partake in the next round.

"Y'all, I don't know if I can handle any more shots. I'll end up puking."

"Oh, Kate! Don't be a puss! You'll be fine! Remember, *you're* the one who said you wanted to get 'crazy' tonight!" Lana says, reminding me of my earlier statement.

Within minutes, April returns with six shot glasses of tequila. A bowl of limes and a salt shaker. *This is a terrible idea!* I think, already feeling woozy.

Davis tucks a strand of hair behind my ear. "Don't worry. I'll take care of you if you get sick." He places a gentle kiss on my neck, just behind my ear. His breath sending chills down my back. He walks back to his side of the table without saying another word.

I look around, stunned. Thankful, no one else saw him do it. My mind races as my body goes into a heated frenzy. The sudden, uncontrollable, desire to ravish him right here in the middle of the bar. *But I don't even like Davis! This has to be the booze, right? Oh, he's good. He's REAL fucking good.* I think as I shake my head. *Trying to pull his Davis charm on me.* I'm pissed at myself for even thinking about him that way. *He's lost his everloving mind if he thinks I'm falling for his sneaky little tricks.*

He watches as I slide the bowl of limes closer. I stare back with an annoyed eye and lick the back of my hand. He grabs it and shakes salt on it. We down our shots at the same time. It's terrible, but I control the urge to grimace. I grab a lime wedge and bite into it, praying for some relief.

Never taking our eyes off each other.

Lana pulls me to her and whispers. "And you tried to bullshit me into thinking I didn't see anything between you two! Y'all are practically eye-fucking each other right here at the table!"

Aggravated, I cross my arms. "Nope! I think he's a disgusting pig. I don't care how hot he is! I wouldn't sleep with him if the fate of the world rested on it!"

"Oh! So he's hot now?"

My eyebrows furrow. "Uhhh!" I growl.

She shakes her head, laughing as I stomp off. "I know you far too well Kate Carpenter!"

Drunk, but determined to not fall for Davis's con, I scan the club for Kyle, spotting him near the bar. I walk over and chit-chat with him and his friends. After introductions and small talk, he asks if I'd like to dance again. I'm not up for it but see Davis back on the dance floor. He's with someone new and of course, she's gorgeous.

Irritated, I say, "I'd love to," as I grab his hand and pull him through the crowd.

I find a spot on the dance floor a few feet away from Davis. We're facing each other, making it hard to focus on who I'm with. Out of spite, I dance on Kyle a little more provocative than I should. Davis is watching and our eyes meet. The music is loud, the bass vibrating the floor. Hot sweat pours off both of us. The colors of the light machine bouncing off our bodies. I'm overcome with desire for him as we stare at each other.

As if he was reading my mind, we simultaneously rush to one another. Leaving our dance partners behind. He's to me in an instant, effortlessly picking me up. I wrap my legs around his waist and we kiss.

Fire rages through my body the second our lips touch. A hard, rough kiss, exploding with passion. The girl he'd been dancing with shouts, "Are you fucking kidding me?" But he doesn't stop. I taste tequila on his tongue as our mouths race to explore every inch of each other.

He pulls his mouth from mine, running it up and down my neck. His teeth find my earlobe and he gives a gentle nip. "I want you," he says. My body instantly reacting to his words.

I turn my head to see his beautiful chestnut eyes. I know this is a mistake, but I don't care. I want him to.

"Let's get the hell out of here," I say breathlessly in his ear.

He sets me down. "No, Kate. I want you *now.*"

Davis grabs my hand and leads me through the crowd, to the long, heavy-lit, restroom hallway. I know I should stop him, but I can't. I *have* to have him. My body is on fire for him.

He locks the door of the single stall bathroom and I'm back in his arms in an instant. I can feel him through his jeans, pressing against my stomach. He lifts me on the counter as I fumble with his belt buckle. The countertop is cold against my bare ass, as he slides my panties off. Electricity rushes through my body as I watch him tear open the foil wrapper. My body is ready as he pushes into me. He wraps his large hands around my waist as we sync in perfect rhythm.

He stops. His hands moving to my face. "You might possibly be the sexiest woman I have ever met." I bite my lip as his hungry eyes show me how much he's enjoying this.

I lay back, using the mirror as leverage. Drowning in the intense pleasure of him. I can't hold back my screams any longer, causing him to moan loudly.

Faster and faster, never taking our eyes off each other. The intensity of his stare almost brings me to tears. His hands squeeze tightly around my waist, pushing harder until he falls breathlessly into me.

We stay paralyzed, panting as sweat drips from our bodies. He lifts his head enough to grab a few paper towels from the machine. He hands me my panties, as a sudden burst of embarrassment floods through me. I try not to let it show as we silently pull ourselves back together.

As we leave, he kisses the top of my forehead. "Promise me we won't let things get weird between us?"

I wave it off. "Pfff! No, of course not." Even though I'm already feeling that way.

He reaches for the bathroom handle. "Are you sure? Because if we need to talk about this…"

I smack his chest. "It's all good, Lurch. It was a random bang among friends. Nothing more. Nothing less." I try my best to say it as convincingly as possible.

Lana gives me the death stare as I scurry back to the table, with Davis a few steps behind me. "Where the hell have you two been?"

I act casual. "We went for some air."

"Oh, right! Air my ass!"

I kick her foot under the table. Which is code for *shut the hell up!* And mouth "I'll tell you later," when Davis isn't looking.

Overwhelmed with what's taken place over the last thirty minutes, I'm desperate to get out of here.

Hoping not to be obvious, I glance at my watch. "Wow! It's getting late. Y'all think we should start heading back?"

Praying they say yes.

"Hell yes! These heels are killing me," Lana whines.

Artie, who's the DD, rounds up Ashley and Santos. As Lana, Davis and I wait for them outside. Except for a few random tourists filing out of the bars, the streets are empty. Making it eerily quiet. The temperatures dropped and can feel myself shivering. Davis swoops Lana and me into each of his arms to keep us warm.

"Oh my God, Davis! Thank you!" she shouts, reveling in his warmth. "You're like a human heating pad."

She was right. His tall, burly, stature is like having our very own Paul Bunyan. It's sexy as hell, but I try to not let it show.

We spot a tipsy Ashley staggering out the door, singing. Artie laughs, as he and Santos, guide her to the sidewalk. "I convinced her to go, but only after promising her we'd stop at the candy store on our way back to the car."

"Chocolate… Chocolate... Chocolate!" she chants.

Lana nods. "Sounds like a pretty good idea, if ya ask me!"

"Candy shop it is!" Santos shouts.

With six bags of different types of Griffin's Chocolates; Ashley, Santos, Davis and I, are once again piled in the back of Lana's tiny Mazda like sardines. I'm on Davis's lap and thankful it's a short drive.

The four of them chat amongst themselves as Davis and I remain uncommonly quiet. His arm is around me and I'm intently aware of his every move. He slides his hand up my back and under my hair. No one else sees as his giant hand grabs the nape of my neck, giving it a gentle squeeze. I close my eyes as my body goes limp under his touch.

What a fool I am for letting this happen, but what we'd done was too incredible to care.

It's after two in the morning by the time we make it back, and the cabin is dark and quiet. Jackson and Jenn are already in bed. We try the best five drunk people could do, to not make a big commotion coming in. But we sound more like a marching band in reality.

"I'm not tired yet. Anybody up for the hot tub?"

Santos is quick to take Ashley up on the offer.

"Sorry, friend. My baby and I are crashing." Artie says, grabbing Lana by the hand.

"Kate? You joining us?" Ash asks as Santos gives me a pleading, *please say no* look.

I glance over at Davis and I can tell he's waiting for me to respond before making a decision. "Y'all two go ahead. I think I'm going to call it a night."

Davis stretches his arms above his head. "Yeah, me too. I think today's adventures have finally caught up to me."

Twenty minutes later, Ash and Santos are in the hot tub as I fumble through the hall closet for my blanket and pillow. My mind spinning from the alcohol. Nerves set in my stomach as Davis heads up the hallway. I stumble into the closet door. He throws his hands up to catch me.

"You ok there, Ms. Long Island?"

"I'm fine. Just fighting with my damn pillow here."

"Why don't you take the bedroom tonight? It's not right for me to be hogging a king-size bed, while you're out here sleeping on a shitty sofa mattress."

It's music to my ears the second he says it. "It *would* be nice to sleep in tomorrow."

I walk in the bedroom, trying desperately to not let the fact we just had steamy, drunk sex in a bar bathroom freak me out. *Do not overthink this, Kate! It was only a hook-up.* Repeating it over and over, as I choke down the awkwardness.

"You know it's fine if you want to sleep in here too," I say, pulling my hair into a ponytail.

"It's a good thing because I was already going to," he says while rummaging through one of the bags of chocolates.

A line forms between his eyes as he studies my face. "Hmm!"

I scratch my nose, suddenly self-conscious. "What?"

"You look pretty damn cute all bummed out. I'm diggin' the glasses."

"Well enjoy it while it lasts. They're only at bedtime. It's contacts ninety-percent of the time."

He pulls his shirt over his head, exposing the thick mass of hair covering his firm chest. He isn't chiseled but his tall frame makes up for it. He fumbles around his rucksack for a few seconds, before pulling out a clean pair of boxers.

He smirks. "These got a little dirty tonight."

I laugh, but my face flushes. I crawl into bed, turning my back while he changes his underwear.

"You don't have to turn away, especially since my Johnson was in your hand less than an hour ago."

I pull the covers over my head. "You're trying to embarrass me."

He turns off the light and climbs into bed, settling in close. My body immediately affected by the intimacy of it all.

"Did you try the chocolate turtles?" he asks, handing over the paper bag from the nightstand.

I grab one out. "I think these are the only ones I missed."

My eyes roll back in my head. "Mmmmm!" I mumble. "Hands down the best one."

"I know! I can't stop. They're addictive."

I lick chocolate from my fingers. "I think we might have to make another trip for more before we head home."

He puffs an exhausted breath. "This has been one hell of a day."

"Yes, it has. When I woke up this morning, I couldn't have imagined what today would have in store for us."

"You have to admit. The weekend wouldn't have been *near* as exciting if I hadn't been here."

I laugh. "This is true. You always add a certain flair to everything we do. Too bad it's flying by. Only one more day, then it's back to reality."

"Well, I guess we need to get Lana busy planning our next big adventure."

Something in the way he says it pulls at my heartstrings, causing my voice to crack. "I honestly can't put into words how much I needed this trip." He understands why without me saying it.

I roll to my stomach and watch him. The moonlight casts a glow across the bed, lighting his smooth-shaven face.

He rubs his hand over the scar on my shoulder blade. "What happened here?"

I close my eyes as snippets of the accident flash through my head. "I was in a pretty bad motorcycle wreck a couple of years ago. Like a freaking idiot, I jumped on the back of Wayne's crotch rocket. Ten minutes later he laid it over right smack in the middle of I-85."

"Holy shit! Are you serious?"

"Luckily, I don't remember much. The lights from the ambulance, mostly. I was shouting for him to slow down, then my memory goes blank.

Sometimes I dream about being in a cold, white room and my clothes are being cut off, so I'm guessing that's a memory too."

"Jesus, Kate. You could have been killed."

I raise up on my elbows. "It could have been a lot worse. Other than being covered in scrapes and bruises, I was lucky to walk away with only a broken arm and the wicked burn that left the scar."

"Was he drunk or something?"

"Oddly enough, no. The hospital tested him for everything imaginable, but they all came back clean. So the cops ruled it an accident."

"I guess it's a blessing you don't remember anything from it."

"Yep. And thanks to the forever reminder of my stupidity, my days of being reckless are over. Although, you wouldn't know it after I went barreling down The Beast today."

He smiles. "You showed it who's boss."

"I've actually been thinking about getting a tattoo to cover it." I gesture to the American flag wrapped around dog tags on his bicep. "I just haven't decided what I want yet."

"There's a great place a couple of miles from Post. I'll take you when you're ready."
We lay quietly as he slowly runs his fingers through my hair.

"Are you having any regrets about what happened tonight?" he asks.

"No. None at all." I roll to my side to face him. "What happened was pretty amazing, and I'd lying if I tried to deny it."

His cocky smirk appears. "It was pretty damn incredible."

"I hope when the sun comes up and the alcohol wears off, it won't change things. We're too good of friends for any weird awkwardness between us, ya know?" I say tongue-tied. "I'm probably not making any sense."

"No, no. I get it and agree with you. We have to make a point to not let it happen."

"Promise me one thing," I ask.

"What's that?"

"Please don't start treating me like one of your conquest girls."

His head tilts. "You aren't some random girl I picked up for a quick lay, Kate. You're important to me. You're one of the few girls in my life I actually like being around."

I appreciate his words, but it immediately causes The Fourth of July to pop in my head. "Can I ask you a question?"

He yawns. "Of course."

"It doesn't make a difference now, but did you lie to me about who called the Platoon Sergeant on me and Lana?"

He shakes his head and breathes out a long, heavy sigh. "No matter how I answer this question, I'm still going to look like the bad guy. I guess I didn't have all the facts straight and honestly, it's still a mystery. The last I heard it was all a big joke, but I still have a hard time believing it."
I roll back on my pillow as I process his words.

"What I *can* say is…I should have kept my mouth shut. It wasn't my place to get involved."

I shrug. "Like I said… it doesn't matter now. It's the least of my worries these days. But it'd been weighing on me a little though."

He pulls my chin towards him. "I'm sorry Max hurt you."

My stomach knots. "He did the right thing by her. Unfortunately, I was the necessary casualty."

He hands over another chocolate turtle, "Since we are having a heart to heart. Can I ask *you* a question?"

"Sure. Anything."

He hesitates.

"Were you with me tonight as some type of revenge thing? In hopes it'll get back to him?"

I roll towards him, wrapping an arm over his chest. "Davis, if I'm being completely truthful, until you mentioned his name a few minutes ago, Max had not crossed my mind all day."

He gives a relieved smile and I'm taken back by his concern. "Would it have bothered you if I had said yes?"

"The idea of being used by a woman to get back at an ex would typically be pretty hot. But the thought of you doing it would definitely sting a little."

"Ya know, as much as I hate to admit it. I think there might actually be a pretty decent guy hidden in that Lurch body of yours."

He chuckles. "Shhhhhh! You can't tell anyone. It might ruin my playboy rep."

I yawn loudly, no longer able to hold my eyes open. "Your secret is safe with me," I whisper as I fall asleep in his arms.

CHAPTER FOURTEEN

It's late morning when I finally drag out of bed, following the smell of bacon. I'm glad Davis is already up, avoiding any uncomfortable, "morning-after" weirdness.

The sun beams through the tall living room windows like a Broadway spotlight. Adding additional pain to my already pounding head. Artie's kicked back watching Seinfeld on the TV.

"Damn, girl! You look like shit."

"I'm not sure which hurts more, my sore body from the rafting, or my head from the ridiculous amount of alcohol y'all let me consume last night."

Lana cuts open a biscuit and laughs. "Breakfast is ready. There's a fresh pot of coffee on and I have Ibuprofen in my bag."

"How come you're not dragging ass this morning? You drank as much as I did."

She crosses her arms. "Nope. No way! I refuse to have any additional conversation until you spill the dirt on you and Davis!"

I gasp. Flailing my hands in a panicked no. "Oh my God! Hush! He'll hear," I whisper.

"Geez! Freak much?" She pitches her dirty knife in the sink. "Calm down. He's not here."

I freeze. "Huh?"

Artie flips aimlessly through the TV channels. "They've been gone a good hour now."

"Ummm… who is *they*?"

Lana plops on the couch beside him. Jelly from her biscuit oozing down her fingers. "He, Jenn, and Jackson went sightseeing this morning. They were taking a drive into the National Park or something."

A tinge of unfamiliar jealousy tugs at my heart. "Oh."

"Yep, Jackson's hoping to see some bears," Artie adds.

"Davis said you told him you wanted to sleep in today, so that's why he didn't wake you. And Ash and Santos are still asleep, and you know I'm going to tell Artie anyway, so you might as well spill it."

I make a cup of coffee and slide into the recliner by them. "Honestly, there isn't much to tell. One minute we were on the dance floor, the next minute we were locked in the ladies' restroom."

"I *knew* it!" she yells and points. "Y'all had goo-goo eyes for each other all night!"

Artie laughs. "I've seen it coming for months. You could cut the sexual tension between you two with a knife."

My lips curls. "Uh. No! I've never once thought of him in *that* way until last night. He's always been a complete asshole."

"Yep! And he would say you were a snobby bitch. You know what they call that?"

I roll my eyes and huff. "What, Dr. Ruth? Please enlighten me."

Artie and Lana look at each other, then back at me.

"Foreplay!" they shout in unison.

I cave, unable to keep from laughing. "You know what? You two can both kiss my ass."

"I'll take the right cheek and Artie can take the left!" she teases.

"In all seriousness, let's not make a deal out of this. It was a one-time, crazy thing between two drunk friends.

It isn't the start of anything."

Artie's face twists. "I promised I wouldn't mention a certain you know whose name. But you know Davis is going to shove this down his throat the second we get back, right?" Artie says.

I shift in the seat. "I don't know why it would matter. I don't have any ties to Max anymore."

He shrugs. "Well, you have to admit, Kate. You did hook up with the one person he couldn't stand being anywhere near you. If you were looking for the ultimate payback. You sure as hell found it."

"Good! Let him find out. I don't give two shits if he knows," I lie.
No matter how angry I am, Artie's right. This was the worst thing I could do to hurt Max.

"Do **not** feel guilty! This is his own damn fault!" Lana snips. "If he would have slapped a raincoat on that thing. Or at the very least… pulled out! *He'd* be the one you had hot bathroom sex with!" Her upper lip snarls. "It pisses me off every time I think about it!"

I puff out a heavy sigh. "No reason to get all worked up about it. What's done is done."

The three of us sit quietly, sipping coffee and watching the Gatlinburg morning news.

"He's miserable ya know?" Lana kicks Artie's foot, signaling him to shut up.

I lift my eyebrows, hoping he will elaborate without me having to ask.

"Jody isn't even there anymore," he says.

"What do you mean? Where is she?"

Lana lets out a long exaggerated breath, clearly not wanting him to share the info.

He lifts a pleading brow and she nods for him to continue.

"She left about a week after they got married, went back to Boise. Left before the ink was good and dry on the marriage license. Now, I'm not saying she trapped him, but she certainly figured out a way to get you out of the picture."

Lana kicks the ottoman. "I fucking hate her!"

"Now he goes to work during the day and sits in his room at night. Making a terrible attempt to appear happy and keep up this sham of a marriage."
I'm not sure if this news makes me happy or makes matters worse. This whole time I'd imagined them moving in together, picking out furniture, painting the damn nursery together.

"If she hasn't been there, how come he didn't call me? Explain everything. Give me a shred of closure?" I ask, more confused than ever.

"Well-LL," Lana draws out. If we're having a Max tell-all…I might as well tell you the rest." Guilt floods her eyes. "The reason he didn't call, was because I told him not to."

I gasp. "Wait! *You* talked to Max?"

"Actually, I saw him. When I went down for my birthday. Jody had already ditched town and he'd been buried in his room for days. I was so angry but seeing how much of a wreck he was absolutely broke my heart. So Artie convinced him to go to the Journey concert with us. Honestly, I think the only reason he went was so he could ask me about you." She pauses to wipe jelly from her mouth. "He told me when he heard the knock at the door the night of the hurricane, he assumed it was us and was about to ring our necks for driving in the storm. *But* it was her. After she dropped the bombshell of all bombshells, he said he snuck out to call you, but the phones had already gone out.

The next day, everything unfolded in a flash. After it was over, she was monitoring every move he made. By then, he knew you knew and was too ashamed to call."

Pain pierces my chest as I fight back tears. "I guess there's some comfort in knowing he at least tried to call."

After processing everything that's been said it dawns on me, there must be more. "Wait. You said you're the one who told him not to call."

"Well, Max got rip-roaring drunk at the concert and had a complete meltdown. It was quite possibly the saddest thing I've ever witnessed. Wasn't it Artie?"

"Yep. Dude balled his damn eyes out."

"He kept repeating how he had ruined his life and what a terrible mistake he'd made. But how he had no choice because his parents would disown him if he didn't step up to the plate." She grabs her heart. "Once he started talking about you, holy shit! That's when I broke down balling. He kept saying how much you meant to him and how he never meant to hurt you. And how he knew you probably hated him." Her tone flattens. "The next morning we went by his room to check on him and he asked if he should call you. But it had been three weeks. You were finally getting back on your feet. Hell, you were finally showering again. I was worried if he called it would be too much for you to bear. Especially, since the ending was ultimately the same. So I asked him not to call." Her gaze falls to the floor. "I'm so sorry, Kate."

I swallow the lump in my throat. "I don't know what to say. I'm honestly speechless right now."

"Please don't be mad," she pleads. "Remember, you made me promise I wouldn't tell you anything about Max, even if you begged me."

"You're right. I did."

"If it helps any, he asks me about you all the time," Artie says, hoping it will help cushion the blow.

My head falls in my hands. Trying desperately to make sense of all this. "Does he know you guys are here with us?"

His lips purse the second I ask. "Yeah. He does. I wasn't going to tell him but Davis made sure he knew. Did it on purpose, of course. Total dick move."

I choke down the guilt festering in my belly and hold my head high. Forcing myself indifferent. "Well. Like Lana said. If he would have wrapped it up, things would be much different today."

I'd be lying if I said there isn't a tad of comfort knowing Max is miserable. Even a small part of me wants him to find out about Davis. I know it's terrible to think this way because it's cruel, and I'm not a cruel person. I know in my heart he didn't ask for any of this to happen to him. So even after everything, I am deeply saddened by the pain he must be going through. Him finding out about Davis will only add to his pain and for that, I am incredibly ashamed.

It's late when Davis and the rest of the group stumble back to the cabin, and it's clear they added getting sloppy drunk to their sightseeing adventure. I'm on the back porch smoking a cigarette when they barrel through the door.

They're all in the living room talking and can't see me outside. Jenn's draped over Davis like a winter coat and he appears to be enjoying it. *What an idiot I am for letting my guard down with him.* He looks around and asks where I am. Lana tells him I've gone to bed and I immediately see the switch flip from good guy to playboy. He's back to being his typical cocky, arrogant, self.

Davis shouts, "Jenn, show me your tits!" Which of course, she immediately does without question.

"Damn! They might be a little saggy, but I still want to motorboat the hell out of em'!"
I cringe as he buries his head into her chest.

Everyone laughs, which only fuels his ridiculous behavior. This is *exactly* how he acted the weekend we first met and I'm reminded of why I disliked him so much. He's in true "Davis" mode and I want zero part of it.

Between the news of Max and Davis being a tool. I'm sad, lonely, disgusted, and pissed off, all rolled into one. The last thing I need right now is Davis thinking I'm upset over him. So to avoid any drama, the best thing for me to do is camp right here until the coast is clear.

Underwear it is! I say to no one, slipping into the warm, bubbly, hot tub. The perfect medicine for my weary bones and aching heart. Steam lifts in the air as I lay back to watch the stars. There isn't a cloud in the sky tonight, creating a magnificent view. The hot tub light changes from blue to green to red, reminding me of the night we threw Chemlights with Max and Drew. I smile as I allow my mind to drift to him. That night feels like it was ages ago. As if it was only a dream. I wonder what he's doing tonight. I wonder if he's worried about me being here with Davis. Guilt sits on my chest again, even though I know it shouldn't.

The sound of the back door opening pulls me back to reality. I slither up as quietly as I can as Davis and Jenn's voices carry from the other side of the porch.

"Did you get the bottle of Goldschlager?" I hear her ask.

Shit, Shit, Shit! I scream in my head. *I'm trapped!*
I have about ten seconds to decide to face Davis or take a dive off this eight-foot-high porch.

The answer is quickly made the second he asked her if she likes to be spanked. *Ew! Davis! Really?* Shuttering at the mental picture.

Water sops from my mint green panties and bra as I shimmy down the latticework, threading my toes in each hole as fast as I can. It's pitch black dark as limbs and brush impale my bare feet at the bottom. *Son of a bitch!* I mouth, trying desperately not to shout. Thankful, the jets are on, masking most of the noise.

"No, ma'am! This is no clothes allowed hot tub!" Davis flirts.

How could I have been so stupid? Smacking myself on the forehead. *I can* **NOT** *believe I fell for his shit!*

As she climbs in I faintly hear her ask, "Wanna stick your head in between these again?"
I roll my eyes. *Seriously, Jenn? You couldn't come up with something a little more original than that?*

"Hell yeah, I do! Get over here!"
I assume they must be making out because they're quiet for a few minutes. Halting me mid-step.

"You know I've always had a fantasy about being bent over a pool table," she says between kisses.

Ew! Ew! Ew! That's it! I'm officially grossed out! I have to get the hell out of here RIGHT NOW!

I tiptoe under the porch as quietly as possible, powering through the pain in my feet; using the latticework as my guide. Leaves grind under my feet as I feel my way along the steep hillside. A downspout crunches beneath me causing my foot to pivot. I slam to the ground shoulder first, clumsily grasping at branches as I bounce down the ravine. Stopped by the force of a tree five feet into the wood line.

I bite my tongue and cringe through the pain. Staying perfectly still to see if I've been heard.

My heart pounds against my chest but I think I'm in the clear. They're still yapping on the porch as I survey the damage. Blood oozes from my busted hands and knees as pain radiates from my right ankle. *Perfect! Just. Fucking. Perfect!*

I quietly roll on my side to pull up and hear a tiny crackle in the darkness. *What the hell was that?* My heart races as I slowly turn my head, swallowing hard. It's *them*. Their beady little eyes staring back at me.

"HELLLLLLPPPPPP!" I scream. "I NEED HELPPPPPPP!"

Three raccoons, eye level, stare straight into my soul as I scream at the top of my lungs. They stand on their back legs and let out a high pitch screech.

"HELLLLLLPPPPPP MEEEEEEE!" I scream again, jumping to my feet. Hobbling up the steep ravine as fast as I can, too afraid to turn back. "RABIES! THEY'VE GOT RABIESSSS!"

Davis and Jenn spring from the hot tub and peer over the railing as Lana and Artie rush out the back door.

"What the hell is going on?" Lana yells as I make it to the bottom of the porch.

She gasps. "Oh my God! What happened?" She asks as I hop the stairs on one foot.

I grasp my side as I reach the top. Water pooling at my feet. "I... hot... fell... raccoons!" Sliding down the porch railing into a ball of exhaustion.

Artie flings his head towards the screeching raccoons, who retreat further into the woods. "Were you out there?"

"I thought you were in bed," Jenn says, using her hands to cover her lady parts.

They're by my side in a flash. "Her legs are bleeding," Davis says.

"It's freezing out here. Will y'all help me get her inside?" Lana asks.

The words are barely out of her mouth when Davis lifts me and carries me towards his room. Lana, Ashley, and Artie right behind him.

"No. I don't want to be in here!" I protest, grabbing at the door frame.

"Too bad," is all he says, before laying me across the bed and scurrying out.

Ash grabs the assortment of throw pillows from behind my back. "He's right. You have no business sleeping on the couch."

Lana's hand flies to her mouth. "It looks like you were in a catfight! What the hell were you doing in the woods?"

I sit in silence for a few seconds, examining the cuts and scrapes on my legs. "My foot's starting to swell," I dodge; too embarrassed to answer.

"Nope! Spill it, sister!" Ashley shouts, propping the throw pillows underneath my foot.

Exhausted, I cave. "I didn't have it in me to deal with Davis's shit tonight," I begin. "I was on the porch when they got back..."

"Dammit, Kate!" Lana shouts. "We all thought you had gone to bed. You could have been kidnapped and we would have never known!"

"It would be awesome if you didn't Mother Hen me right now," I plead as a now dressed Jenn, joins us.

"Ok. And?" Ashley says, shooing Lana's mothering moment. "How in the world did you end up in the woods?"

Davis strides back in with an ice bag, wet washcloths, ointment, and Band-Aids before I'm able to answer.

"Please don't stop on my account," he says as he and Lana begin cleaning my cuts.

"The Cliff Notes version is… I tripped over one of the cabins downspouts, which caused me to go head first down the hill."

"And the raccoons?" Artie asks.

"I happened to roll right where those three little bastards were waiting for their nightly hand out. They scared the living shit out of me… which scared the living shit out of them. I screamed bloody murder… they screamed bloody murder. I think I even peed myself a little."

They're trying not to laugh, but Lana snickers a tad, unable to hold back. Which sends everyone else following in suit. I join in, able to find the humor in it now.

After a few jokes are thrown around the room and they have me cleaned and bandaged, Davis says, "It's getting late. We need to let her get some rest."

Lana sighs. "Oh, I guess you're right. But don't think for a second I'm letting you off the hook for the complete version of this story, missy!"

She hugs me goodnight. "Tomorrow. I promise," I say. "Thank you for the help. I'm sorry if I spoiled everyone's night," I call out to the group as they file out of the room.

"You're staying with her tonight, right?" Lana asks Davis as they make their way out.

He furrows his brow. "Well, yeah. Of course."

"Don't act so shocked I would have to ask, Davis. You did *just* have your tongue down Jenn's throat."

"I've got her. Don't worry."

Davis is the last person I want to deal with after all this and pray Jenn will keep him busy. They're in the hallway talking, but I can't make out what they're saying. I assume she's hoping to continue where they left off before I ungraciously interrupted them.

No such luck! I think as Davis heads back into the room, shutting the door behind him.

I tug at the covers. "I thought you two had a date on the pool table?"

He thinks I'm trying to be funny and laughs. "Heard that, huh?"

"Unfortunately, yes. *All* of it. And quite frankly, I've never been more grossed out in all my life."

"Wait. Are you mad at me?"

"Nope. Being mad would imply I actually give a shit and I don't."

With a confusion slapped across his face, he sits on the side of the bed. "What's going on, Kate?"

"Davis…I promise I'm not trying to be a bitch here, but I scaled an eight-foot porch wall to avoid having to talk to you. That was *before* I careened down an embankment, got busted up, and the shit scared out of me by three hungry ass raccoons. I can assure you after all that, I'm in no mood to talk. So please, for the love of Pete… go have your bang fest with Jenn and leave me alone."

"I don't understand. I thought we made a promise to one another we weren't going to let things get weird. Not let what happened change anything."

"Yep! And what a fool I was for thinking it could happen."

"If this is about Jenn, I promise we were only cutting up. I don't want her."

"Oh, don't flatter yourself into thinking this is some weird jealousy thing. This is **not** about Jenn and it's **not** about last night. This is about you being a disgusting man whore, who can go from nice guy to chauvinistic asshole at the drop of a hat.

I don't even know which one is the real you. And to be honest, after what I witnessed tonight, I don't care who the real you is."

He huffs. "I think you're being a tad dramatic. I'm a nice guy who knows how to have a good time."

"Yes. Because telling someone they have saggy boobs is the perfect example of you being nice."

Davis laughs at the boob comment and it does nothing but piss me off even more.

"Please just go," I beg.

"Being the cocky asshole is who I am. You know this, Kate. I don't know why it's bothering you all of a sudden."

"It bothers me because I realized how much of a freakin' idiot I am for falling for your silly tricks. When deep down I knew you were only using me to get a rise out of Max."

He doesn't say anything, leading me to believe my suspicions are right. "But it's ok. Because I'm pretty sure deep down, I was too."

He pulls his pillow from the bed and walks out of the room without another word. I fight the urge to feel bad about what I've said. He's an asshole and needed to be called out for it. But he's right, it's unfair of me to judge him for being exactly who he is. He uses women. What on Earth would make me think I would be any different?

My ankle is sore but I'm feeling better after a good night's sleep. Davis and I do not speak as everyone packs the cars to head home. We stop in Pigeon Forge to eat breakfast, giving everyone a chance to say their goodbyes. With everything that's unfolded this weekend, we thought it best for the girls to ride back together, instead of splitting up again. Lana cries as Artie wraps his arms around her one last time.

Plans have already been made for him to come to Athens in a few weeks, but they're still upset to leave each other.

I'm waiting in the car when Davis walks up. "Kate? Can we talk for a second?"

I don't speak, only shrugging my shoulders to convey some shred of a response.

He crouches in the door. "I'm sorry about last night."

I let go of the anger and relief floods my heart. "I'm sorry too. I did exactly what I didn't want to happen. I made things weird."

"No, it was completely my fault. I vanished on you without a word and when I finally show back up, I'm all over one of your closest friends. It was wrong of me to do."

"It's ok, I promise. It was all a big, dumb, drunken, mistake. Let's promise not to let any of it screw up our friendship," I plead.

"Of course. Yeah. I don't want that either," he says.

"I mean, you get on my nerves. But I've kind of gotten used to having you around," I tease, hoping to lighten the mood.

He smiles and throws out his hand. "Friends?"

I grab it. "Friends!"

"We gotta get on the road, D!" Artie calls out and I can tell he's thankful for the interruption.

"Us too," I say. "Lana will be losing her mind if we get too far off schedule. You know she's the on-time these days."

He says his goodbyes to Lana and the girls, then gives me a gentle kiss on the forehead. "Goodbye, Kate."

As we pull out of the parking lot, Lana asks, "What was that all about?"

I shake my head. "It was nothing. Just making things right."

I'm glad Davis and I had an opportunity to clear the air before we left. We have great chemistry but it could never be more than friends. Max is the one who holds my heart and probably always will.

The drive is long and mostly quiet. The only conversation we've had since we left is about how well Ashley and Santos had hit it off and how he plans to come to Athens with Artie in a few weeks.

"What do you have planned for when they come?" I ask.

"I'm thinking maybe a trip into Atlanta. He's never been to Six Flags. Maybe catch a Braves Game. It'll be Artie's twenty-second birthday, so I want to make it as memorable as possible."

"He'll love it! I'm so happy for you two. I can tell he adores you."

She flashes a bashful grin. "He told me he loved me last night."

"Dammit, Lana! We've been in the car for two hours and you're *just* now telling us!" I yell, poking her in the shoulder.

"I'm sorry," she laughs. "I didn't want to make a big thing of it."

"But it *IS* a big thing! It's huge!" Ashley adds.

"I guess I was worried I would jinx it if I said it out loud."

"Why, silly?"

"I'm excited and terrified all at the same time. I keep worrying the rug's going to get pulled out from under me. You know what terrible luck I have with guys. They either bore me in a week or they're only looking for the dumb, trophy girlfriend."

"Don't think that way, Lana. He would never do anything to hurt you. He's so different from anyone you've ever dated. He's got the kindest heart." I assure her.

"I know. It's just...."

Mid-sentence, the car shutters. Puh, Puh, Puh. Then silence as it begins to coast.

"Ummm… what the hell was that?" Jenn asks.

"Please, God! Tell me we didn't run out of gas?!" Ashley says.

Lana yells in a panic as she pulls the car onto the side of the interstate. "It showed we had five more miles!"

Jenn smacks the back of her headrest. "For Christ's sake, Lana! You can't let it get that low! Why didn't you stop at the last exit?"

"Please don't yell at me! My brain was on Artie. I guess I wasn't paying attention!"

"I am going to kill you!" Jenn says, screaming now.

"Ok, y'all! Yelling isn't helping. The guys can pick us up and take us to get gas," I say calmly.

Lana cups her face. "They got ahead of us when we stopped to pee at the Georgia Welcome Center."

"What about James? They'll be behind us soon, right?" Ashley asks.

I puff out an exhausted breath. "No, James and his group weren't leaving until this afternoon. They're probably just now getting on the road."

"Oh, no! What the hell are we going to do?" Lana pleads as the three of them start squabbling among each other.

I try to think of a solution over them and the loud vehicles whipping by, jostling the car.

"Please stop arguing and let me think for a minute! Jesus!" I shout, throwing my hand up to hush everyone.

"The McDonald's billboard said two miles ahead, so we aren't far from an exit. Maybe we can hitchhike to a gas station?"

"Are you crazy!?" Jenn screams. "We could get murdered!"

"Well, we have three choices, Jenn… we can either hitchhike, walk, or sit here like four idiots until James passes by. Pick your poison, because whichever one we pick is going to royally suck!" I snip, still pissed off at her for last night.

She rolls her eyes and huffs, but knows trying to catch a ride is our best option.

We all climb from the car. "Maybe if we start walking someone will eventually stop," Ashley says as a loud boom of thunder claps overhead.

"Isn't this perfect! We just *had* to break down right before a thunderstorm hits!"

"Shut up, Jenn! Your attitude isn't helping anything!" I yell. Finally losing all patience with her.

"Oh, oh, oh! A cop! Y'all… help me wave! It's a cop!" Ashley points and jumps, as we all spot him coming up the opposite side of the interstate.

We watch as he flies past us. "Please turn around! Please turn around!" Lana begs as we watch, praying he spotted us.

Cheers erupt when his brake lights flash and he slows to turn into the median emergency lane.

Minutes later the Sheriff's cruiser pulls behind us. The young deputy steps out, straightening his belt as he stands. "You ladies breakdown?"

"YES! Praise The Lord you saw us!" Jenn shouts. "Our dumbass friend here, let us run out of gas!"

He chuckles loudly as we gather around him. *Damn! He's hot!*

"Officer…" I glance at his name badge. "Mullins. You don't happen to have a gas can on you, by chance?"

"I don't, but I'll be more than happy to run you girls to a gas station and back. There's a Shell station about two miles from here."

Without hesitation, we take him up on his offer. "Y'all jump in!"

Jenn sits in the front seat of Officer Mullins white Crown Vic, while Lana, Ashley, and I take dibs on the back. We continue to thank him and sing his praises as we make the short drive to the gas station.

We get the gas we need and after a quick break, the stress from the ordeal finally calms.

"Us in the back of a cop car! First time for everything!" I tease as we wait for Jenn to get back from the restroom. We look around the back of the cop car and get the biggest kick out of the metal barrier and no door handles.

"I don't know how we've managed to stay out of the back of one these, with all the crazy shit we've gotten ourselves into over the years," Lana says.

Ashley grabs the barrier and pretends to escape. "It's like something out of a movie!"

"I know! No one's going to believe this actually happened," I add.

"Ooo! Ooo! I have my camera! We can take pictures!" Lana says, fumbling through her purse.

Officer Mullins chuckles as he snaps a picture of the three of us holding our hands up in a surrender pose.

"I can honestly say, I can't think of a single time I've had anyone actually excited about being in the back of a police car."

It's late evening by the time Lana and I pull up to our apartment. "Another wild weekend comes to an end!"

I smile and nod. "This was definitely one for the Kate and Lana record book!"

CHAPTER FIFTEEN
Georgia vs. Auburn Weekend

"Warrrrrrrr Eagle Hey!" The kickoff chant of the Auburn Tigers fills the large stadium, as the time clock to the oldest rivalry in the Southeast begins counting down.

"God, I had forgotten how much I hate Auburn until I pulled into this ridiculous cow town."

"Don't be hatin' on my school, Lana!" James yells, popping his orange and blue shaker on the top of her head.

I wave the flask I snuck in. "Take a few nips and you'll forget all about your hatred."

"Can't we ditch this game and head on to Columbus?" she whines.

"No, you cannot!" James balks. "You can go three more hours without your precious wittle snooky wooky!" For added annoyance, he and I make kissy noises in each one of her ears.

She shoos us away. "Y'all suck almost as bad as this freakin' school does!"

It's been three weeks since our crazy Labor Day weekend and Lana and I have been going nonstop ever since. Classes are in full swing and the ones I'm taking this semester are kicking my ass. I've done everything I can to keep my mind off all things, Fort Benning. I've forced myself to attend all the Georgia home games, drug Lana to a few parties, and even went home to pull a few shifts at DiMaggio's. But with her still dating Artie, and Santos and Ashley seeing each other now, it looks like I won't be closing this chapter of my life anytime soon.

James pulled a few strings to get me, Lana, and Ashley free tickets to the Auburn / Georgia game. And since our schools were playing each other it was almost impossible to say no. Lana jumped at the opportunity to be forty minutes away from Fort Benning and began making plans the second she heard the news.

I, on the other hand, had absolutely no desire to be anywhere near Columbus. Between Max and the whole Davis thing, it's best if I sit this visit out. I intend on getting rip-roaring drunk, hitting a few parties and ending the night on my brother's lumpy sofa.

"Yuck!" She shivers. "Is this whiskey?"

"Yep! Bottom's up!"

"There is no way in hell I can drink this shit!"

I laugh and shrug. "No problem. More for me!"

A flask of whiskey and four beers later, we've made it to the fourth quarter of a fantastic match up. The crowd goes wild as Auburn kicks a field goal to tie up the game.

"I think Ash and I are going to head out. Try to beat the traffic."

"You're not actually going to leave with the game tied, are you?"

"I don't give eight shits about this game, Kate! You know football bores the hell out of me. What I do give a shit about is my hot-ass boyfriend and partying with all our crazy-ass friends. Which *you* could be a part of if you'd put on your big girl panties!"

I roll my eyes, annoyed at her words. But let the idea of going bounce around my loopy head. I'm tipsy enough to call her bluff. "Screw it! Let's go."

I continue to consume JD as we make it to Columbus in record time. Thankful I'm too buzzed to overthink my decision to tag along. As the large beige building comes into view, I scan the parking lot for Max's Harley and relieved to see it isn't here.

The thump of loud music and laughter bellows through the halls the moment we reach the building steps.

"I bet that's our crew making all the noise," Lana says, perky for the first time all night.

A guy manning the front desk greets us with a friendly smile. "You must be Lana and Ashley?"

They both flash big smiles of excitement. "Yep! That's us!"

"Artie's been down here at least a half a dozen times looking for y'all." He laughs. "Feel free to head on up."

I watch as Lana and Ash fly up the stairs two at a time. "He didn't mention a third," he quizzes.

I fan the air. "Oh, don't mind me. I'm just the tag along."

He flashes a smile exposing a mouth full of crooked teeth and throws out a hand. "I'm Kevin!"

I knew the "Hot Guy Train" in this building would eventually have to make a stop at Unattractive Station. I think as I try not to stare at his acne and unibrow.

"Kevin?" I ask, taking his hand. "Like plain ole Kevin? No crazy nickname or last name only?"

He laughs. "It's Griggs ninety-percent of the time. So it's nice to be called by my first name every now and then."

"Well, Kevin. It's nice to meet you. I'm Kate." I release his hand. "So you got stuck with CQ Duty this weekend, huh?"

"Yeah," he groans. "And it's been the longest day in history. I had to miss all the good football games."

"We just left the Auburn-Georgia game. It was a nail-biter all the way to the end."

He shakes his head and groans again. "I heard! I hate I missed it."

"Wait! Are you the guy from Alpharetta?" I ask as the night we met Max flashes through my head.

"I am," he chuckles. "I wasn't going to mention it on account you girls were probably still in elementary school when I was there."

"Oh, come on now. You can't be *that* old," I tease. "Maybe you know my brother, Eric Carpenter. He graduated in 89."

"Holy shit! Yes! Eric's your brother? What a great guy. Please tell him I say hello."

"I sure will!" I say, floored. "It's crazy what a small world we actually live in."

"It most certainly is," he agrees.

I glance towards the second-floor entry. "Well, I guess I better get upstairs before they send the Calvary after me."

"I only have an hour left. Maybe I will pop by when I'm done."

"You should! If we keep digging, we may find out we're long lost, cousins!" I shout, trekking up the stairs.

I clear the landing as nerves flood my body. Sweat gathers on my neck as I peer down the hall towards Max's room. *Calm down! He's not here!* I remind myself.

I make my way the opposite direction, following the loud music. The door's open to the packed room. "There she is!" Lana yells, buried in the sea of people piled on the twin size bed.

I'm welcomed in with hugs and high fives, including a few from the ladies I'd met on my "latrine date."

I spot Davis the second I walk in, but we keep our hellos casual. We make eye contact, but don't speak until I've made introductions to everyone else. He's sitting on the bed with Lana, Artie, and another girl, who I don't know. He stands as I make my way through the small crowd.

"This is a nice surprise," he says in my ear, pulling me in for a bear hug. "They told me you weren't coming."

"Oh, you know Lana," I say, poking her in the knee. "She always figures out a way to talk me into things."

"You can have my spot," Davis says. "It's a little tight in here right now."

"Thanks," I say, popping beside Lana, who's already pulling back the tab of a beer for me.

"Whose room is this?"

"It's Davis's," Lana whispers. "And the blond girl who jumped up behind him… she's been glued to him since we walked in."

"She's pretty," I admit. "Looks a little trashy, though. Which of course is right up Davis's alley."

Davis's room has a loveseat on the right wall and his small bed pushed against the far back wall. Upside-down buckets have been made into makeshift seats and in the corner, sits an expensive stereo system with a pyramid of empty beer cans on top. Other than a calendar with Ms. September sprawled across a Corvette, there isn't anything else displayed.

Twelve of us are piled into his little room. It's hot and loud, but everyone appears to be having fun. With the exception of Davis, who seems frustrated and isn't making himself the center of attention like normal.

"Goldie Locks is following Davis around like a shadow," Lana notices.

"I know. He looks pissed off."

Davis looks over while we're talking. "You ok?" I mouth.

He shakes his head slightly and rolls his eyes towards the girl. "She must be getting on his nerves," I whisper to Lana.

Lana motions to Davis to come over. Which he immediately does. "Why don't you sit right here?" Lana pats the bed, scooting over so there's an open spot in between us.

"You look miserable."

"You have no idea," he groans.

"Lady troubles?"

He lets out a deep huff. "She's a friend of Shepard's." He gestures over to one of the girls on the couch. "I met her at a club a few weeks ago and she's been stalking me ever since."

I raise an eyebrow. "I know what you're thinking and *no*. I didn't hook up with her. So you can stop giving me that look."

It's the first time he's smiled since I arrived.

I grab his chin and shake it. "I guess it's that irresistible charm of yours."

He laughs. "I forgot how much I miss having you around."

As expected, it didn't take Goldie locks long to take the hint. Her and several others head to another party being hosted on the third floor.

The four of us sit on Davis's bed, with Ashley and Santos on the couch, cutting up for what seemed like hours. Laughing so hard at times my sides hurt.

"You know what I have been thinking about for weeks and would give my left arm to have right about now?" I ask.

"Davis on the bathroom counter again?" Lana jokes, sending laughter booming through the room.

My face turns bloodshot red, but it's too funny to not laugh at. "No! Smart-ass!" I glance over at Davis, who's getting a kick out of it as well. "I've actually been thinking about those damn chocolates from Griffin's Candy Shop."

"Oh my God! Yes!" Ashley shouts.

Davis nods. "Yep! Those turtles were out of this world!"

I match his nod. "Yes, they were."

"I don't think I got any of those. Y'all must have been hogging them," Lana says.

I smirk as my mind drifts to us lying in bed, passing the bag of chocolates back and forth. I glance over at Davis and know he's remembering it too.

"How about a celebratory shot, toasting to great friends and great laughs," Santos says passing shot glasses to everyone. We clink them together and I throw it back. The disgusting licorice flavor burning its way to my stomach. *Well, this was a mistake!*

"Um, Kate? You ok? You're looking a little green."

I don't answer right away, my stomach churning. "Nope! Last shot. Bad idea!" I yell, sprinting to the latrine. Praying I make it in time.

Being a true best friend, Lana steps in the stall to help. She holds my hair back as a night's worth of JD and Jaeger shows itself in the ugliest form. I rest between wretches on the cold green tile, swearing off liquor forever.

Twenty minutes and an empty stomach later, I drag back to Davis's room.

"Feel better?" Santos asks.

"My head's pounding, but better."

Davis squints his eyes. "Sorry I couldn't hold your hair back this time," he slurs.

"Looks like I'm not the only one who drank a little too much tonight," I say, kicking him on the foot. "I think maybe it's time we all call it a night."

Artie checks his watch. "Holy Shit! It's two-thirty in the morning."

Lane smiles devilishly. "Take me to bed or lose me forever!"

"Well, I guess that's your cue, Goose!" Santos teases, recognizing the *Top Gun* quote.

I crouch beside Davis. "Mind if I crash on your couch?"

"You can take the bed. I'm good rightttt here," he says, awkwardly patting his hand on the couch.

"Are you sure?" I ask. Thankful, neither one of us is in any condition for any potential late night hook up. Things are getting back to normal and I don't want to risk it with another Gatlinburg repeat.

After our goodnights, the couples head to their perspective rooms on the floor. Leaving Davis and me alone for the first time. He's awake but appears to be in a drunken fog.

"Crap! I'll be right back. My bag's in Lana's car and there's no way in hell I can sleep with my contacts in." I catch her before they make it to Artie's room.

Thanks to my barf fest, I've sobered up some, but still stagger as I make my way to the car. I scan the lot again for any sign of Max and catch myself slightly disappointed he's still out. "I guess he's with *her*," I say out loud to no one.

By the time I finally make it back to the room, I'm dead tired and in desperate need of Ibuprofen and a bed. I try to open the door, but it's locked. I'm forced to knock and stir Davis from his cozy position.

"Sorry, didn't mean to make you get up," I say when he opens the door, wearing nothing but his boxers.

He hiccups. "These damn doors open from the inside, even if it's locked. It's annoying as shit. So don't close the door all the way if you have to leave again."

"Oh, that's right. I remember Drew telling me about that."

"I bet I've locked myself out at least two dozen times," he slurs, before staggering out for a last-minute bathroom run.

I shuffle through my bag for my contacts case and spot an eight by ten frame, lying face down on the dresser. So of course, I do what any nosey person would do and flip it over...

Department of the Army Certificate of Achievement
Sgt. John Patrick Davis
In recognition of your outstanding performance in Artillery
Regiment Combatives
Fort Benning, Georgia. February 10, 1994
Your achievement reflects great credit upon yourself, your
unit and The United States Army

Hmm! He looks like a John. It fits him. Curious, I slip open the door to his wardrobe. His uniforms are neatly hung across the wooden rod. His formal ones still in dry-cleaning plastic, tucked in the back. I run my fingers across his medals, patches, and ribbons, hanging in a plastic organizer on the inside of the door. Polished boots line perfectly across the bottom. I spot a thick stack of papers on the top shelf and thumb through a few. They're all certificates, similar to the framed one, all acknowledging different work achievements.

I change into my favorite oversized Snoopy T-shirt and settle into Davis's bed. It's comfortable and I can smell his cologne on the sheets. I lay thinking about the words I've read.

How did I go this long and not know his first name is John? Or that he is a freaking Sergeant? I've known this entire time he was in the Army, but reading his accomplishments is oddly eye-opening. He's always so damn cavalier about life. Learning he's such a decorated member of the military shocks me for some reason. He may play it off, but it's evident he takes a lot of pride in what he does.

"Thanks for letting me crash in here," I say as he slips back into the room.

"I know you probably feel weird being here," he says. Both of us know why, without having to say Max's name. "So always know you can crash in here anytime you like."

I don't respond. There's no point. But I am appreciative of the open invite.

The music is still on, but not as loud as it had been earlier. Led Zeppelin is playing and he's badly singing along to "Stairway to Heaven."

"I think I hear a dog howling outside."

He cracks a smile. "You making fun of my singing?"

I chuckle as he flips off the light and stumbles back to the couch. We lay in silence, listening to the music. Finally allowing exhaustion to set in.

The ridiculously long song ends and I couldn't be happier it's finally over. But seconds later, the first few guitar riffs begin to play again.

"Uhhhh? Do you have this song on repeat?"

He chuckles. "It definitely sounds like I do."

"Oh no, no, no!" I say, shaking my head. "You're going to have to turn this shit off. My head's pounding hard enough as is."

"Ok, ok. I will," he mumbles. "Let me listen through the end and I'll turn it off, I promise."

I cave to his compromise. "Fair enough."

I listen for a few and begin to doze off.

"Hey, Kate?"

Startled, I rub my eyes and yawn out a sleepy, "Yeah?"

"I'm glad you came tonight," he mumbles. "It was good seeing …"

"Davis?"

No answer.

"Davis!" I yell. Louder this time. "You're going to have to turn off the music."

He still doesn't budge, so I try throwing a pillow at him. *I'm going to fucking kill him!*

After a failed attempt to turn the music off, I lay staring at the ceiling, as the song plays over and over. Sounding louder and louder with every note. And now, to make matters worse… he's snoring. *Errr!* I can't figure out his high tech system, the remote's nowhere to be found, and I can't reach the back to unplug it. *This can't be happening! It's like Chinese water torture in here!* I toss and turn, trying desperately to drown out the noise. I throw my arm, the pillow, and the blanket over my head, but it's useless. *"Stairway to Heaven" my ass! Stairway to HELL is more appropriate!*

It's three in the morning, I'm wide awake, annoyed and dying to pee. I fling the covers off and jump from the bed. Leaving my glasses behind, but grabbing a cigarette from my secret stash before slipping out. Thankful the restrooms are right across the hall, so I can slip over as I am.

I sit in the chilly stall, smoking my cigarette, reveling in the joy of complete silence.

Dreading the thought of having to go back into my own personal hell. I rest my head against the cold metal partition and watch a tiny spider pop in and out from the adjoining stall.

I savor every minute of my Led Zeppelin reprieve and reluctantly make my way back across the empty hall. I reach for the handle when it hits me…

"Oh shit!" I yell out, trying to turn the locked knob. *Son of a… I completely forgot about the damn lock!*
I tap on the door, hoping by some miracle I can wake Davis without waking the entire floor in the process.

Tap, Tap, Tap.
No answer. Nothing but the sounds of that damn song.
I tap harder this time. TAP, TAP, TAP.
Nothing.

I wait quietly for the song to end and knock during the few seconds break before the loop begins again.
Nothing.

Don't freak out! I tell myself, realizing I'm standing in the middle of the bright hallway, barefoot, in only a T-shirt and panties. Unable to see three feet in front of me without my glasses, I give it one last shot; knocking as loud as I can. Dismissing any concern for the surrounding neighbors.
Nothing.

"Dammit!"

I give up and make my way to Artie's room, hoping desperately I can at least get one of them to answer. Unfortunately, between no glasses, the booze, and pure exhaustion, I'm not a hundred percent sure I have the right door.

You've got to be kidding me! They all look the same. White walls, white doors. One after the other. I knock lightly, praying it's the right room.

No answer, so I knock harder. Panic begins to set in, worried I might be stuck out here until God only knows when. I lean against the wall and collapse to my feet as tears begin to stream down my cheeks. *I should have kept my ass in Auburn.*

I make a sad attempt to look at the bright side. *The fluorescent lights are bright enough to land a plane, but at least it's quiet.* Defeated, I curl into a ball and close my eyes, desperately trying to push past the pounding in my head enough to doze off.

It feels like it's only been minutes when the faint sound of laughter carries through the hall. *Am I dreaming?* The voices get closer and louder. *No, I'm not dreaming!* Forcing my eyes open as they make their way up the stairs. I squint to see who it is but I can only see shadows without my glasses. They're walking towards me as embarrassment sets in. *Perfect! As if this couldn't get any more humiliating.*

"Whatcha doin' out here all by yourself, doll?" One of the guys whispers loudly down the long hall.

I take a deep breath and attempt to play it cool. "Oh, I accidentally locked my silly ass out." Quickly wiping tear stains from my cheeks before they get any closer.

When they make it to me, three fuzzy images come into focus and by their boisterous behavior, it's clear they've been out partying.

Two of them stoop around me. "Well, aren't you a pretty little thing," one says, making me slightly uncomfortable.

"How long have you been sitting out here?" the other asks.

I'm not up for the small talk, but I'm in no position to be rude. "I'm not sure. I ran to the restroom and came back to a locked door."

"Oh yeah, they'll open from the inside, even if they're locked on the outside," the one standing chimes.

No shit, Sherlock! Or I wouldn't be sitting in the fucking hallway in my underwear, like an idiot!

I bite the urge to be a bitch and opt for the sweeter route. "Yep, learned the hard way, I guess." Forcing a smile.

"You couldn't get Artie up?"

Well, at least I had the right room.

"No, I tried knocking about fifty times, but was worried I'd piss off the entire floor if I kept it up."

"Well, you can come crash in our room if you like."

"ABSOLUTELY NOT!"

The four of us whip our heads towards the voice approaching. It's only a silhouette, but I know exactly who it is. *Just when I think my night can't get any worse.*

"Where the hell did you go, Maxi?"

"I had to piss," he snips.

"Come meet our new friend!"

He's five feet away from me now, finally coming into focus. So close I can smell him.

"What are you doing out here, Kate?"

I look up, but I'm unable to speak. I want to sink into the floor as every fiber in my body fights the urge to cry.

"Oh, you know her?"

I meet his gaze for a split second, then it falls to his shiny gold band.

"I do," he says. "She's a friend of mine." His voice wavering at the end.

There is something in his choice of words that instantly infuriates me, causing my heart to grow ice cold. *Friends, huh?*

"She locked herself out," one answers for me. The other adding, "Poor things been sitting out here for an hour."

Fueled by jealousy and pain, the sudden need to lash out takes over. "If the offer still stands to crash in your room…," I say, popping to my feet.

"Hell yeah, the offer still stands! Um, do you have purple underwear on?"

As if I'm not even here, Max begins spouting orders. "No!" he says firmly. "I'll crash with y'all. Kate can take my room."

The others realize quickly Max is in no mood for a debate. The plan is non-negotiable, without any regard to what I might have wanted to do. But I'm too tired and mentally drained to argue about it.

Annoyed and confused, I stomp off in the direction of Max's room. He grabs me by the wrist and begins walking towards another door. The tears I've been fighting flood my eyes the second he touches me.

He's moved since I was last here. This room is bigger and he's personalized it more than the other. I stand in the center looking around, wondering if he's going to take the opportunity to explain everything now that I've *literally* been delivered to his doorstep.

The awkwardness between us is as loud as the music in Davis's room. Without saying a word, he grabs a change of clothes from a laundry basket. I turn my back, not knowing if he plans to change in here. Instead, he hands over a pair of gray Army athletic shorts, clearly wanting me to cover up.

A framed five by seven, photo of Max and a girl who I can only assume is *her*, is sitting on the small window ledge above his bed. They're smiling in front of a Christmas tree, both appearing ridiculously happy. I close my eyes, desperately trying to keep my anger in check. I turn around when the door creaks open. He's leaving and I can't stop the urge to hurt him as much as I am.

"How's the wife, Max? Been busy picking out china patterns and baby names?"

He looks over with pain in his eyes and I immediately regret saying it. I feel terrible but refuse to let it show. I turn away and climb into his neatly made bed as he closes the door without saying a word. I lay engulfed in his world and cry myself to sleep.

I manage to get a couple of hours of sleep and for a brief moment, wonder if I dreamt the entire night. But I'm quickly hit with a five by seven reality check. Their ridiculous smiles taunting me as I crawl from Max's bed. I feel like death, smell like a whiskey factory, and now noticing I have a tiny chunk of barf stuck in my hair. *I'm living an actual nightmare!* I have to get out of here. Leave and never step foot in this God-forsaken place again.

I look over to see what time it is, but it's blocked. *What the hell is that?* I lean closer and spot a small white envelope with "Kate" written on the outside, propped against the alarm clock. My hand shakes as I slowly reach for the letter. He's been in here this morning. He was right here beside me, close enough to touch and I didn't know. Never heard a sound. I stare at my name as a million thoughts of what it might say flood my mind. I tear the corner open but stop. Too afraid to read his words.

It's nine-thirty in the morning and I'm desperate to get home. I'm thankful Max is nowhere in sight and the door to Artie's room is open. He and Lana are lying in bed, comparing feet sizes when I walk in.

"Damn! Rough night?" Lana asks.

I shake my head. "There are no words."

An hour and two, weepy, lovesick goodbyes later, we're finally headed north. I wait until Lana and Ashley finish telling all about their amazing, perfect, loving, make me want to rip my ears off, night, before letting them in on my disastrous eight hours.

"Well, you won't believe this… *but*… I slept in Max's room last night," I blurt.

"WHAT!?" Lana shouts, running two wheels of the car off the road.

It takes me over an hour to catch them up on the entire ordeal. And by the time I finish, I'm as angry, hurt, and confused as ever.

"So you haven't opened the letter yet?" Ashley asks.

I pull the envelope out of my purse. His small, neatly written, handwriting staring up at me.

"Don't stare at it, Kate! Open it!" Lana demands.

"I can't. Not right now. I just…"

"Well, it sounds like he still cares for you," Ash says gingerly. "So much so he'd risk having you in his room so you didn't have to sleep with strangers."

"But why not take the opportunity to talk to me? It was like I was delivered on a silver platter and he *still* didn't have the balls to explain things."

"Maybe he was too ashamed or embarrassed. Maybe that's why he left the letter instead."

I don't respond. I sit in a mental fog as my mind and heart pull me in a million different directions. I trace the A and the R of the word Army, printed on the shorts I couldn't bring myself to part with.

CHAPTER SIXTEEN
Artie's 22nd Birthday

They say time heals all wounds, but for me maybe a small white envelope holds the key to healing mine. A week has passed and I have yet to muster the courage to open the letter Max left for me. It's sitting on my dresser, begging to be opened. But I'm too afraid. Too afraid it will be the closure I so desperately need, but do not want. Closure would mean having to admit it's over. The pain is what keeps him real. A constant reminder, that even though it was only for a brief moment, he was mine.

A hard knock on our apartment door shakes me out of my daze.

"Lanaaaaa!?"

"What?" she yells, from the bathroom.

"I think Artie's here."

"He's not supposed to be here for another hour."

"Well, someone's knocking!"

"Can you get it, pleaseeeee? I just got in the shower!" she whines through the door.

I'd been dreading this visit from the moment it was planned. It's incredibly hard to keep the jealousy monster contained as is. Having to witness it in the confines of my home is downright torture.

I swing the door open. "Welcome to the nuthouse!"

Artie greets me with a huge smile and a hug.

His chin drops. "Holy shit! Look at this place!" he says as he and Santos walk in.

"Between this sweet ass apartment and all the lavish weekends you two go on, y'all are officially spoiled rotten!"

"Rurnt! As they say in the South!" Santos jokes.

"What can I say, our parents love us!" I say admittedly, scanning our beautifully furnished two-bedroom apartment, overlooking the swimming pool.

"Where's my gorgeous girlfriend?" he asks.

A familiar jolt of envy punches my gut. "She's in the shower and Ash should be pulling up any minute."

Artie grins devilishly. "She's in the shower, eh?"

I shake my head. "The bathroom is down the hall, third door on the right, ya big perv!"

Santos and I bust out in laughter when Lana screams a few seconds later.

"Those two are a mess," he chuckles.

"They're definitely two peas in a pod, that's for sure."

We take seats in the living room and continue to make small talk for as we wait for the others.

"You excited about Six Flags tomorrow?"

"You better believe it! I've been in Georgia over two years and this is the first time I've been able to take leave to go."

"I guess Ashley's persuasion helped motivate you."

"She's pretty damn awesome, I won't lie," he admits.

"Well, I have no doubt you guys will have a fantastic time. The weather is supposed to be nice and since school's back in, it shouldn't be too terribly crowded."

"Wait. You're not going with us?"

"Nah, I'm sittin' this one out. I'm not up for the whole fifth wheel thing. I'd be riding all the rides by myself, which would only remind me of how pathetic my love life is." I laugh to cover how true the statement actually is.

"Well, shit. I wish we had known you were bailing on us. We could have brought Max to keep you company."

"Um, I know this won't come as a huge surprise. But ever since the whole marriage and baby thing…Max and I aren't exactly on speaking terms."

An odd expression sets on his face. I open my mouth to ask him about it when Lana and Artie rumble down the hall.

"Kate! For the last time… You will **not** be the fifth wheel!" she shouts, rounding the corner of the living room.

I smile. "Thank you for wanting to include me. I appreciate it, but I'm not feeling it. I'm thinking about heading home for the weekend. James will be there, and since I bailed on him at the football game a few weeks ago, thought it would be a good time to make it up to him."

"I miss your crazy ass brother! I keep forgetting how close he is, now that he's at Auburn. We all need to plan a trip to visit him," Artie says.

"He was talking about a big Halloween party his fraternity is throwing. Maybe we can plan to go that weekend?" I suggest.

"Hell yeah! The one night a year I get to dress slutty without the shame! Count me in!"

Artie lifts an eyebrow. "Not too slutty, Lana Michelle Mathews. I have a hard enough time keeping guys off your sexy ass as is."

She throws her hands on her hips. "Oh, it's totally happening, Samuel. Ryan. Armstrong!"

I crinkle my nose. "It's so weird to hear your actual name, Artie."

He laughs, poking Lana in the side. "Yeah, her and my mom are about the only ones who call me Sam anymore."

"There she is!" Santos says, grinning ear to ear as Ashley walks in the door.

He scoops her in his arms. "You up for a Halloween party in Auburn, babe?"

"Can we get one of those ridiculous-looking couple costumes?"

"You better believe it!"

"Then I say you've got yourself a date!"

The five of us bum around the apartment for a few hours, catching up on all the latest news since we were last together. I pass around the pictures we had taken on Labor Day and we all have some good laughs reminiscing. The guys get the biggest kick out of us telling the "non-Lana" version of our running out of gas fiasco.

"Something was clearly wrong with the car. The gas thingy showed we still had a quarter of a tank left," Lana says, trying not to laugh.

"You know you go to hell for lying, right?" Ash teases.

Artie fans the shot of the three of us in the back of the cop car. "At least y'all got some cool pictures out of it."

"Just another crazy day in the life of Lana and Kate," I say.

"Here's an interesting picture," he says, showing the room the picture Davis and I took at dinner, the night of our infamous hook-up.

I snatch it from his hand. "Give me that! All this picture does, is remind me how much his arrogant act got on my nerves."

"If my mind serves me right, he got on something else that particular weekend as well!" Lana teases.

I snarl to keep from laughing. "You're both assholes! You know that right?"

"Speaking of Davis…why didn't he come with y'all?" Ashley asks.

"He wanted to, but his sister's getting married this weekend. We actually dropped him off at the airport on our way through Atlanta," Santos says.

"Well, tell him we said hello. And make sure he knows about the Halloween plans."

"And speaking of guys Kate's hooked up with..." Lana smirks.

I open the fridge to make a glass of sweet tea. "Oh, Lord. Here we go."

"Since you're being a titty baby and running back to Alpharetta for the weekend. You have to promise to stay the hell away from Wayne, ok?"

"Well, yeah. Of course," I groan. "I have zero desire to be anywhere near him this weekend, or any weekend for that matter."

"Don't pretend this is coming out of left field! You know if you go out, someone will tell him where you're at and he'll show up."

"Is Wayne the dickhead who got in the fight with Max and Drew?" Artie asks.

"Yes! And ever since Kate's dumbass got drunk and slept with him two months ago, he's been calling here non-stop."

"Hey! I was in mourning! I had a reason for being a dumbass!"

Lana points her finger. "Stay the hell away from him! I mean it!"

"Geez! Ok, Mom!" I snarl, throwing a cube of ice from my glass at her.

It's late Friday afternoon and I'm headed home to Alpharetta. It's early October now, the leaves are beginning to fall, and it's finally cold enough to pack the shorts and tanks away until spring. Although Lana made two more attempts to convince me to stay, I couldn't do it. I'm thrilled beyond words my two best friends are happy and in love. I can't find the strength to fester in the middle of it all weekend.

I lied about James being home. It was the quickest excuse I could think of at the time. I'll fess up once I get back on Sunday. What's worse, my parents are out of town and Jack didn't need any help at the restaurant. So there's actually no true reason I should be heading home, other than to escape the love nest. I bring Max's letter with me, hoping maybe I'll find the strength to open it at some point.

The radio's dialed to the local classic rock channel as I make my way through the heavy traffic. As the Alpharetta exit appears in the distance, my stomach flutters when I spot the large green interstate directional sign. *Columbus-133 Miles.*

I bite my nails as thoughts of Max and the letter race through my mind. My knee bounces on the steering wheel; my willpower to avoid his words, crumbling. I can't stand it any longer. I have to know what he's written. I exit, finding a place to park at my favorite Shell station. My hands shake as I pull the letter from my purse and slowly rip the envelope.

There isn't a day that passes I don't think of you.
I hope one day you'll be able to forgive me.
I love you,
Max

I gasp. *He loves me?*

As if it was a sign, the first few notes of "Hotel California" begin to play loudly through the speakers. The same song that played the night we met. The one we sang at the top of our lungs. Our hands swaying in the air without a care in the world. The night my life was forever changed. I read his words again and know what I have to do. Without a second thought, I throw the car in drive. Following my heart...

I was at complete peace with my decision the entire drive until I pass through the gates of Fort Benning. *What the hell are you doing, Kate?* I slam my fists against the wheel. *Errrrrrr! No! Don't think!* I keep repeating it as his building comes into sight. My stomach's a ball of nerves as I pull into the parking lot, spotting Max's motorcycle parked a couple of spaces over. I turn off the engine and close my eyes. Taking long deep breaths to steady the shaking in my hands.

I pull the rearview mirror down to check my make-up, realizing I hadn't prepared for this little venture south. As I rub lip gloss on, I notice a black gentleman standing in the doorway of the main lobby entrance. *Shit!* I yell out, crouching in the seat even though he's too far away to see me. It's the Sergeant Jackass who ran us off on Memorial Day. He's in street clothes, but I recognize him in an instant. I stay slouched in the car trying to wait him out. But after twenty minutes with no sign of him leaving, I'm forced to move to plan B.

Sweat pools on the back of my neck as I cross the lot, trying desperately to blend in. I say a silent thank you when I find the side door unlocked and slip up the back stairwell. My bearings are off, but manage to find the correct direction of Max's room. Passing over the open atrium, I peek down to the check-in desk below. Jackson's manning the phones, as he and Sgt. Jackass shoot the breeze. Their laughter echoes across the tall ceiling as I slip past them unnoticed. I walk the long hall, the stark white walls and bright lighting bring back horrible memories of my last visit and the disappointment on Max's face when I lashed out at him.

I take a minute to calm myself when I make it to his room. I pull sweaty hair off my neck and do a quick armpit check. *Thank God, for extra strength deodorant!*
My heart pounds against my chest as I knock.

"It's open!" Max yells through a small crack in the door. I close my eyes, trying to find the courage to push the knob. *Pull it together, Kate!* The door swings open as I reach for it. A small gasp escapes as his mouth falls. Speechless, we stand blinking at each other. He takes a step forward and wraps his arms tightly around; burying his head into my hair. I smell his cologne and feel my knees weaken under him.

He pulls his arms back to grab my face. He feels around in disbelief. "Am I dreaming? You came back?"

"I came back," I whisper. Fighting the urge to cry.

We're interrupted by the sound of voices coming up the stairs. "Get in here," he says, taking me by the hand to pull me in. His arms back around me the second the door shuts.

"I hope it's ok I'm here."

"Of course it is," he says with a huge smile. "You have no idea how happy I am to see you."

I let out a nervous laugh. "I won't lie. I almost talked myself out of it when I pulled into the parking lot. But knew I'd regret it if I did."

He shakes his head in disbelief. "I think I'm in shock." His voice grows serious. "I mean after everything that happened last time."

I peel from his embrace. "That's kind of why I'm here. I thought maybe with everyone gone, it might be a good time for us to clear the air."

"Yeah, I heard about the big birthday plans," he says as we both take a seat on the edge of his bed. "It about killed me when I saw them all leaving out earlier."

"Why?"

He gives a knowing look. "Pure, heart-shattering, jealousy."

A twinge of pleasure races through me as he says the words. But bury it, since he's the whole reason we're in this situation in the first place. I bite my lip, mustering the courage to have the conversation we're both dreading.

My eyes drift to the floor. "Why didn't you call me Max?"

"I'm so sorry," he says with a heavy breath. "I know you deserved to hear it directly from me. It's just…I knew if I heard your voice…even for a second, I wouldn't have been able to go through with it. And I *had* to. I *had* to do the right thing. There was no other option." He shakes his head in irritation. "Not to mention she was watching me like a damn hawk!"

I don't interrupt, hanging onto every word. "By the time she left, I was too embarrassed to call. As the days and weeks passed, it only got harder. I would pick up the phone to call you, then talk myself out of it. Too afraid calling you to explain would mean admitting it was over. And I wasn't ready to let go yet." He taps his feet nervously on the tile floor. "I'm so sorry. The last thing I ever wanted to do was hurt you," he admits, finally looking at me as tears fill his eyes.

"If it hadn't been for the storm, we would have been here when she showed up. We had barely made it out past Atlanta before we had to turn around. It was either divine intervention or a terrible twist of fate. Either way, it was obvious we weren't meant to be here."

"You have to know what I said in my note is true. Not a day goes by I don't think about you." He grabs my hands and squeezes.

"Hell, everything reminds me of you. No matter how hard I've tried to put my feelings for you aside, they're always there."

His face goes rigid as he springs to his feet. "I think that's what pisses me off more than anything about this whole screwed up situation! It's that she knew! She knew I was over her and had fallen for someone else. She knew the only thing that could tear you and I apart was to cook up a damn pregnancy story. And like a fucking idiot, I fell for it hook, line, and sinker!"

Stunned, I throw my hands in the air. "*WHAT!?*" My chin dropping to my knees.

His eyes go blank. "She lied, Kate. Didn't you know?"

"I… uh…" My mouth is physically unable to make words.

"I figured that's why you were here. That Artie told you."

My hands glue to each cheek. "No. Neither one of them said a word. They were acting a little off, but no." I shake my head. "How could she do this?"

He paces the room, his fist balled on his hips. "Her best friend, Kristen told me. I had never met her. Never even knew Jody had any close friends until then. She called out of the blue and said she had something important to tell me. That she couldn't live with herself knowing someone was being used so badly. I guess it's been about two weeks now, right after you were here." He sits back beside me and continues. "She said Jody admitted she wasn't pregnant, and since we were living apart, she would fake a miscarriage at some point."

My eyes widen. "Are you kidding me!?"

"Evidently, she thought I would feel so sorry for her about the miscarriage, I wouldn't have the heart to divorce her in her 'terrible time of need'."

"Thank God her friend was an honest enough person to rat her out!"

"Kristen told me she was pissed off I had met someone, but it ultimately boiled down to money. Since she was discharged from the Army, she'd been freaking out over how to pay bills and her military insurance was about to run out. She couldn't find a job that paid more than minimum wage, so she concocted the whole pregnancy lie to get my paycheck and benefits."

I punch the bed with both fists. "What a straight. Up. Evil. Bitch! What kind of sick sociopath does that?"

"I'm having the marriage annulled, Kate," he blurts. I sit back down and grab my temples.

"I'm clueless, Max. How exactly does that work?"

"I was too. But thanks to her, I've had to get a crash course in ending botched marriages. It's different from a divorce, where both parties acknowledge the marriage. An annulment will be like it never happened."

A loud knock at the door startles us. A male voice with a strong northern accent yells. "Hey man, ya ready to go?"

My head whips around. "Oh shit, Max! I'm so sorry. I should have known you were going out," I whisper.

Not whispering and without hesitation. "Nope! There's no way in hell I'm going anywhere tonight unless it's with you."

He jumps up to open the door. "Should I hide?" I panic, scanning the room for a place to dive.

He laughs. "Well hell no, silly woman! Why would you ask that?" he asks, flinging the door open.

I don't recognize the person and I catch him off guard when he spots me. "Oh! I didn't know ya had company!" he says, wide-eyed.

"Coop… this is Kate." I stand as he introduces me. "Kate… this is Cooper. He's from Jersey."

"It's a pleasure to meetcha," he says, extending his hand out.

"You too, Cooper. Thank you."

"Wait a minute," his right brow raising. "Are you *the* Kate? The Alpharetta Kate?"

Max beams with pride. "Yes. She. Is!" My heart melting at the sound of *"the Kate."*

"Well, I guess this means you won't be joining us tonight, huh?" he says with a chuckle.

"Sorry man! We've got a lot of catchin' up to do."

"No problem, Maxi. Catch up wich' ya girl. We can go out another night." Cooper throws his arm out to shake Max's hand. "Kate, I'm glad to finally put a face with the name. I've heard so much about ya, I feel like I already knows ya!"

"Oh, Lord! I'm afraid to ask," I say, slightly embarrassed.

"All good. Promise," he chuckles. "The story of you rolling into the family of raccoons had me laughin' for days!"

"Yep! Those little bastards wanted to see me on a dinner plate."

Max smiles but his eyes drop to the floor. He wasn't there for that trip and his discomfort is apparent. We say our goodbyes and Max walks out with him.

My curiosity gets the best of me when I hear whispers. I slip closer to eavesdrop, but can't make out what everything they're saying.

"I thought he was in Alpharetta?"

"No, I don't think so. He told me he was flying home for his sista's wedding," Cooper replies.

They're talking about Davis and I panic. The mere thought of having to have a conversation about the whole Davis thing makes me cringe.

I bolt back to the bed when feet shuffle up the hall. "You hungry?" he asks, closing the door behind him.

I grab my stomach. "Starving!"

"Me too! How about we go grab some dinner? I know we still have a ton more to talk about, but at least we can do it with full bellies."

"That works!"

"What are you in the mood for?" he asks.

"Well, are you wanting to go through a drive-thru or…"

"No way! Nope. No more Waffle House. No more Taco Bell. I'm taking you on a real date. Where dinner isn't served over a counter, wrapped in paper." He cleans a pile of CDs off the floor. Unable to contain my toothy smile.
Is this real life? Am I actually sitting in Max's room deciding on where we should go on our date?

"Well, I can't go like this. I look like a ragamuffin!"

He wraps his hands around my wrist and pulls me to my feet. "I'm not going to pretend to know what a ragamuffin is. But I can promise you, you've never looked more beautiful than you do right this second."

I feel my cheeks go hot. He's nuts but I resist the urge to disagree with him. Opting for a simple, "Thank you" and a smile instead.

His face grows solemn as he pulls me close. Staring at me as if he's trying to read my mind. His eyes begging for forgiveness. "I'm so sorry I hurt you."

"I was never angry at you for doing what you did. Stepping up to the plate is the type of man you are," I admit. "Did I like how it all unfolded… Absolutely not. It was as if my heart had been ripped from my chest."

He closes his eyes as guilt floods his face. I grab each cheek, forcing him to look at me. "But you did what you had to do. I would expect nothing less from you."

Tears swell in his eyes as he wraps his arms tightly around me. So hard I can feel his heart pound against my chest. "I can't put into words how it felt when I opened the door and saw it was you."

"If it was anything like how I felt… then I have a pretty good idea."

CHAPTER SEVENTEEN

It only takes a few minutes to get cleaned up in the all, too familiar, female latrine. Luckily, I had packed a cute long sleeve top and a pair of black boots, throwing them on with the jeans I'm already wearing. After a quick touch up of my hair and makeup, I'm ready. It wasn't the best I've ever looked, but definitely an improvement from the sweatshirt, tennis shoes, and ponytail I showed up in.

Max is waiting for me in the hall. His button-down is tucked in and he's replaced his flip-flops with brown Doc Martens. I had almost forgotten how ridiculously hot he is.

His eyes raise as I walk towards him. "Damn Kate. You look…" He shakes his head. "Fantastic!" He grabs my hand and twirls me, causing me to blush. "Shall we?"

I wrap my arm around his elbow as he leads me down the hall. Braking as we hit the main atrium stairs.

"Max! No! Wait!" I whisper loudly. "I snuck in. They don't know I'm here!"

He laughs. "It's fine. It's only Jackson."

"If I need to remind you, you said the *exact* same thing, right before a *very* large, *very* mean, Sgt. Jackass, screamed at me and told me if I ever came back here they would call the MP's!"

"Kate? Is that you?" Bellows from the first floor.

"Yes. It's her. And she's being paranoid up here. She thinks Sgt. Brently is going to get after her again."

"It's all good. He left twenty minutes ago."

Confusion riddles Jackson's face as he rounds the bottom of the stairs. "What are you doing here? Did y'all bring the birthday festivities here?"

I let out a big sigh of fake aggravation as I stomp down each stair. "No. They're all still in Athens. It's only me."

"Oh!" he says, surprised. "Well, it's good to see you," he says, giving me a quick hug when I make it to the bottom. He makes a terrible attempt to hide the shock of me and Max together.

"Good to see you too. Did you get things worked out with Gigi?"

He smiles a big toothy grin. "Yep! She's actually going to be moving here."

"That's great, Jackson! I can't wait to meet her."

"Thanks! Y'all headed out?"

"Yep, grabbing dinner. But unless Kate wants to ride on the back of my Harley, which she would look sexy as hell on. I'm going to have to bum a ride off her."

His words make me grin and I can no longer pretend to be irritated at him. "Well, since you've already taken my dad's car for a spin and got it back in one piece. I guess it will be ok for you to drive mine too."

"Y'all have fun. Don't worry about me. I'll be sitting here with my thumb up my ass for another three hours," Jackson yells from the front entry.

"It was Drew, by the way," Max blurts.

"Huh?"

"The large, mean, jackass who yelled at you. It was Drew.

He called me a few weeks ago to see how I was doing and finally admitted it was him. He wanted to play a joke on Lana. The fact you happened to be in the bed with her was a case of shitty timing. I was so pissed off about it when it happened, he was too afraid to fess up to it."

"That little shit! I'm going to beat the crap out of him if I ever see him again."
I dig through my purse as we reach the car. Max follows me to the passenger's side door, and I assume he's waiting for the keys. My heart soars when he opens the door for me instead.

"So, where are we headed?" I ask as he climbs into the driver's seat.

"There's a great little steakhouse on the east side of Columbus with an amazing view of the city. It's usually pretty busy this time of night but I thought we could get a few drinks. Maybe sit out on the patio while we wait."

"Sounds perfect, Max." I smile, unable to hide my excitement.

He grins. "What is it?"

"It's just… I can't believe I'm here. With you. And we're going on a date of all things."

"It's answered prayers."

Max was right. The view was absolutely breathtaking. The restaurant is packed to the gills and buzzing with action. He fights the crowd at the bar, while I find a cozy spot on the patio for our thirty-minute wait. The night air is chilly, but the outdoor heaters are keeping things comfortable. Benches and high top tables line the patio as patrons watch a three-person jazz band playing on a small outdoor stage.

Max searches through the sea of people, a bottle of beer in each hand. A group of older women are staring at him, but he doesn't seem to notice. They turn and watch him as he makes his way past them, waiting to see where he goes.

"Max!" I shout and wave. The ladies give the stink eye when they spot me. I can't help but smile, I'd probably be doing the same thing if the roles were reversed.

"Whoa! Look at this! You got an awesome spot," he says, sitting at the small bistro table.

"We lucked up. A couple was sitting here, but the hostess called their name right as I was walking by."

"I came here a few weeks ago with Coop and the guys. There was a two-hour wait and it was standing room only out here. Thankfully, the food made up for every minute of the wait."

"Cooper seems nice. You guys look like you're pretty close."

"Oh yeah. He's awesome! A real lifesaver through all this Jody shit. I don't know what I would have done without him."

His words hit me hard. He's been here all alone this whole time. Going through all this pain without his closest friends. Forced to hear about everything he's missed out on. All because of a lie.

The band begins to play a slow, instrumental version of "Every Breath You Take" by The Police. The crowd grows quiet, as Max and I watch in silence, enjoying the moment.

He stands and extends his hand. "Dance with me, Kate." Without hesitation, my hand is in his as we walk the few steps to the small dance floor.

He pulls me close, wrapping me in his arms. He places his cheek to mine and whispers, "God, I've missed you."

I feel my body tremble as we melt into one. Other couples have joined us, but I am too enraptured in the moment to look. His hand is holding the back of my head as we slowly sway back and forth to the music. If I could stop time, it would be at this exact moment. As the months of pain and sadness in my heart begin to lift and pure happiness fills its place.

I swipe a tear from my cheek as the song comes to an end. The ladies from earlier are watching. I enjoy the envy in their eyes as Max leads me back to the table.

"I know that song is actually pretty creepy, but that was amazing. Even with the stalker undertones," Max teases.

"It felt like a dream," I admit. "I was worried I would wake up when the song ended."

He grabs my hand. "If this is a dream, I pray we never wake up."

The wait for our table flew by and before long we're seated and enjoying a basket of delicious homemade yeast rolls. The restaurant has a ranch-style vibe with low lighting, woodsy décor, and dark beams lining the cathedral ceiling. The smell of steak fills the room as music from the band outside, pipes through the speakers. Adding to the soft hum of conversation carrying throughout the room.

"So what do you think Lana and them are up to tonight?"

"Well, when I left, they'd all sat down to two large Domino's Pizzas. So we definitely have them beat on the dinner choice," I joke, licking honey butter from my fingers.

"What did she say when you told her you were coming here?"

"Well…here's the thing about that." I smile through gritted teeth. "She doesn't actually know I'm here. No one does. I was on my way to Alpharetta when the car kind of drove itself here."

Max chuckles. "Well, remind me to tell your car thank you when we leave."

"I still can't believe no one told me about what was going on. Lana and Artie tell each other everything, so she must know."

"I'm sure it's mostly my fault. I made Artie and Santos promise they wouldn't tell. It needed to come from me. But I wanted everything finalized and completely in the past before calling you. I wanted us to start off on a clean slate. I'm shocked they were able to keep it from you."

"I'm still kicking her ass, regardless!" I tease. "Maybe I'll even keep my little journey here a secret as payback."

Our server arrives with our food. Hot steam billowing from the tray on his shoulder. He presents two sizzling fillets, topped with Béarnaise sauce, garlic mashed potatoes, and sautéed mushrooms.

My eyes widen as I take it all in. "Oh, Max! This looks divine!"

"It will taste as good as it looks too."
The server asks us to cut into the meat to ensure they're cooked as requested. My eyes roll back in my head as I take my first bite.

"Impressed?"

"Absolute perfection!"

The table grows quiet as we both devour our first few bites of the incredible meal.

"Can I ask you a question?" Max asks as he uses the white linen napkin to wipe Béarnaise from his mouth.

"Of course."

His brow furrows and I can tell he's hesitant to ask. My stomach drops, knowing instantly what he's about to ask.

"It's about Davis..."

Yep! Just as I thought… Fucking Davis!

My head lowers, dreading this conversation. "I'm so sorry, Max. I honestly don't know what I was thinking."

"No. No. It's not about that. I mean, it's a little about that. But only when you're ready to talk about it."

I tilt my head. "Then what's it about?"

"Is he at your place this weekend?"

I'm taken back. "No," shaking my head. "He's not. I haven't seen or spoken to him since the miserable lockout night. Santos said they dropped him off at the airport on their way through Atlanta. Said his sister's getting married. Why?"

"It's not important," he says in a calm even voice. "The only important thing is you and me and this incredible night."

I know I should leave it alone, but my curiosity gets the best of me. "No, please tell me. We need to get all this out and past us. Why would you think he was with us?"

"Because he told Kevin he was headed to your apartment this afternoon."

I shrug. "I have no idea why he would say that."

"Oh, I have an idea," he says spitefully. "Another ploy to further my jealousy. I guess he had to come up with something new since he'd driven the whole Gatlinburg trip in the ground."

Him acknowledging Gatlinburg sends a rush of guilt through me and I'm sure it shows.

I drop my head. "Max. I was hurt and lost and…"

"Hey, Kate. No," he pleads. "Please, look at me." I'm not mad at you. How could I be after everything I put you through?" He grabs my hand from across the small table. "All I care about is making things right between the two of us now."

I let out a breath. Relieved it doesn't seem to be hindering his decision to want to be with me. I sit thinking for a few seconds. *Maybe it's time for Max to be the one with the adventure stories again.*

"Up for a little payback," I ask slyly.

He lifts an eyebrow. "What did you have in mind?"

"How would you feel about a little trip to Atlanta tomorrow?"

He grins. "Oh, how I've missed you, Kate Carpenter."

Max and I finish our dinner and spend the rest of the night catching up on every single detail of our lives since we were apart. We drive to a small hole in the wall bar where the beer is as endless as the laughs.

"Yep! You kicked my ass!" Max admits as I sink the black eight ball into the right corner pocket.

"Girls always say they can play pool but never actually can. I have officially been proven wrong."

I laugh. "I have a pool table at home and two extremely competitive brothers."

He slides behind me and wraps his arm around my waist. "I won't lie.

You bent over the pool table, making one perfect shot after the other, was quite possibly the hottest thing I've ever witnessed."

I turn around to see his beautiful blue eyes, studying every line and curve of his face. "Thank you for tonight."

Even with all the pain and heartache we've both experienced over the last four months, it was as if a day hadn't passed between us. We're as comfortable and natural together as we'd ever been. Tonight is about him and me. Nothing else matters. In our own world and although there are others around, they fade into the background. He places a hand on each cheek and pulls in. Our lips touch, but he waits to kiss me. I can feel his warm wet lips, as he gently grazes them back and forth over mine. I can't wait any longer, grabbing the back of his head and plunging my mouth to his. His tongue dancing around mine, causing me to whimper. Overcome with emotion, tears fall from my eyes. It's not until someone asks if we're done with the table, we're finally able to peel ourselves apart.

I slip into one of Max's Army T-shirts as we finally make it back to the barracks. "Get your sexy ass over here!" he demands, flipping the covers back to his small twin size bed.

"Just a head's up. If I wake up to some big, scary, black dude screaming at me, they'll be carrying the both of you out of here on stretchers!" I tease as I climb in.

"Well, after the beat down you gave me tonight at pool, I wouldn't dare."

It's late and Max and I have a big day ahead of us tomorrow. Although we know we could stay up talking all night, we both agree we need to get some sleep. After finalizing our plans, I snuggle into a cozy spooning position, resting my back into his chest. It's quiet and within minutes I can feel his breathing go heavy. I stare at the ceiling and replay the events that unfolded today. I smile, realizing this is the first time I've been genuinely happy in months.

CHAPTER EIGHTEEN

I'm already awake when the clock begins its loud five am wake up call.

"You ready to make the Scream Machine our bitch today?" I ask as Max slams the off button on the alarm.

"Damn right, I am," he says between a sleepy yawn.

"It's been ages since I've been on a roller coaster. Probably since Senior Skip Day back in high school," I admit

"Oh, a whole two years ago?"

I chuckle and I drag from the comforts of his arms. "Five years if you must know. But it wasn't my senior year. I just felt like skipping."

"There's a Six Flags less than thirty minutes from my hometown. My parents would buy my sister and I summer passes each year and let it be a built-in babysitter. We'd ride roller coasters over and over to see which one of us would barf first," he chuckles.

"Well, I've never puked before, but I should probably forewarn you… I'm a screamer."

Max grins devilishly. "Oh really? Maybe we should skip the whole Six Flags thing then."

I shake my head. "I guess I walked right into that one, huh?"

"Yep! Ya sure did. But man, at the mental picture I have right now."

After quick showers, packing, and a stop through the Hardee's drive-thru, we're Atlanta bound.

The gang was planning to be at the park when the gates open so we needed to be there waiting when they arrived. If not, it might be damn near impossible finding them once they're inside.

The sunroof's open to the beautiful, Saturday morning fall sky. The *Eagle's Greatest Hits* plays loudly, helping the two-hour drive go by in a flash. Max looks amazing, as always. It's the most casual I've seen him out, with blue jeans and a long sleeve, Dallas Cowboys T-shirt. I let him drive. One arm resting on the steering wheel, the other on the gear shift. His gold-rimmed Ray-Bans reflecting the warm sun. There's something insanely sexy, watching him shift gears through the busy Atlanta traffic.

We pull into the massive Six Flags parking lot. "Great timing!" he says.

"Made it with fifteen minutes to spare. I can't wait to see the look on Lana's face."

"No. Freaking. Way!" Lana shouts as we see the group near the entrance gate. Chins drop as everyone turns She runs towards us, her hands covering her jaw dropped mouth.

"Holy shit! Holy shit! Holy shit! I can't believe you're here!" she shouts.

"Well, now that I'm completely deaf!" I tease, throwing my arms around her.

"How…When…How did this happen?" Looking back and forth to me and Max.

"Thank you, Lord!" Artie yells with relief. "It took every ounce of me to not break!"

Lana snaps her head towards Artie. "You knew they were coming?"

"Oh! No. I had no clue about this. The part about Max and no more Jody is what I'm talking about."

"WHAT?!"

I'm dumbfounded. "You mean you didn't know?" Shocked Artie was able to keep it from her.

"Umm, no. He didn't!" she says, giving Artie the death stare. "Because if he had, there's no way I would have kept it from you."

Artie points. "*See!* That's exactly why I didn't!"

I laugh. "He clearly knows you pretty damn well now."

"Well, you better tell me every last detail," she demands.

"It's a longgggg story. Thankfully, we have all day to catch you up on everything."

By ride number five the gang had been brought up to speed on the Jody fiasco and as we wait in the winding line at Splashwater Falls, I give a quick run-through of my unexpected trip south. Purposely leaving out details I want to keep between me and Max. As we wait in the slow-moving line, Max wraps his arms around me from behind, giving me a gentle kiss on the side of my neck.

"Having fun?" he asks.

I look around at this wonderful group of friends laughing and playing as Max's strong arms engulf me. "I couldn't have dreamt of a more perfect day."

Splashwater Falls is one of the most popular rides in the park. To avoid walking around in wet clothes, we waited until it was the warmest part of the day to ride it. What we didn't take into consideration was Lana + water + white t-shirt = Boob's McGee.

"I've never been so embarrassed in my whole life!" Lana yells over the hand dryer she's using to dry her shirt.

I bust out laughing again from a nearby restroom stall. "I about died when that old lady shook her finger at you and said this was a family establishment."

Ashley and I make it to the bank of sinks at the same time, still cracking up over the sight of Lana fanning her sopping wet shirt away from her skin. "Not to change the subject, because trust me… I could laugh about this one for days. But since we have a few minutes…"

"Oh my God, yes!" Ashley adds, already knowing what I'm about to say.

"You're pretty fearless, but I would have *never* thought you'd have the balls to drive to Fort Benning by yourself and knock on his door!"

"Oh, I was scared shitless. I don't know what came over me. I don't know if it was the letter or maybe because I'd left you guys and saw how happy you all were. Or maybe it was fate. All I know is one minute I'm in an ugly sweatshirt with day-old makeup and dirty hair, drowning in my sorrows. The next minute, I'm in Max's arms dancing to The Police at a fancy Columbus restaurant."

"Well, this is by far the happiest I've seen him since the Fourth of July," Lana says as the dryer cycle finally comes to an end.

"This is by far the happiest we've seen *you* since the Fourth of July," Ashley adds.
I smile, realizing how right they both are.

"Since we have a sec. I've been dying to ask you this all day. Has he mentioned anything about Davis?" Lana asks.

I grimace. "No. Well, yes, sort of."

"Sort of?" Ash repeats.

"It's kind of hard to explain. We sort of grazed the surface of the whole Davis subject. I know at some point we are going to have to have a full-blown conversation about it.

But for now, Max wants to enjoy a drama-free weekend."

"But didn't you say Max is going to ride back with Artie and Santos tomorrow?" Lana asks.

"Yes… It makes the most sense."

"Well, there will definitely be some drama then."

"Oh, that's right!" Ashley pipes. "The guys have to pick up Davis at the airport tomorrow."

Lana shakes her head. "Those two packed in a car with each other for two hours. Eeesh!" She grimaces. "It's not going to be pretty."

It's after six in the evening; eighteen rides, twelve carnival games, three giant teddy bears, and one wet t-shirt later, we've made our way to the last ride of the day. The most famous coaster in the park… The Great American Scream Machine. It was the first roller coaster I'd ever ridden as a kid and saving it for last had become a bit of a tradition.

Lana and Artie are in the first row. Followed by Ash and Santos, with Max and me in the third row. We buckle in as the single row bar is locked into position across us. Our heads are jolted back as the cars spring forward. In seconds, we begin the slow climb. The sun is setting, the flashing lights of the rides below, sparkle in the evening air. Max grabs my hand and gives it a quick kiss, taking in the view.

The metal tracks rattle against the wood beams. Click… Click… Click… Silence, as we crest the top. Our hands fly in the air, the guys cheering in anticipation. In a split second, we're falling. Immediately feeling coaster stomach, cheering as we make it down and quickly back up another.

Commotion coming from the front row grabs my attention. *Did their bar come loose?* Panic rises, but I calm when I see Lana laugh. *Did Artie throw up?* Max notices too and is curious to know what's going on.

"I wonder what happened?" he shouts over all the screams.

We make it to the end of the ride; the cars slowing as we creep back into the station. The coaster noise finally quiet.

"Get me out!" Artie screams to the pimply kid at the coaster controls. "Hurry the hell up! I… I… I gotta get out of here, NOW!"

Lana's still laughing as Artie springs out of the seat the second the safety bar is released. We sit stunned and clueless as he slings his shirt off. "Ow, Ow, Ow! Shit! Ow!"

He pulls his pants down as far as they'll go. Doing a crazy man's dance the entire time. Lana's trying to speak, but the words are incoherent. She's laughing too hard. Tears are rolling off her cheeks as drool literally falls from her mouth.

We, along with everyone else in the station stare in bewilderment. As if it were in slow motion, a giant red wasp falls from the back of Artie's bright yellow boxer shorts. Our eyes grow wide and chins drop as Artie stomps his foot over the paralyzed insect; swearing the entire time.

The place erupts in laughter and instantly I regret not bringing my camera. Because the sight of Artie standing there in his skivvies is beyond priceless.

We make it off the station platform, into a small corner of the ride's exit. Where the breathless, half-naked Artie is finally able to explain the course of events that have unfolded.

"That son of a bitch flew straight into the side of my head when we made the first big fall. Must have hit so hard it injured himself because he fell between me and the seat. I could feel it, so I leaned forward to let Lana swat it away. But when I moved it somehow managed to fall right into the gap of my jeans. I tried to grab it, but the bar and seatbelt were too tight. The little bastard stung me in my ass crack the *entire* time!"

We can't help but laugh, but the second he pulls his boxers back to examine the damage, our laughter turns to concern. Seven large stings are quickly swelling.

"Holy Shit, Artie! You're not allergic to wasps are you?" I ask.

"No. Thank God! Or I would be totally dead right now!" he jokes.

"Dude! The entire top part of your ass is already double the size it should be. Maybe we need to get you to the ER," Max says, concerned.

"It hurts like hell, but I think I'm ok. Maybe we can stop at a drug store and get some ointment or something."

"It wouldn't hurt for you to get some Benadryl in you too," I add.

Bruising has set in Artie's butt and halfway up his back by the time we make it back to the apartment. It looks incredibly painful as he lays on his stomach with a large ice pack perched on his ass.
We feel terrible about laughing at his condition, but every few minutes someone cracks a joke, sending everyone into another round of hysterics.

"Oh yeah! Laugh at the injured guy!" A groggy Artie groans.

"This is payback for all the raccoon jokes I had to endure over the last two months!"

"Y'all leave him alone!" Lane spouts. "My poor baby has a broke tooshy," she says in her best baby voice. "Why don't we get you to bed?"

"Yes. Now that you've managed to wipe all the drool from your chin and the tears from your eyes. You can finally help him," Ashley teases.

Lana gives a guilty smile. "I'm sorry… I know it was terrible I was laughing. But it might have been the funniest thing I've ever witnessed. He was jumping in his seat like he was bull riding, hollering 'Ba, ba, ba, bee!' over and over again."

Laughter fills the room yet again as the defeated Artie drags his sore, swollen, ass to bed. Holding the ice pack in one hand and shooting us the bird with the other.

"Yet another crazy day with the infamous Alpharetta Girls," Santos says, cuddling up to Ash on the couch.

"Yes, it was." she agrees. "I'm so glad you two were able to be a part of it. It wouldn't have been the same without y'all."

"You mean there was no way in hell you could have fully described the whole wasp down the ass crack thing, without actually being there?" Max jokes.

She laughs. "Exactly!"

It's getting late and I can tell Ash and Santos are ready for some alone time. So Max and I take the hint and call it a night. We walk into my bedroom he begins exploring. Picking up pictures, the art, my CD collection, and lastly my most prized possession…

"What's this?" he asks, holding the small open box.

"It's my grandmother's engagement ring. She left it to me when she passed away."

"And I'm guessing it'll be yours too?"

I nod. "That's the plan."

He reads the small card lining the top out loud…

"My Dearest Katherine,

May only a worthy soul and kindred spirit place this ring on your deserving hand.

Love, Grandma June"

"My grandmother was a true romantic. When we were packing her things, we found a box full of old love letters she and my granddad had sent each other while he was overseas fighting. They were the sweetest words two people could ever share."

"Y'all must have been close."

"*Very* close," I admit. "I guess I've always imagined having a love like theirs one day. That's why I keep the box out. It's a daily reminder true love does actually exist, and they made it look so effortless."

Max places the ring box back on the dresser and walks towards me. "It looks like she wasn't the only true romantic in the family." Pulling me in for a tight hug.

"Do you know how awesome you are?" I ask, glancing at his handsome face.

He smiles and sweeps my hair off my shoulders. There's something different in his eyes. It's desire and it sends an instant charge rushing through me. His mouth is on mine, kissing me hard and with so much passion, my legs go weak. He slowly unbuttons my shirt and slides it off one shoulder at a time. He reaches down, placing a soft, gentle kiss on my neck, before moving to my chest. I can feel his breath on me and I am instantly aroused. He unclasped my bra and I instinctively throw my arms over my breasts when I feel it loosen. Uncomfortable with how exposed I am.

"Max?" I whisper.

He looks at me with loving eyes. "Yeah?"

"Every inch of my body is dying to be with you right now. But my heart is telling me the right thing to do is wait. Wait until we have all this Jody stuff officially behind us."

Desire fades, replaced with disappointment. But I can tell he knows I'm right.

He lets out an exhausted sigh. "You're probably right. I don't want any of my past mistakes flooding over onto us. And if it means waiting, that's what we'll have to do."

We lay in silence, enjoying the simplicity of the moment. It had been the perfect weekend. No words are needed. Max pulls the covers over us and we fall asleep, entangled in each other's arms.

CHAPTER NINETEEN
Halloween Weekend

The girls have already checked into one of the four rooms we have reserved at the Days Inn, around the corner from the Auburn campus. We're busy perfecting our costumes as we wait for the guys to roll into town.

"Last time I talked to Artie, there were two more joining us," Lana says, rolling up her thigh-high pantyhose.

"Hell yeah!" Jenn shouts. "That brings the total to nine. It will be hot guy palooza around here!"

"So who all's coming?" I ask.

"Well, let's see… of course, there is Artie, Max, and Santos. Jackson and Gigi. Kevin and Palmer. Both of them are bringing dates, and some new guy named Cooper."

"Oh, I've met Cooper! He's so sweet. A Yankee. But sweet."

"Who the hell said they could bring dates?"

Lana scoffs. "For Pete's Sake, Jenn! Don't be such an asshole. Between the guys we're bringing and an entire fraternity house, you won't have any trouble finding someone to love on tonight."

"Soooo, that's it?" I ask. "No six-five, loud, arrogant, pain the ass to worry about?"

"Honestly, I have no clue. I invited him, but since the whole blow-up with him and Max, I don't know."

Wrapped in my terrycloth bathrobe, I crawl into the bathroom vanity to put my makeup on. Enjoying the last few minutes of peace before the festivities commence.

Curiosity still lingers if Davis will show tonight. I can't help but feel bad. As much as he drives me crazy, I hate the idea of him getting left out. Then again, he's never had to worry about attention from women, so I'm sure he'll have no trouble fending for himself. Since the blow-up Max and Davis had on the way home from Atlanta, they've been working to mend fences. Staying angry isn't an option. Especially, since most of the issues were simple misunderstandings. Max took responsibility for everything else. Blaming himself, even though it was ultimately Jody's fault. He had annulment papers served to the lying bitch two days ago, getting him one step closer to putting this nightmare behind us. I haven't seen him since our Six Flags weekend and even though we talk every day, my heart aches for him.

"Well? What do you think?" Lana asks as she straightens the ears of her Playboy bunny costume in the mirror.

"You look hot! Artie's going to shit a brick when he sees you."

"He better! I didn't squeeze my ass in this damn thing for nothing."

"You two get out here! I have a surprise to tell you!" Ashley yells from outside the bathroom. "Hurry!"

"Ok! Ok! We're comin'! Calm your tits!" Lana yells. Ashley's holding a large bottle of champagne in one hand and a stack of clear plastic cups in the other as we make our way back into the room.

Lana does a shimmy. "Oh, hell yeah!"

"I wanted to celebrate for a minute with my three best girlfriends before all those icky boys come in and ruin it," she teases with a tearful smile.

I hug her neck. "I can't think of anything more perfect."

She pops the top of the cheap champagne, catching the run out with her mouth.

"Let's all make a toast!" she says, pouring each of us a glass.

"If we are going to do this! We're going to do this right!" Lana says, decidedly. "Get your asses up here!"

She grabs Ash by the hand and pulls her onto the motel bed. Jenn and I climb up behind as they hand over our cups.

"I'll go first!" Lana says, throwing her cup in the air. "Cheers to having the three greatest friends a girl could ask for and to having a night to remember!"

We raise our cups and smile, knowing how fortunate we are to have each other.

Jenn is next. "I know I don't get to see y'all as much now that I'm all the way in Podunk, Arkansas. So cheers to always knowing I have the most amazing friends to come home to!"

We wrap our arms around her and hug her tight. "Awe, Jenn! We love you! No matter how far away you are."

"Ok, Kate! Your turn!"

"Oh goodness, my turn, huh?" I'm lost for words for a few seconds. "Ok, cheers to always following your heart and believing there is such a thing as a happy ending."

"Damn straight there is!" Lana yells as we giggle over my ridiculousness.

Jenn points to Ashley. "And last but not least..."

Ashley raises her cup in the air. "Here's to wishing me the best of luck. Since December 15th...I will be moving to Columbus!"

Our cups tap together as the words compute in our brains. "No freakin' way!" Lana yells, jumping on the bed. Champagne spilling onto the pillows.

"Yes, freakin' way!" she squeals. "Since I'm graduating from nursing school at the end of the semester, I had to start looking for jobs. St. Francis Hospital was hiring. Nicholas and I talked it over. It made the most sense, so I applied."

I pull her over for a hug. "Oh, Ash! I'm so happy for you. I can't think of anyone more deserving!".

"Are you guys going to live together?" Jenn asks.

"God, no! We're nowhere close to being ready for that. Besides my mother would kill me. I rented an apartment about ten minutes away from Post. Giving us a real shot at making a go of this."

"So what you're saying is we now have a place to come crash, instead of those horrible barracks?" Lana says.

"Exactly!"

Jenn shakes her head. "I had no clue Santos's first name was Nicholas until now."

"Maybe we should call each other Carpenter, Mathews, Roy, and Holmes to confuse the shit out of them!" Lana jokes.

"What's Davis's first name?" Jenn asks, putting the finishing touches to her costume.

She shrugs. "Ya know? I've never thought to ask."
I'm about to tell them but for whatever reason, stop myself.

Lana adjusts her cleavage in the mirror. "Well, since we are on the subject of the future," she beams. "Artie's taking me home to meet his parents for Christmas!" She turns and squeals.

We join in on the squeals as a bang on the hotel door stops us mid-cheer. I look at my watch. "Shit! I have to finish getting dressed!" I run to the bathroom, snatching rollers from my hair.

The sound of silly best friend laughter, shifts to the loud, boisterous noise of Army Soldiers filing in. Hearing them sends a rush of nerves through my belly; second-guessing my ability to pull off the cop costume I picked out. Especially, since sexy has never been one of my strong suits.

That's always been Lana's department.

I slip on my thigh-high black boots and slide the fake handcuffs and baton on each hip of the tiny costume. Leaving the aviator sunglasses I borrowed from Jenn, as the final touch. After a quick touch up of my cherry red lipstick, it's time to make the big reveal.

The room goes eerily quiet as everyone turns. "HO–LY SHIT!" Lana shouts. "You look smokin' hot!"

"Look at those legs?" Jenn adds.

Max is frozen in the doorway, wide-eyed.

I hug him. "I don't even know what to say right now," he mutters. "You look…Wow!"

I laugh and do a little spin. "Thanks! I'm way out of my comfort zone, so I hope you're pleased."

"I don't know about taking you into a house full of fraternity brothers looking like this," he teases.

Artie ties the jacket of his Hugh Hefner costume. "Should we get going?"

The cheap motel is walking distance from the frat house, so everyone can drink tonight without the worry of driving. One by one we file out of the rooms. Some in couple's costumes, some only in masks. A few, including Max, who aren't dressed up at all.

We gather in the parking lot to wait on the stragglers. Santos bangs on the door two rooms down. "Yo, Tarzan! We're leaving! Come On!" he yells through the door.

I laugh. "Oh, Lord! Who's Tarzan?"

Max grimaces. "I meant to tell you…"

The door flings open and out pops Goldie Locks wearing a tiny Jane costume. Davis dressed as Tarzan, towering behind her. Max glues on a smile. "…Davis came with us."

I'm thankful I have on sunglasses to shield my embarrassment. And to help hide how irritatingly hot Davis looks. *Act natural! You can do this!* I repeat over and over in my head.

"Hey, Skeeter!" Davis shouts. Catching me a little off guard by his casualness. "You left these in my room. Figured you'd want them back."
I stare at my shoes. The ones I had to leave behind because I had inadvertently locked myself out.

The four of us stand uncomfortably silent as he passes over the black flats. "No, this isn't awkward at all," I say out loud. Trying desperately to make light of the situation, while his date throws eye daggers at me. "I'm going to run these back to the room real quick." Gesturing to the shoes, hoping to hide how mortified I am.

"Skeeter?" Max quizzes.

"Yep! Gotta love those flat-chested nicknames."

Disgust washes across his face. "I'll kick his ass if he ever calls you that again."
Why do I have the feeling this is going to be a longgggg night?

James is waiting for us when we walk up the sidewalk of the heavily decorated Pi Kappa Phi house.

"Please God, tell me that isn't my sister!" James yells throwing his hands over his eyes when he spots me. "If dad saw you in this, Katie… he would ground you for life!"

Davis mumbles, "No shit!" under his breath, but I'm the only one who catches it.

"Well, I guess it's a good thing he's not here!" I say, ignoring the snide Davis remark.

James's eyes brighten introducing me to his beautiful date. "This is Julia. Julia, this is my sister, Kate. And well, this is all her friends!"

He laughs, giving hugs and high fives as everyone files up the stairs behind me.

"Well, don't you two look cute!" Lana brags, noticing their Gangster and Flapper Girl costumes.

"I can't take any of the credit. It was all Julia's idea."

"Well, she did ya good!" Lana said, winking.

"Welcome! Welcome! Welcome!" A loud booming voice yells from the doorway. "You must be James's sister?" The toga-wearing fraternity brother asks.

"That's me!"

"He told us you were coming but failed to mention how hot you were."

I raise an eyebrow. "Well, it would be pretty creepy if he had."

"Told ya! I'm not going to be able to leave your side for a second." Max teases in my ear.

James waves us in. "Y'all come on in! Make yourself at home. The kegs are in the back. It's a buck a cup if you're in the mood for beer. If not, here's a bar in the game room."

Our group of sixteen causes quite a reaction when we walk in. The guys definitely stand out from the typical frat crowd. It didn't occur to me when we accepted the invitation, but these two incredibly different worlds might have a difficult time meshing together. Unfortunately, it's a little too late to worry about it now. We have no choice but to trust everyone can play nice, now that we're all here.

"You don't think there will be any issues tonight, do you?" Lana whispers as if she's reading my mind.

I sigh. "Let's hope the brothers and soldiers can all live in harmony for the night."

"What can I get you to drink?" Max asks.

My face twists. "Ehhh, I'm not sure what I'm feeling tonight. Don't wait on me. Go grab yourself something."

Max lifts my hand, giving it a small kiss before heading in the direction of the keg.

"Yo, wench! Fetch me a beer!" Davis shouts in the direction of Jenn. Who's dressed up, *well…* as a beer wench. Which, of course, she immediately does.

A shirtless Davis has a brown Tarzan loincloth covering his junk, soars over the crowd. I don't turn his way but I can tell he's in rare form tonight.

He stretches his back. "So much college pussy… so little time!" he shouts to Kevin.

"I guess Davis is back to being an annoying, arrogant, self-centered, asshole," Lana huffs with an eye roll.

"He's kept it in check the last few times we've been around him, I had forgotten he's the most vulgar man in America," Ashley says.

A girl sashays past carrying a full bottle of Boone's Farm, dressed as a naughty Cowgirl. "Hey, Hun! You looking for a bull to ride?" he flirts, even though Goldie is standing right beside him.

"Never mind. Make that the most vulgar man on the *planet!*"

The cowgirl raises an eyebrow. "Only if you can last longer than eight seconds."

Please, God, tell me I didn't witness that! I think as Max returns, red solo cup in hand.

He eyes me. "What's that look for?"

I blow it off. "Oh, it's just these damn boots. They're already killing my feet."

He pulls me in close, wrapping his arms around my waist. "Well, does it help to know you look sexy as hell in them?"

I force a grin. "Beauty before comfort, I guess."

The annual Halloween Bash is going off without a hitch. The DJ has the packed dancefloor jumping as black lights and fog fill the air above them. The bass of the music so loud I can feel it under my feet.

James challenged Max to a keg stand competition, while Artie, Lana, Ash, and Santos play cards with a group of frat brothers. Everyone appears to be having a great time. Everyone that is, but me. I don't know what's wrong with me tonight. I'm trying to have fun, and Max is being so sweet, but I feel "off" for some reason. Maybe it's this tight, itchy, costume or maybe I can't shake the discomfort of having my boyfriend and his friend I screwed, in the same room together. Thankfully, it doesn't faze Davis. Between Goldie Locks, Jenn, and half of the female student body at Auburn, he's well occupied. I roll my eyes as they hang on every ridiculous word he says.

"What are you doing sitting here all by your lonesome?" Jackson asks. "*And* with two empty hands? Who are you and what have you done with our friend Kate?"

"Thank you. I needed a good laugh," I admit.

"It's so good to finally get to spend time with you, Gigi" She slides onto Jackson's lap. "He talks about you incessantly."

"I know!" she beams. "It's nice to finally have a face to put with all the crazy stories."

Jackson shifts closer. "Can you keep a secret?" he asks, loud enough only she and I can hear.

"Well, yeah! Of course, I can!"

Both ready to burst, he whispers, "We're engaged!"

I clap my hands together. "Oh, Jackson! What wonderful news!"

"We still have a few more family members to tell, so shhh!" he says, putting his finger over his lips.

I gesture locking my mouth and throwing away the key as Max makes his way back into the room.

"That brother of yours is a hoot!"

"I'm glad you two are hitting it off."

"Hell yeah, we are! I schooled him on keg stands, so he's challenged me to a game of pool for redemption." He high fives James as he walks up behind him.

"You ready, man?"

"Wanna play teams, babe? I could use those kickass skills of yours."

Ugh! Aunt 'Flow' must be on her way because I'm not in the mood for any of this tonight.

"Sure. But why don't you two go ahead and play a round. I'm going to run back to the room real quick and change my shoes. I am officially over these boots."

"Well, let me go with you. You don't need to be walking by yourself."

"Oh, I wasn't going by myself. Jenn's going with me."

"No, it's ok. I want to."

"It's fine. I promise. We'll be back in a flash," I insist.

"You sure?"

I give him a smile and a quick kiss. "Yep! Promise! Be right back."

I do want to change my shoes but the truth is… I'm *dying* to smoke a cigarette. An unfortunate vice I haven't mentioned to Max. Not that I think he would care, I just haven't felt the need to tell him.

I search aimlessly around the loud fraternity house for Jenn. Who I finally spot sucking face with a masked Zorro and don't have the heart to interrupt. Lana and Ashley are knee-deep in their card game, so I decide to make the short walk alone.

I shed my boots as soon as I hit the sidewalk. Thankful for the immediate relief to my aching feet and ringing ears. It's a perfect October night. Chilly, but not cold as college students, decked out in their Halloween costumes, stumble from party to party on the busy AU Fraternity Row. I walk the three blocks back to the motel, enjoying the few minutes to myself.

Thankful for the break, I light the end of a Marlboro Light and sprawl across the empty double bed. Dreading the idea of having to go back to the party. I lay staring at the ceiling, thinking about Ash moving to Columbus, and Lana and Artie spending Christmas together. It's all becoming so real for everyone. It saddens me a little to hear them all talk about the future while Max and I are still learning what each other's favorite color is.

I'm startled by a knock on the door. *Dammit!* I scream in my head, knowing it has to be Max.

"Commm-ing!" I shout, quickly running to the bathroom to flush my cigarette in the toilet. Spraying hairspray to mask the smoke.

I fling the door open and gasp, staring for a few seconds before speaking. "What are you doing here, Davis?"

"I saw you leave."

"Ohhh kay? *And?*"

"You have no business walking around here by yourself, especially looking like *that.*"

He says the last part with disdain. As if the sight of me dressed this way disgusts him and it instantly pisses me off.

"Oh, my bad! Maybe I should have gone with the whole slutty cowgirl look instead."

"That's not it and you know it!"

"Really? Tell me, Davis. What is it?" I sneer, getting angrier by the second. "That's the second time tonight you've made a snide comment.

"Why is it ok for every girl on this fucking campus to be dressed in costumes the size of postage stamps, but I dare wear one and you judge me for it?"

"Because!" he yells.

"Because, why?"

"Because they aren't the ones I'm in love with!" His stunned face appears as shocked for saying it as I am hearing it.

His admission renders me speechless. My shoulders rise and fall as I try to catch the breath that's evaded my body. He stares. So focused on my eyes I worry he can read my mind.

"Please say something," he pleads.

I don't know what to say. I turn back into the room and grab the black flats he had given me earlier. "I have to get out of here." I shove past him, too afraid to have this conversation. "I can't do this right now."

He snags me by the arm right before I clear him and spins me around. "He doesn't know you like I do, and you know it! He doesn't challenge you like I do. And y'all sure as hell don't have the heat you and I do!" He growls the words inches from my face. So close I can feel his breath.

I snatch my arm from his grip. "Let go of me, Davis!"

I take a few step, but the cold, pebbled asphalt forces me to stop. With my back towards him, I slide on one shoe at a time.

"I know you feel it too, Kate."
I close my eyes. His words punching my gut. But I refuse to turn around.

"Oh my God!" Lana yells as I make my way through the door. "Where the hell have you been? Max walked straight through the back porch screen door and took it completely off its hinges! Fell flat on his face! It was the funniest thing I've seen since Artie had a wasp in his ass!"

"Yeah, yeah, yeah! Laugh at the drunk guy!" Max slurs. I grimace when I spot a small cut near his right eyebrow.

"Oh no, Max! Are you ok?"

"I'm fine," he says. "Just remind me to never let your brother talk me into keg stands again!"

My entire group is three sheets to the wind, including Max. Seeing him like this is strange. Not that he doesn't deserve a night of complete inebriation. He's typically so controlled and methodical in everything he does. Him letting loose feels foreign to me.

I'm trying desperately to wipe what happened with Davis from my mind. Chalking it up to him trying to stir things up again. He doesn't return right away, but when he does, he's no longer sporting the tiny Tarzan costume and has changed into dark jeans and an untucked Polo.

"I wondered where you went," Goldie Locks says when he makes his way into the game room.

Lana puts two and two together in her head and gives me a knowing eye. I pray Max is too drunk to make the connection as well.

"Are y'all ready for an ass-whippin'? I ask James and Julia as they return from the dance floor.

"I think your boyfriend might be a tad too tipsy to play another round," Julia says, gesturing over to Max, who's fallen asleep on the dingy, 1970s couch.

"Ah! It definitely appears so," I agree, shaking my head at the sight of him. "I should probably get him back to the room."

"No way, Katie! You're not getting out of it that easy," James teases. "He'll make it another twenty minutes. Which is plenty long enough for me to kick your ass."

"I'll play Max's spot," Davis volunteers from behind me.

James smirks. "Perfect! It's settled."

I look at Max, trying desperately to telepathically wake his ass up, to no avail.

James racks the balls as Davis scours through the wall of pool sticks for one that fits his tall frame. His cavalier attitude irks me and after the night I've had, I am in no mood for it.

I walk over to Goldie Locks, her face lighting up as I hand her my pool stick. "Why don't you play my spot? I'm going to call it a night."

James laughs and yells, "Chicken shit!" as Davis side-eyes me.

Artie and Santos help me get Max back to the room, who passes out the second his head hits the pillow. As I pull his shoes off, I joke with the group. "Oddly enough, I saw tonight going much differently in my head."

Artie looks down at Max. "Don't be too hard on him, Kate. After the hell he's been through the last four months, he needed this."

"That's for damn sure!" Santos agrees.

"Oh, I'm not mad. I'm thrilled he had a good time. I just feel bad I was a big fuddy-dud tonight."

"No kidding!" Lana interjects. "You were a bit of a killjoy! Is it your time of the month?"

"It's not, ya bitch. But I do feel like I might be coming down with something."

After everyone has settled into their rooms, I leave a sleeping Max and step outside to smoke. I know Lana's comment about being a killjoy was true, but I can't find the energy to care as I collapse on the curb of the motel parking lot.

"Please, don't be getting sick," I say out loud to no one, in between coughs. My throat stinging with each drag of the cigarette.

"You ok?"

My head snaps up, "Dammit, Davis!" I grab at my chest. "You gotta stop sneaking up on me!"

"Sorry. I was headed back to the room and heard you over here coughing up a lung."

"I'm fine." My voice cracks, followed by an outburst of coughs.

"Oh, you certainly sound it."

"I think I might be getting sick. Which would explain why I've been so blah tonight. *If* you must know."

"Got anything you can take?"

"I think so," I say, too tired to keep up the attitude. "I'm pretty sure I've got some Motrin in my bag."

"I can run to the gas station and get you some cough drops."

"Thank you, but I think I'm ok. I just need to get to bed."

He puts his hand on my forehead. "Holy shit, Kate! You're burning up."

Grabbing my hand, he pulls me up and walks me back into the room. Max is out cold, but Lana and Artie are still awake.

"Lana, help me get her into bed!" Davis says, assertively as we walk in.

Startled, she jumps up. "What's wrong?"

"She's running a fever. If you'll get her into bed, I'm going to run and get her some medicine." He bolts before I have time to protest.

By morning my sore throat and headache have shifted into what feels like full-blown flu. I managed to get a couple of hours of sleep, but my hacking cough wakes me and Max, both up.

"You, ok?" he asks between a sleepy yawn.

He is caught off guard to find me laying in the other bed. "What are you doing over there?"

My voice is gone, but I manage to force a throaty reply. "I got sick after you went to bed last night. I have a fever and didn't want to risk getting you sick too. Lana and Artie stayed in another room so I could have this bed."

His eyes widen. "Oh God, Kate! I'm so sorry."

He's to me in a split second. His eyes scanning my face. He cowers his head. "I shouldn't have drank so much last night. I would have been…"

"Max, no!" I say, grabbing his hand. "I wanted you to have a good time."

"But I could tell something was wrong. You weren't yourself. I thought maybe it was because Davis came with us."

"I didn't want to be Debbie Downer," I squeak out, grasping at my throat from the pain.

He grimaces. "Is there anything I can get you?"

I point to the dresser on the far side of the room. "Would you pass me the bag of cough drops?"

Motrin, Nyquil, cough drops, a box of Kleenex, and two bottles of orange Gatorade, line the small four drawer dresser. Max's head lowers when he turns and sees half the CVS pharmacy sitting there. He's even more disappointed in himself now.

It's best for everyone if I don't mention who bought it all, choosing a more open-ended approach. "They ran and grabbed me a few things last night."

He sucks in a big breath and shakes his head. "Dammit! I can't believe I wasn't here for you. I'm so pissed at myself."

"It's no big deal, I promise," I say, reassuring him. A knock at the door is an appreciated distraction. Max opens it to a fully dressed and ready to go, Lana and Ashley.

"Morning, Drunkard!" Lana teases, causing him to feel even more guilty. "We figured we'd get your sickly ass on home," she continues as she barges into the room.

As much as I didn't want to leave Max, the thought of going home and getting into my own bed was the best words I could hear.

"Ok," I mouth, forcing myself to an upright position.

"No, no, no," Max blurts. "Lay back down. I'll pack your stuff."

Too tired to argue, I do as he says. Maybe helping me pack will ease some of his frustrations for missing out last night.

I'm laid out in the back seat as Lana and Ash talk about how much fun they had last night and their upcoming holiday plans. My fever's back as I drift in and out of sleep. Finding yet again, I'm the odd man out when it comes to matters of the heart.

CHAPTER TWENTY
Thanksgiving

I glide into the kitchen with my nose in the air. Breathing in the mouth-watering aroma of Thanksgiving dinner cooking.

"Whoa, Mom! The turkey smells fantastic!"

"Thank you, honey! Not too much longer and it'll be ready."

"Need any help?"

"I think I have everything under control. You go relax. Oh! By the way… Happy Birthday!"

I roll out my lip. "Awe! Thanks, Mom."

"How does it feel to be twenty-one?"

"Good," I admit. "Strange. But good."

She wraps an arm around me as I sneak a deviled egg from the table. "It's good to have you home, sweetheart. I think this might be the longest you've ever stayed gone."

"I know. I'm sorry. Classes have been a nightmare this semester."

Max flew home to Texas yesterday to spend the holiday with his family. I met him at a Ruby Tuesday's outside the Atlanta airport for a quick lunch before his flight. Between him having CQ Duty and a big project due for my marketing class, it was the first time we'd seen each other since Halloween. I've missed him, and even though it was only for a little while, feeling his arms around me was exactly what I needed.

Mom doesn't know I'm seeing him again. I don't know why I've been so hesitant to tell her. Maybe it's fear she won't be able to forgive him for what happened over the summer. Or maybe it's simply because I'm not ready for her to know. Until the annulment is finalized, I think there will always be a part of me waiting for the ball to drop.

"You headed to Lana's later?" she asks.

"I was thinking about it. Artie and a few of his friends are in town having Thanksgiving at her house. So figure I should pop over and say hello for a while."

"Be sure to tell her mother I say hello and remind her I put her down to bring her sweet potato casserole for the Ladies Christmas Luncheon."

James slides his chair back from the dinner table. "That. Was. Amazing!"

"Yes, it was! I think you've outdone yourself," I agree.

"Don't run off yet. There's a red velvet birthday cake with twenty-one candles that need to be blown out!"
I'm stuffed, but I make room for cake. Enjoying every minute of the family time, that's been long overdue.

"How are things going with the lovely Julia?"

"Really good, actually. She's invited me on a ski trip with her family for New Year's."

I raise my eyebrows. "Wow! That's exciting. It must be getting serious."

He grins and continues shoveling in cake.

After some much-needed quality time with the family, I slowly but surely make my way to Lana's house. Her driveway is packed with cars when I pull up. Jackson's, mustard-colored, truck, standing out like a sore thumb against the luxury cars Lana's family drives.

I stare at the house, hoping to find the courage to go in. I shouldn't have come. Davis is here and I'm not sure I'm ready to face him. I've spent the last three weeks wiping his late-night Halloween confession from my brain. I care about him and I know deep down he's a good guy; even if he chooses to let the world believe otherwise. But my focus is Max. It's always been, Max. This is our time to finally make a true go at something real.

A twinge of nerves flutters in my belly as I head through the back door. Everyone is sitting around the long, perfectly decorated, dining room table.

"Katie!" Lana's mom shouts when she spots me. "It's so good to see you!"

"Happy Thanksgiving, Mrs. Mathews. My mom sent over a pie and wanted me to remind you about the casserole for the luncheon." My eyes lock with Davis and he gives me a small side smile.

"That's so sweet of her! Patty makes the most amazing pies," she tells the room.

"Well, this was perfect timing," Lana says, standing from the table. "We were just finishing up."

The group shifts from the formal setting upstairs to the large comfy den in Lana's finished basement.

"Anyone want a drink?" she asks, opening the fridge to the small wet bar.

Artie unbuttons the top button of his jeans. "Not me. I'm too stuffed to drink."

"It's been so long since I've had a home-cooked meal, I'd almost forgotten what one tasted like," Kevin says, sprawling out across the sectional sofa.
"I need a nap after all that food."

Lana flips the TV to the Cowboys and Packers game.

"How were things at your house, Kate?"

"Wonderful, as always."

Thoughts of Max flash in my head when I see the Dallas Cowboys on the screen.

"Is James and Eric home?"

"Hmm?"

"I asked if James and Eric are home."

"Oh, sorry." Snapping back to Earth. "James is, but Eric won't get to come home until Christmas. His new job has him crazy busy."

"Who's Eric?" Davis asks.

"That's her older brother. He lives in Charlotte," Lana says.

The room grows quiet and within minutes Lana, Artie, and Kevin are sound asleep. Jackson's outside on the cordless phone talking to Gigi. Leaving just me and Davis together.

I cut through the awkwardness in the air. "I guess they're all in a turkey coma.".

"Appears so."

"Didn't want to head home for the holiday?"

"Well, I wanted to, but the tickets were so damn expensive. Since I saw everyone at the wedding, I figured it would be best to save up and go home for Christmas."

"At least you were able to get a home-cooked meal."

Davis nods. "Yeah, it was nice of Lana to invite us all here."

"Are y'all heading back tonight?"

"We're supposed to."

Our heads both shift to the three sleeping beauties.

"Well by the looks of it right now, I would put my money on staying."

"Definitely looks that way."

It's obvious Lana has forgotten it's my birthday, and I'd be lying if I said I'm not slightly disappointed. I was looking forward to walking into a bar and ordering my first beer, *legally*. But her hands are full and I know she would never purposely forget. She's going to feel terrible when it finally dawns on her.

After a few minutes of watching the game, I break the silence between us. "I didn't get to thank you for helping me the night of Halloween. I can't remember the last time I've been so sick. If you hadn't gone to the store, God only knows how bad it would have gotten."

"I'm glad I was able to help. I could tell you were sick. I could see it on your face."

We both go back to watching the football game until he blurts. "By the way… about what I said… I didn't…"

I interrupt him. "It's ok. I knew it was the booze talking."

"Yeah," he nods. "Sorry about that," he says with a chuckle. "You know me, always stirring shit up when I've got a few in me."

"No biggie," I say, hoping to end the topic by turning the attention back to the game as Dallas runs it in for a touchdown.

I'm home fixing a plate of Thanksgiving leftovers when the phone rings. "Kateeee! It's for youuuu!" James shouts across the house.

"Hello?" I say, trying to juggle the phone and plate at the same time.

"Happy Thanksgiving, Beautiful!" Max says warmly. His voice already making my lackluster birthday a little better.

"Well, aren't you the sweetest boyfriend ever!"

"Did you have a good day?"

"I did! Pigging out on leftovers as we speak. You?"

"I had a fantastic day. Right up until two hours ago." His voice growing serious.

"Why? What happened?"

"Jody happened!"

It turns out, Jody's been dragging her feet with the annulment and has been calling Max incessantly, begging him to reconsider. When he stopped taking her calls, she made another one of her infamous out of the blue, "show-up's." Only this time, it was at Max's parents' house. Giving them an Oscar-winning performance, swearing to them the pregnancy wasn't a lie and how she loved him with every inch of her soul…blah, blah, blah.

"Then, as if it couldn't get any worse, she proceeds to tell them the only reason I'm walking away from our marriage, is because I'm being 'brainwashed' by a spoiled rotten brat, who does nothing but party."

His words are like taking a knife to the heart. The idea of his parents thinking negatively of me, without even knowing me, brings tears to my eyes. "If I could get my hands around her fucking throat," I growl between clenched teeth.

"I know. I didn't even want to tell you, but knew it wasn't right to keep you in the dark."

"Well, I'm glad you did. But I hate the idea of your parents thinking I'm some sort of wild child."

Max is silent, and for a second I worry we've been disconnected.

"Hello?"

"I'm still here," he says and I can tell there's something he isn't saying.

"What is it?"

"I had hoped to have everything finalized before I told them about us," he says reluctantly.

"Well, I hope now that the cats out of the bag you were able to take up for me?"

"I… uh… I," he stammers. And I know instantly he didn't. "I thought it best to say we were friends for now. I don't want to take any chances of Jody using it as ammunition."

Tears have now turned to sobs. I'm not sure why I find his confession so upsetting. Especially, since I haven't told my parents either. But my reason is because Max hurt me and they had to see me heartbroken for months. Not because he was some sort of "dirty little secret." Maybe I'm being a hypocrite for being upset because I understand why he hasn't told them. But his inability to admit to our relationship crushes me all the same. Leaving me to question everything. *Am I breaking up a marriage? Am I a spoiled brat who does nothing but party?*

I hang up the phone confused, angry, and most of all, feeling as if I will never truly be worthy of Max. Our relationship has been one obstacle after the other. Nothing's been easy. From night one, when Wayne and his crew jumped him and Drew, it's been a constant ongoing battle. It's like the forces of nature don't want us together.

I'm upset and consider heading back to Lana's to vent but talk myself out of it. It's not the time to involve her. Instead, go for a more "drown in my sorrows" approach and head straight to DiMaggio's.

It's eight-thirty and the tiny pizzeria is packed. "Dang, Jack! This place is hoppin' tonight!" I shout, slithering through the line at the cash register, that's caused a traffic jam at the front door.

"Sup, Kate?"

I cringe at the voice coming from the bank of booths. *Great! Just when my birthday can't get any worse. I run into Wayne and his Merry Band of Rejects!*

I plaster on a smile. "Hi, guys. Good to see you," I lie. "Did y'all have a good Thanksgiving?"

"Ha! We sureeee did," Wayne slowly says between squinted, bloodshot, eyes.

"Uhhhh, are y'all high?"

Wayne chuckles. "We went for a more herbal menu this Thanksgiving."

"Well, I guess a lone turkey is walking around thanking you right now," I say sarcastically, as they continue their Beavis and Butthead laughs.

"Not parading around town with those fuckin' GI's tonight?" Wayne asks, turning to his boys. "Y'all remember when I knocked half that fuckers teeth in?" Throwing his hand up for a high five.

"Well actually, you didn't," I huff. "And no, I'm not parading around town with them tonight."

"It's a good damn thing. I would hate to have to knock the rest of his teeth in."

I consider leaving, but I'm hell-bent on buying a beer on my twenty-first birthday. I escape the ridiculousness and find a stool at the long pub-style bar.

"Damn, Carlos! I can't get over how busy it is. I guess everyone's had their fill of Thanksgiving food."

"Well, and the fact we are one of the few places in Alpharetta open today." He blows hair off his forehead. "We've been going nonstop all night!"

I reach across the bar to grab a bowl of peanuts. "More tip money to spend on Christmas, I guess."

"Feel free to throw on an apron and start slingin' some dough."

"I'd love to, but I have a date with a tall, frosty, beer mug tonight!"

Jack sneaks behind me and grabs my shoulders, giving them a gentle squeeze. "Kate, I love you. But there's no way in hell I'm losing my liquor license so you can have a date with Mr. Budweiser."

I grab my ID out of my wallet and slide it across the bar. "It's Mr. Coors Light, actually."

Carlos picks up my driver's license. "Well, I'll be damned! Let's pour this girl a drink! She's twenty-one today!" He shouts it across the restaurant and I smile, appreciative of the acknowledgment. Especially since it hasn't been the best of birthdays.

I wipe foam from my lip and about to call it a night when the bell on the front door jingles. I turn around to the sound of singing. My heart bursts as Lana, Artie, Ashley, Santos, Jackson, Kevin, and Davis, walk towards me holding balloons and a slice of my mom's pecan pie with a single candle in the middle.

"Happy birthday to you. Happy birthday to you! Happy birthday, dear Kate! Happy birthday to you!"

I close my eyes and make a wish. Tears swell as I blow out the candle. Lana throws her arms around me. "I'm so sorry I forgot. I'm a terrible best friend!"

"Awe, it's ok! Don't worry about it. It fell on Thanksgiving this year. Everybody had a million other things going on."

She shakes her head. "Nope! That's no excuse!" she says as Ash and Santos wrap around me for a sandwich hug.

I look around as everyone finds a seat at the bar, so grateful to have each one of them in my life. What a perfect way to end the night.

I take a bite of pie and feel a familiar hand on my lower back. "Happy Birthday, Kate," Davis whispers in my ear.

I don't look up, worried he'll see how flushed his touch has made me. "Thank you, Davis."

Wayne's giving us all the death stare and worry there might be trouble.

I whisper. "You remember my dumb, hillbilly, ex?"

"I didn't get the pleasure of meeting him personally, but yes, I remember him. Why?"

"Well, I don't want to make a big deal of it. But he's sitting over there," I say, gesturing Wayne's direction.

An evil grin splashes across his face. "Is that a fact?" he says, looking over.

"Don't turn around!" I laugh, grabbing at his face. "They'll see you and think it's an invitation for a fight."

"I'm six-five, two hundred and twenty pounds, Kate. Anyone dumb enough to fight me deserves to get their head kicked in."

He has a point.

We watch as Davis walks over to Wayne's table. Looking even more enormous with them sitting. A few words are exchanged, but it appears Davis is doing most of the talking. It's too loud in here for us to hear what's being said. Wayne glances over at me, then back at Davis.

"Oh God, here we go!" Bracing myself.

To my surprise, Davis throws money on the table as Wayne and his crew head toward the door.

Lana yells, "Holy shit! Are they leaving?" as we watch them leave with their invisible tails between their legs.

"I simply informed them we're having a party and asshole exes aren't invited."

"Hell yeah, ya did!" Santos shouts, giving Davis a chest bump. "First rounds on me!"

The holiday weekend went by in a flash and by Sunday evening Lana and I are back at our apartment, working on a week's worth of laundry.

I twirl a pair of bright pink thongs. "These are clearly date night panties."

"Give me those, ya perv!" Lana says, snatching them out of my hand.

"Artie has a thing for thongs."

"What man doesn't have a thing for thongs?"

She laughs. "Very true!"

"It's good to see you guys doing so well. It's obvious he's crazy about you."

"We actually got into our first big fight Thanksgiving night. So bad, I thought we might break up."

"Why? What happened?" Floored at the idea of them arguing.

"It was a stupid misunderstanding. I made a comment about this being the first Christmas I've ever had away from my parents, and he took it as me regretting my decision to go to Oregon with him. Next thing I know we're in a huge blowout."

"Was this after y'all left DiMaggio's?"

"Oh, no. It was before. But after Carlos called and reminded us about your birthday, the argument was put on the back burner. By the time we got back home, it was all water under the bridge."

"Well, that's good to hear," I say relieved, filling my laundry basket with stacks of clean towels.

"I wondered how you finally remembered it was my birthday."

"Yes! Thank God he called! I felt bad enough as is. If he hadn't, I would have never forgiven myself," she admits. "Nor Davis."

"What do you mean?"

"Oh, I thought he was going to kill me when he found out," she says, heading back to the dryer to pull the next load out.

"Really?" I shout.

"Oh, yeah!" she yells. "Actually the pie and balloons were his ideas. He refused to show up empty-handed."

She returns to the living room with her arms full of whites. "If I didn't know better, I would swear he still has a thing for you," she adds, dropping the clothes in the middle of the room.

I consider telling her about mine and Davis' run-in at the motel the night of Halloween, but it's best to leave it be. She would probably tell Artie, who would turn around and tell Max, causing a chain reaction none of us need right now. Especially, considering Max and I are already dealing with enough drama in our relationship. Adding Davis into the mix again would only make matters worse.

"What should we do about dinner?" I ask, putting up the last of the laundry.

"I'm all Thanksgiving'ed out. How does pizza sound?"

"Eh, I don't know." I shrug. "I was kind of craving Chinese."

"Sounds good to me. I'll buy if you go pick it up."
I call in our order and throw on a pair of sweats and a hoodie to make the three-minute walk to the Chinese place around the corner.

"Be right back!" I yell towards Lana's room.

I open the front door and jump out of my skin.

"Max!?"

His fist is raised, about to knock. The other hand clenching a vase full of gorgeous red roses.

"Holy shit!" I leap into his arms. "What are you doing here?"

"I took an earlier flight so I would have time to come by and see you," he says, wrapping his arms tightly around me. "I know I upset you and needed to make it right."

I kiss the side of his neck. "You have no idea how happy you've made me!"

"Were you headed out?"

"No. I mean... yes. Sort of. We called in an order for Chinese and was on my way to get it. Up for a walk?"

He gives me a little side grin. "How about I take you over on my bike?"

My heart begins to race. "Uhhh, I don't think..." He grabs my hand and pulls me into the parking lot.

Max standing beside his black and red bike is quite possibly the sexiest thing I've ever seen. The image could easily be the cover of a Harley Davidson magazine.

He grabs a spare helmet out of a small trunk. "I promise to take good care of you," he says, patting the top of the black leather seat.

He's such a big fan of motorcycles, I haven't told him about my wreck yet. I don't have the heart to tell him I hate them.

"Mind if I take a rain check this time? It might be hard to hang on to you and all the food."

He's disappointed but lets it go. "Sure. We can go another time. When we've got enough time for a real ride."

I can hardly wait.

"Look who decided to join us for dinner!" I say to Lana as we walk back into the apartment, carrying two brown paper bags full of Chinese food.

She laughs. "Oh, Max! Funny seeing you here!"

"Wait!" I look back and forth at them. "Did you know he was coming?"

Max pulls out a small wrapped box from his bag. "Since my girlfriend didn't tell me I was missing her birthday, her best friend pulled the slack."

"Oh, Max!" I say, grabbing at my heart.

He reaches over and gives me a sweet kiss. "Happy Birthday, Baby!"

I beam as I tear open the box. A ridiculous grin plastered across my face as I pull out tissue paper, exposing the navy blue, Dallas Cowboys ball cap.

"I know how much you like wearing your hair in ponytails. So thought you'd look even hotter sporting them with the help of my Cowboys."

"Oh. Thanks. Max," I say appreciatively, hoping to hide my confusion.

"You're welcome. But I should bend you over my knee for not clueing me in your birthday was coming up."

Max has physical training at six in the morning, so he had to get on the road. I'm thankful he surprised me. It was a sweet gesture, especially after we had ended our conversation on such a bad note the other day. We still have a lot of obstacles to work through, but it definitely seems like he wants to try.

CHAPTER TWENTY-ONE
Christmas Break

Another semester is officially in the books. The break has been nice and much needed after four incredibly intense finals. After admitting to my parents I'm seeing Max again, I helped Ashley move into her new apartment in Columbus. I spent four amazing days with him as we helped her settle in. It was the longest I'd been able to stay and took full advantage of our time together. No partying, no distractions, just us. Doing normal couple things. It gave us the opportunity to learn more about each other. It was exactly what we needed. Especially, since we're going to be spending Christmas apart.

Lana and Artie left for Oregon yesterday. I won't see her again until New Year's Eve. There's a huge military ball Fort Benning hosts each year and we've been invited. We spent the entire weekend combing through racks of dresses at every boutique in Atlanta. I thought shopping for prom was tough. It pales in comparison to the insanity of ball gown shopping. Thirty-two dresses later, we finally found gowns we love and we can't wait to wear them. I've never wanted Christmas to fly by so badly in my life.

"Sweetheart? Would you mind wrapping this last-minute gift I picked up?" Mom asks, dropping Walmart bags on the kitchen table. "Eric waited until this morning to ask for a new electric razor."

"Sounds pretty typical of him," I say. "Is all the wrapping stuff in your bedroom?"

"No, I've got it all piled on the pool table downstairs.

I rummage through the bags for the razor. "Speaking of Eric, when's he supposed to be in?"

"I'm expecting him any minute, actually. He left Charlotte at eight this morning."

The Christmas Story is playing on the big screen as I make the finishing touches to my wrapping job.

"Katie Bug? You down here?" The voice of my eldest brother bellowing from the staircase.

It's been over nine months since Eric's been home and my heart leaps as he rounds the corner of the den.

"ERIC!" I shout, running over for a hug. "Oh, I've missed you!"

"How's my favorite sister?"

"I'm your only sister, dork!"

"Well, you know dad. He was pretty wild in his younger days. There might be a little Carpenter bastard running around somewhere in the world."

"You're terrible!" I say, smacking him on the arm. "It's good to have you home, but you're terrible!"

"What's with the ball cap?" he asks, smacking the bill. "I thought you said they make your head itch."

"Ehhh, I know. I'm trying to push past it." Suddenly feeling itchy as I straighten it back in place.

"I hope that was my new razor you were slapping a bow on. Mine crapped out on me this morning."

"No, it's actually a big lump of coal."

"Well, it would probably be more appropriate," he admits.

I jump on the end of the sectional sofa and run the volume down on the TV as Eric plops on the other end. "So what's with the Cinderella dress I saw hanging in your room?"

I flash a big toothy smile. "It's my gown for the New Year's Eve ball my honey is taking me to."

"Ah, that's right. Your military guy. The one you met at the beach, right?"

"Yep! That's the one."

"And isn't he the same guy Wayne beat the shit out of?" he asks, trying not to smirk.

My smile falls and is replaced with irritation and a side-eye. "I wouldn't go as far as saying he beat the shit out of him. But yes, there was a confrontation."

"Classic!" Eric says, laughing. Purposely trying to annoy me. "And what was the deal about you jumping off a porch to avoid him and got chased by raccoons?"

"Oh my God! Don't ever listen to James. He *never* gets stories straight."

"So you didn't jump off a porch?"

"Well, yeah. I did. But to avoid Davis, not Max."

Eric scratches the side of his head. "So you jumped off a porch for another guy?"

"I haven't seen you since Easter. You've missed a ton. Maybe I should start from the beginning."

"It would definitely help!"

An hour and a half later, I had finally brought Eric up to speed on everything that's happened since our crazy Memorial Day weekend. I fill him in on almost every sordid detail of the last six months, with the exception of Davis and the bar bathroom. There are some things my brother doesn't need to know about his little sister.

Eric's brow furrows. "So let me make sure I have all this straight. Max… the one taking you to this ball next week… is *still* married?"

I grimace. "Well, technically, yes. But that's only red tape."

"Uh-huh," he says. "And this other guy... Davis. The one you say is a big douchebag. He told you he was pretty sure it was either Max or the Drew guy who had you and Lana ran off…. and it ended up being true?"

"Well, yeah. But it was a misunderstanding. Drew was just trying to be funny."

"And he warned you Max was still seeing this other girl. The one he ended up marrying?"

I'm getting irritated with where this is going. "Yes, but he blew it *way* out of proportion!" I snip.

"And even though he knew you were head over heels for this Max guy… he rescued you from bars, defended you when you were being hit on… bought medicine when you were sick… made sure you had presents on your birthday *and* stayed by your side after you went tumbling down a ravine?"

"Well, if he wouldn't have been such an asshole, I wouldn't have been in a position to go flying down a damn ravine in the first place!"

"Katie, I love you and I support whatever you do. But if you honestly think what he said on Halloween was because he'd been drinking. You're a fucking idiot."

My mouth drops. "But *he's* the one who apologized and said he was trying to stir the pot."

Eric flings his hands in the air. "Of course he did, ya dumbass! He was saving face! I mean, come on! Wouldn't you if you were in his shoes? He's played second fiddle in your eyes for months. I'm sure he wanted to bow out gracefully after you walked away from him like you did."

Heat radiates from my cheeks. "You don't know him, Eric! He's a complete dick ninety-nine percent of the time.

A vain, womanizing, male chauvinist pig, who's screwed everything this side of the Mississippi!"

"Who's screwed everyone this side of the Mississippi?" James asks as he makes his way into the den.

"Sup, Little Bro!" Eric says, standing to give James a hug. "Katie's been filling in all the holes of her Fort Benning adventures."

James nods. "I'll give her credit. They're a pretty cool group of guys."

I smirk. "See! Even James agrees they're awesome!"

"Don't get me wrong. It definitely sounds like they're great. But it doesn't change my opinion of Davis."

"What about Davis?" James asks.

"I was telling Katie I think he's got a thing for her."

James chuckles. "Hell yeah, he does! Dude's Coo-Coo for Cocoa Puffs over her."

My smirk falls and is replaced with annoyance. *Not him too!*

"No. He's. Not!" I shout.

"Don't play dumb. He held your freaking hair back while you barfed your guts up. No guy is going to do that unless he's batshit crazy over them."

"Yep! He's right. Only true love would move a man enough to watch a girl upchuck," Eric teases.

"And it only got worse after the two of them did the deed in Gatlinburg," James adds.

"Ohhhh really? You conveniently left that little tidbit of info out of your story!" Eric shouts and points. "She said they *just kissed.*"

I fling a pillow at his head.

I'm irritated and refuse to be subjected to any more of this. "You know what? I'm done with this conversation. Davis is completely irrelevant." I stand to leave.

"Y'all have no clue what you're talking about."

"We're right and you know it!" James yells as I make my way up the stairwell.

Hearing, "and you know it" sends flashes of Halloween spinning through my brain. *"He doesn't know you like I do and you know it. He doesn't challenge you like I do. And you sure as hell don't have the heat you and I do."*

"No!" I growl. Stomping away like a child as I will away thoughts of Davis. I refuse to let those few random moments of kindness cloud my judgment.

Taking every measure possible to avoid my brothers, I spend the rest of the night confined to my bedroom watching old Christmas movies. Glancing over occasionally at my dress hanging from the closet door. The royal blue, strapless gown with silver crystals on the bodice. Elegant ruffles tier down the long full-flowing, Cinderella skirt. I fall asleep with thoughts of Max in his dress blues. Me proudly clutching his arm as he guides me through the crowd.

"Merry Christmas Eve!" I gush, handing my mom a cup of coffee as she makes her way into the kitchen, wearing her adorable Santa PJ's and matching house shoes.

"Oh goodness, Katherine! Are you making breakfast?"

"Yep!" I beam. "I had a great night's sleep. It's Christmas Eve… the whole family is home. The least I can do was make us a big ole Carpenter breakfast."

"Well, thank you, sweetheart!" she says, kissing me on the cheek. "And Merry Christmas Eve to you too."

I'm trying desperately to hide the fact I haven't heard from Max in three days, have terrible menstrual cramps, and thanks to my stupid brothers… I spent the entire night dreaming about Davis, instead of my actual boyfriend. *Ugh!*

Eric rubs his eyes as he drags into the kitchen. "Is that sausage I smell?"

"Your sister's making breakfast for us this morning," Mom says proudly.

"I'm going to spit on his," I mumble under my breath.

"I'll go wake dad and James," he says, giving me the evil eye as if he heard me.

After slaving over the stove, breakfast is finally ready. The table overflowing with scrambled eggs, bacon and sausage, pancakes, toast, and OJ. It all looks pretty damn good if I do say so myself. Then again, it's hard to screw up breakfast.

"You've outdone yourself Katie Bug!" My dad's voice booming through the kitchen, taking his seat at the head of the table.

"Run and grab the paper off the porch, James. I want to read the latest on The Whitewater investigation and that son of a bitch, Clinton."

"Oh, Joe! It's Christmas. Can we at least try to refrain from the profanities?" Mom snips, gesturing over to the baby Jesus in his manger display.

His lips purse. "Yes, Dear," he concedes. "But I'm sure the Shepard's and Wise Men would agree he's an S.O.B. too!"

James barrels back into the house, slamming the door. "Burrrr! It's gotten cold out there! I grabbed yesterday's mail while I was out there too," he chatters, dropping mail and a small, elongated, package on the counter.

"What's this?" Mom asks.

He stuffs a sausage link in his mouth. "No clue," he mumbles. "It's for Kate."

"For me?"

"Well, unless there's another Kate Carpenter, who resides at 1519 Brookdale Drive. I'm pretty sure it's yours," Eric says sarcastically. Showing the name to the table as he hands it over.

The package is wrapped in brown shipping paper and although addressed to me, there's no return address, but postmarked Columbus, Georgia.

I roll out my lip and pull the box to my heart. "Awe! It's from Max!"

"Oh, Maxipoo! My whittle boo, boo, boo!" My brothers chant.

"Don't be jackasses!" I say curtly. "Sorry, Mom." Remembering her Christmas rule.

I knew better than to open the present in front of my brothers, so I wait until we're done with breakfast and safely back in my room before opening it. The curiosity was killing me as I had to sit there, staring at it through the entire meal. Yet helping to relieve some of my earlier concerns about Max not calling.

I flip the package over and slowly peel the paper off. Confusion sets in as I see an ingredients list and a calorie chart. *What the heck is this?* I think, ripping off the remainder of the paper.

My hand flies to my mouth as the words register in my brain. "Griffin's Candy Shop–Gatlinburg's Award-Winning Pecan Turtles."
I flip open the small folded card taped to the top...
I know how much you loved these!
Merry Christmas,
D-

CHAPTER TWENTY-TWO
New Year's Eve

I've spent the last six days in emotional turmoil. No matter how hard I try, I can't stop thinking about Davis and it's pissing me off. He's always there! Needling in the back of my head like an annoying gnat I can't shoo away. I could beat the living shit out of my brothers right now. My only hope is when I see Max today, it will help reset my brain back to its original Davis disdain programming. Reminding myself Max has done as much, if not more, incredible things as Davis. *So what he bought me chocolates? Max drove all the way to the beach to spend one night with me. Possibly the most romantic thing anyone has ever done for me.*

"You're awfully quiet today," Lana says, noticing I've barely spoken since we got on the road to Columbus. "Everything ok?"

"Yeah." I smile. "A little nervous about tonight, I guess."

"Don't be nervous! It's going to be a fairy tale come true," she beams. "We will be the hottest three chicks there. Of course, I'm Cinderella and you two are the wicked stepsisters," She winks and grins.

"So the guys are picking us up from Ashley's?" I ask, trying to make some shred of conversation.

"Oh! I completely forgot to tell you. Santos rented a limo!" She squeals. "I told him it was probably a good thing because there's no way in hell all these big ass ball gowns would fit in a regular size car."

"That's awesome! We'll be rolling up like big shits."

She throws her hand up for a fist bump. "Damn right we will!"

It's five o'clock and it looks as if the Ms. America pageant is being hosted right smack in the middle of Ashley's apartment. Makeup, hair rollers, dresses, slips, and pantyhose are strewn under a cloud of hairspray and perfume.

"So who all's riding with us?" I ask, trying my best to sound nonchalant.

Ashley slips her gown over her head. "It's just us six."

"Really? I thought maybe Jackson and Gigi might be joining us. Or Davis."

"Jackson's still on leave, so they won't be there. Davis is going but not with us."

I grab my hairbrush. "He taking Goldie Locks?" I ask, casually.

"Nope. He's actually dating someone now."
Shock floods my face as Lana joins the conversation. "Crazy, huh?"

"Oh, I met her! Her names Cherish and she's a sweetheart!" Ash adds.

"Artie said she's very pretty too," Lana says, slipping on red heels that match her gown perfectly.
He's dating someone? Since when does he date? And what the hell kind of name is "Cherish?" What is she? A fucking greeting card?

"And speaking of Davis," Ash says, pulling me from my thoughts. "Wasn't that the sweetest Christmas gift ever?"
My brow crinkles.

"Oh, it was!" Lana beams. "Absolutely the best chocolates on the planet!"

My heart sinks a little, but try to not let it show. "He sent y'all turtles too?"

"We all got a box. He had ours shipped all the way to Artie's house in Oregon."

"Who knew he was such a nice guy after all!" Ashley adds.

After the news of someone new and finding out the chocolates weren't only for me, I begin to feel like a complete moron. *See! He doesn't like me.* I could kill James and Eric for even putting the notion in my head.

"It *was* sweet of him. But don't let him fool you. He's still an asshole, ladies!" I say headstrong.

"Who knows? Maybe this new lady in his life is bringing out the best in him."

The doorbell rings as the three of us rush to finish getting dressed. "Dammit, Kate! I knew I should have snagged that dress. You look amazing!" Lana says.

"We *all* look amazing!" I shout. Finally finding a burst of excitement knowing Max is here and my mind is back to who is supposed to be on.

"Hello?" Santos yells, cracking the door open. "Can we come in?"

"Of course!" Ash shouts as we make our way down the apartment hall.

Standing in the living room, the six of us stare at each other. I had envisioned this moment a hundred times, but nothing could have prepared me for how exceptional they look. Especially Max, who fits perfectly in his tailored dark blue jacket with gold buttons and cords.

"You look amazing, Max!"

"You too, babe! Wow!"

"Pleased?" I ask, making a turn in the middle of the room.

"Pleased doesn't even come close to describing how beautiful you look. I'm in awe."

It's exactly the reaction I was hoping for and it helps settle the reservations I've had about him in an instant.

"Ladies, you all look beautiful," Artie says. "We will be the three most envied men in Columbus tonight."

Santos opens the door. "Shall we?"

A bottle of chilled champagne and six crystal flute glasses awaits as we pile into the limo. We watch Artie pop the cork, handing a glass over, one by one.

Max grabs my hand and gives it a little squeeze. "Guess what?"

"What?" I ask, curious about this look he's giving.

"I love you."

He places a gentle kiss on my exposed shoulder, right above my scar. My eyes widen. I'm lost for words as butterflies dance in my belly. He's never said it out loud like this and it leaves me feeling more panic than peace.

"You never told me how you got this," he says, kissing my scarred shoulder.

Before I have a chance to respond, Artie begins a toast, interrupting the moment. "To an amazing night and to having the three most beautiful women on our arm!"

"Cheers to that!" Santos concurs as the group clinks glasses together.

It's early, but the parking lot is already full as the limo creeps towards the front of the community center. The line to go in is backed through the front doors.

"This is so exciting!" Lana squeals as we file out of the car.

Max grabs my hand to help me out, noticing I'm fumbling with my dress. Still speechless, I'm barely able to say "Thank you."

We make our way to the front steps. "Uhhhh, is *that* a receiving line?" Lana asks, pointing to the long line of officers at the banquet room door.

Artie tries not to laugh. "Baby, I told you you'd be meeting my Superiors."

"You did. But failed to mention it would be the first thing we did and all of them at one time!" she says, fanning her armpits.

All three of them laugh at the worry plastered across our faces. "It's no big deal. We promise," Max assures. "Shake hands and smile pretty. It's that easy."

He was right. It was simple introductions that got easier as we filed through the line of distinguished officers and dignitaries, all draped in metals. An attendant directs us to a photo area, complete with backdrops and cheesy props.

"Now *this* is more like it!" Lana says, jumping straight into her best prom pose.

Santo's points to the last photography stand. "Look! There's Davis!"

Standing in front of a baby blue background and a hideous fake column, Davis and his date pose for the camera. He looks incredible in his uniform. The perfect depiction of a real-life Prince Charming. Trying not to stare, I force my eyes off him to size up his date, who's as beautiful as he is.

The photographer asks them to gaze at each other instead of the camera. He's looking at her affectionately and it sends a charge of envy coursing through my veins.

He whispers something in her ear and it makes her laugh, as the photographer snaps a picture. They look amazing together and it affects me deeper than I'd like to admit.

After our turn in front of the camera, we make our way into the ballroom. The lights are dim as white tulle and twinkle lights swoop and zigzag across the ceiling. Rows of long tables draped with white linens and beautiful New Year's Eve themed floral arrangements line the room. A podium with the U.S. Army emblem and a DJ table are set up in each corner of the stage. Silver confetti sprinkles across the large dance floor as hundreds of balloons hover in a net above, awaiting their midnight descend.

Max spots Cooper from across the room and waves. "There's Cooper! He's saving everyone seats."

"Oh good!" I say, giving my own wave. "If you don't mind, I think I'm going to run to the ladies' room before we settle in for dinner, if that's ok?" I point back through the ballroom doors.

He smiles. "Of course! I'll meet you over there." He gives me a quick kiss before rushing over to the table, full of boisterous comrades.

Artie and Lana are finishing their pictures and I take the opportunity to snag her. "Mind if I steal your date, Artie? You know how us girls always have to pee in pairs!" I attempt to sound casual while internally freaking the hell out.

I grab Lana by the arm and pull her into the ladies' room. "What's wrong?" she asks, knowing something's up.

"Max told me he loves me," I blurt.

"Awe, Kate! That's wonderful!" she says, grabbing at her heart.

"Is it?"

"Max is amazing! Look at everything you've both gone through to get here. You're finally getting everything you ever wanted. Why the hell are you questioning it?"

I shake away the worry, bound and determined to not overthink this.

"You're right. You're absolutely right!" I say, adjusting the top of my dress in the mirror.

"It's just nerves," she says, smoothing a piece of loose hair in the back of my head. "Falling in love is scary. Trust me, I know. If it were easy, there wouldn't be such a thing as heartache. But for true, unconditional, heart-pounding, knees weakening, do anything for each other type of love… it's a risk worth taking."

I grab each side of the sink and close my eyes. I let out a long, deep breath to calm myself. "I feel better now. Thank you." I wrap my arms around her. "I guess all I needed was a best friend pep talk."

"That's right! Now go out there and get your man!"

The Color guard is lined up in the lobby, queuing the opening ceremony. Lana and I slip in quietly as the attendees rise for the Posting of the Colors. Goosebumps shoot down my arms as the soldiers march across the room, carrying flags to their designated post, followed by the singing of the National Anthem. It was awe-inspiring to watch these amazing servicemen we've come to know and love, honor and respect the moment in such a gracious manner.

After an incredible speech by the Commander and about a dozen toasts later, the buffet line is finally open. It brings a close to the formalities of the night, allowing the New Year's Eve festivities to officially begin.

"Now it's time to get this party started!" a soldier yells across the room, causing the entire hall to erupt in celebration.

"Ready to eat?" Max asks.

"Absolutely! I'm starved!"

He leads me on his arm through the crowd of people and it was exactly as I'd imagined. I smile pretty as heads begin to turn.

"They're all staring at you," he whispers. "Jealous their dates aren't as hot as mine."

My face flushes. "I'm sure it's the dress, Max. But thank you."

The line for food is long and I'm already regretting my shoe choice the longer we wait. Every few seconds, friends of Max's walk up and have typical boyish banter hellos, along with the respectful date introductions. Leaving me to make idle chit chat with each one's boring wife or girlfriend.

I spot Artie, Lana, and Ashley and Santos, further back in line. I consider waving them up but fear the stink eye from the rest of the line.

Max continues gabbing with friends like high school girls as we make our way through the buffet. Making sure to check on me every few minutes, trying to include me in the conversations as much as possible.

"So you're the infamous Alpharetta girl we've been hearing so much about?" a dapper older gentleman asks.

Max says. "Kate, I would like you to meet my Commanding Officer, Captain Michael Mooney."

"It's a pleasure to meet you, sir."

"You said she was beautiful, Maxwell, but that didn't do her justice," Capt. Mooney says, causing me to blush.

"I've heard about all those crazy adventures you've all been on. It helps this old married codger live vicariously through these young bucks," he says, grabbing Max by the shoulder.

"Oh, I bet they've embellished things a tad. We're pretty boring ninety-five percent of the time," I tease.

Four more introductions later, we're finally back at the table and grateful to give my aching feet some relief. While Max reminisces about old Army stories with the table, I catch myself scanning the room for Davis. I shouldn't be, but I'm a tad disappointed he's nowhere to be found.

I'm finished with my meal by the time the rest of our group joins us. All victims of the same delays Max and I were.

"It's about time y'all got here!" I say, thankful for familiar faces.

"Thank God we're not being tested on who's who, because I lost track after the hundredth person," Lana huffs.

"No kidding!" Ashley adds. "I don't know how you guys keep up!"

I take the last swig of my wine as they dig into their meals. "I'm going to run to the bar. Anyone need a refill?"

Before I'm out of the seat, I've got orders for three beers and a jack and coke. I'm in the bar line as the DJ fires up the music, causing another celebratory outbreak. I glance towards the doorway and spot Davis. He sees me and it sends a charge of unexpected nerves.

He's walking over. His gaze drops to my dress, then back up. His face indifferent and cold, as if I'm a total stranger.

"Sup, Skeeter?" he says, flatly.

He hasn't called me that in months and it catches me off guard. "Oh. I'm…I'm good, Lurch. How are you?"

"I'm fantastic!" he says, stoically. "Other than my poor date getting her hair caught in my metals." He waves his hands around his head. "She's in the bathroom having to get it all primped back up."

"I saw you guys earlier. When you were having your pictures made. She's pretty."

"Damn right she is. She's fuckin' beautiful."
The bartender stacks the drinks on the bar as I wait for his typical rude, female degrading punchline, but it doesn't come. *Damn, I guess he actually likes this one. He didn't make one sexist remark.* It's a first and I'm not sure how to feel about it.

"Three Bud Lights, a Jack and Coke, and a glass of Pinot Grigio," the bartender says, staking them across the counter.

"Damn, Skeeter! Looks like Max will be holding your hair back tonight."
I open my mouth to speak, but the words don't come out. Swallowing hard as I stare up at him.

"I thought you might need some help, Kate," Santos says, tapping his elbow to mine.

"Huh?" Snapping me out of my internal torment.

"Carrying the beers?" he repeats.
As I turn to grab the drinks from the bar, I hear Davis say, "There's my girl!" and it's like taking a bullet. I close my eyes to gain my composure before turning around. *Lord, please don't make me have to meet her. Pleaseeee!*

"Kate… I want you to meet Cherish."
I glance at the ceiling. *You couldn't help me out this one time, Lord?*

I screw on a smile and turn around. Thankful my hands are full so I don't have to shake her "beautiful" fucking hand.

"Hiiii," I say. Desperately trying not to sound condescending. "It's nice to meet you. I've heard such great things about you."

She throws Davis a loving smile, and it makes me want to barf. "Thank you, Kate! You too! Davis goes on and on about you guys!"
So I'm just one of the "guys" now, huh?

"Amazing dress, by the way. You look stunning!" she says with a sweet smile. Making me want to punch her in her perfect white teeth and hug her at the same time.

"Sorry I can't shake your hand," I say, motioning to the glasses. "It appears I'm playing bartender tonight." I glance up at Davis, trying my best to play it cool. "I better get these back to the crew before good ole Jack ruins my dress."

By the time I return, everyone's finished with their meals and has moved from old Army stories to the night we first met. "Yep! We thought long and hard about driving the car straight into the ocean," Max says, causing everyone to laugh.

"I would have gone and gotten those, silly woman!" Max says as I sit. "I turned around and you were gone."

"Oh, I didn't mind. You guys were enjoying yourselves. I didn't want to interrupt."

"Thankfully, Davis is head over heels for Cherish or I might have gotten all worried when I saw y'all chatting," he teases.

"Nope," I say wryly. "Nothing to worry about. He's still annoying as ever."

"Speak of the devil!" he says, standing to shake Davis's hand. "It's about time you two joined us."

"We were actually coming to get you assholes on the dance floor."

"Hell yeah!" Lana shouts. "I'm ready to get my boogie on with my honey."

I let the wine ease my conflicted mind. Refusing to let this Davis thing ruin my night. I have a wonderful man, who told me he loves me. Someone who's genuine and kind and adores me. I'm incredibly blessed and feel guilty for letting doubt enter my mind. *So what I've had to watch Davis and Ms. Perfect dance and cut up together all night?*

"Taking a breather?" Ashley asks as she and Santos return to the table.

"Yep, I had to give my poor feet a rest."

"I have a pair of flats in the car if you want to borrow them."

"Ashley, you may be the smartest woman I've ever met and I love you."

"Ut-oh! *Someone's* a little tipsy."

"Nah, I'm good. Just enjoying the night." She cocks a knowing eye. "Ok, maybe a smidge tipsy," I admit, motioning a smidge with my fingers.

"Where are they at, Ash? I'll run and get them," Max says.

"They're in a bright purple gym bag, lying right on top. You won't miss them."

"Thank you," I say and truly mean it. "You're a good man." Kissing him as he leaves.

Max is barely out the door when the DJ makes the "twenty minutes to midnight" announcement and shifts the music to a slow song. Couples who've been sitting, file gracefully to the dance floor. As I sit at the empty table alone, watching. Trying to act casual but feel like a dumbass.

"Angel Eyes" by The Jeff Healey Band fills the room, bringing a sudden calm to the rambunctious crowd. A sea of dark blue uniforms sways in perfect time to the song.

Davis is out there with little Ms. Perfect. His tall stature towering over the crowd. I shouldn't look. It's not right and borderline creepy. I fidget with a hangnail on my finger, trying desperately to keep my eyes off the dancefloor. But a few of the guys begin to sing loudly and it grabs my attention. I look up and my eyes lock with Davis's.

Memories we've shared these last six months flash through my brain like still photographs. We stare at each other as the words of the love song echoes through the room. Cherish grabs his face and pulls him to her. They kiss. A long, passionate kiss that causes pain deep inside my soul.

My chest goes heavy as I'm no longer able to deny what my heart already knows. I can't sit here pretending everything's ok. It's not right. Tears begin to pool, as I jump up and dash towards the door, stumbling a little on my dress as I go.

"Kate!" Max shouts across the lobby. "Come over here! I've got someone who wants to meet you!"

Dammit! I scream in my head, trying to quickly pull myself together for another unwanted introduction.

"Remember this guy?"

My eyes widen as mean, Sgt. Jackass turns around and flashes a huge smile. *This can't be happening right now!*

"Sgt. Brently, this is Kate. You two have already met once," Max says, trying to be funny, even though I'm completely mortified and I'm sure it shows.

"I've been wanting to apologize to you ladies for months." Extending his hand out. "I'm so sorry if I scared you and your friend."

He's still intimidating, but I muster the courage to shake his hand. "It's ok," I say, with a nervous, shy, smile.

"See! I told you he wasn't the big bad ogre you thought he was," Max tease, adding to my humiliation.

"We better get back inside," Sgt. Jackass says. "It's almost midnight."

"Oh crap! You're right," Max says, looking at his watch. "You ready?"

"Mind if I borrow you for a second, first?" Gesturing for him to stay.

"Sure. Everything, ok?" he asks, handing me Ashley's shoes.

"I'm sorry to keep you from the party. I had a couple of things I need to say and it can't wait."

"O…K," he draws, straight-faced.

"Tonight. When you told me you love me…" I take a deep breath, gathering my thoughts. "Those were words I've spent the last six months praying I would hear from you. Praying we'd one day have the opportunity at something wonderful."

"And we've finally been given a chance," he says.

"Yes. I know. The problem is…during those months I was pining away for you. Thinking we'd never be together. Someone else was there lifting me out of my own personal hell. Making things better again. Allowing me to simply feel *normal* again."

He shakes his head and scowls. "Let me guess… Davis?"

His hands ball into fists. "Please don't get angry!" I plead. "Davis has done nothing wrong. He hasn't said one inappropriate thing the entire time we've been back together. This is all me."

"I find that hard to believe," he snips.

"If I'm being truthful, Max. He's been my rock these last six months, by my side through everything."

"Don't be so naive, Kate. All he's done is cause trouble between us. And please don't flatter yourself into thinking it was because of you. It wasn't! This whole time, all these damn problems he's caused… they were because of me. His weird sick competitive side. He *always* has to win."

"I'm sorry you feel that way. But I don't believe it. Davis is a good man and more loyal than any of us give him credit for."

"He doesn't care about you. Hell, he's already moved on to another victim. You were nothing more than a chess piece in his sick little game."

"Maybe so," I admit as tears stream down my cheeks. "Maybe it's inevitable for me to fall for unattainable men."

"That's not true! You had me, heart, body, and soul!"

"Really, Max? Do I?" I snip. "Tell me. How the hell can I truly have someone's heart, body, and soul when they're *STILL* married!?"

"That's not fair, Kate! You know I've been busting my ass to get everything finalized!"

"You're right. You have. But it doesn't change the fact I'm dating… A…. Married… Man!"

I'm irritated now. Frustration and booze causing bitterness. "Besides, I've been so busy trying to be perfect in your eyes, I've hidden most of the real me. I hate motorcycles! Terrified of them!" I turn my shoulder towards him. "This scar is from a wreck I had on one and was too afraid to tell you. Because you love them and I didn't want to let you down. And I hate wearing heels! They're the most uncomfortable things ever invented. Oh… and I smoke! I'd smoke a pack a day if Lana would let me!"

The countdown to New Year's begins behind us and I pause. Ten, Nine, Eight…

The interruption gives us both time to let go of the anger. My voice calms. "I've fought so hard for us this whole time because truthfully, I thought it was meant to be. That the stars had somehow aligned perfectly that hot summer night, just so we could meet." Three…Two…One. "I thought it was fate that brought us together."

"Auld Lang Syne" begins to play as balloons cascade over the crowd in the distance.

"It *was* fate. But not for the reason I thought."

He shakes his head. "So it's over. Just like that?"

"I don't know if I'm a chess piece in one of Davis's little games. But it's not right to either one of us to continue pursuing this. Especially knowing my heart belongs to someone else."

There's nothing more to say. He's angry, but I believe deep down he knows something is missing.

We wrap our arms around one another for one last long embrace. We're saddened things have to end like this but both relieved to not walk away enemies.

Tears fall as he walks back into the ballroom. I watch my friends laugh and sway back and forth to the New Year's song, adorning 1995 crowns and blowing party horns. I don't have the heart to interrupt their happy moment.

I'm thankful for the taxi's lined outside the community center. Allowing me to slip out gracefully, without ruining everyone's night over my complicated love life.

I have the driver drop me off in front of Ashley's apartment and send one more prayer above that the door will be unlocked.

"Thank you, Lord!" I shout as the door swings open. With some effort, I finagle out of my dress. Leaving it in a crumpled pile on the bathroom floor. I wipe mascara from under my eyes and pull the rhinestone headband from my hair. Staring at my reflection, I pray I've made the right decision.

There's a pack of cigarettes hid in my purse and I've never needed one so badly in my life. I throw on a pair of sweats and grab a beer from the fridge. Taking up residence on the stairwell of the apartment breezeway. It's cold, but the crisp air feels good against my cheeks.

CHAPTER TWENTY-THREE

I take the last drag of my cigarette as the limo pulls up and prepare myself for the million questions I know are coming.

"Max told us what happened," Lana says, sitting beside me.

"Did he tell you I'm in love with Davis?"

"Nope. He left that part out. But I already knew."

"You did?"

"Kate, you've been my best friend since we were kids. I know you like the back of my hand. *Of course,* I knew. But I also knew you needed to figure it out on your own. Davis may be the world's biggest pain in the ass, but he has a heart of gold. And no matter what, he *always* put you first. Even when you weren't looking."

I let her words sink in. *God, I hate it when she's right.*

"When did you become so wise?"

She wraps her arm around me. "Well, when you have the world's greatest best friend, you pick up a thing or two."

I lay my head against hers. "Thank you."

"You're welcome," she says, brushing off her butt as she stands. "Davis is kind of like the prickly guy you're always going on and on about."

"Huh?"

She waves her hands. "You know…the one from that book. The Darcy guy."

"Well, I blew it! I had months to tell him how I felt and now it's too late.

He's with little Ms. Perfect and seems genuinely happy."

"He cares about you deeply. Maybe if you tell him how you feel…"

"Nope. No way! Can't do it! I physically can't take any more heartache."

"But aren't you worried you'll have the shoulda, woulda, coulda's?"

I stare off and sigh. "I'm sure I will, but I can't risk messing things up for him. It's not right."

"Are you sure?"

"I am."

"Then I guess it doesn't matter he's just pulled up." My head shoots to the parking lot. My stomach flipping as the car door slams.

"I need to get out of this dress," she says as Davis walks up. An uncomfortable silence fills the air as we watch her leave.

"Where's Cherish?"

"I took her home. She has to work in the morning, so I couldn't keep her out late."

"Happy New Year," I say, trying not to sound as sad as I feel.

"I heard you missed it."

"I couldn't ring in the New Year with him, knowing it would have been a lie."

"I'm sorry, Kate. I know it wasn't an easy thing to do."

"It was tough, but it needed to be done."

"You ok?"

I shuffle my feet across the concrete stair. "I will be." There's silence as I try to muster the courage to say everything my heart wants me to say. But my brain stops me.

"Thank you for the chocolates."

He smiles. "You're welcome. Did you enjoy them?"

"So much I could barely zip my dress tonight," I admit.

"They arrived late and was worried it might not get to you in time, so I had to…"

"I blew it, didn't I?"

"Hmm?" His heads cocks. "What do you mean?"

"Us…me and you. I waited too long."

He doesn't say anything for a few seconds. "Kate…"

"It's ok, Davis," I interrupt. "It's… It's my own fault." I look away, embarrassed. "I spent months fighting feelings for you because I had convinced myself I was supposed to be with Max. That he was my destiny. All because *he* was the one I met on the street that night. But as the weeks and months went by, you became everything I wanted him to be. I was broken. A version of myself I didn't even recognize anymore. Yet you *always* saw the real me." My voice trembles, but muster the courage to continue. "You were right the night of Halloween. Max doesn't know me like you do. He doesn't excite me, or challenge me, or make me feel safe and cared for like you do. And you and I had more passion in one night together than I've had in my entire life."

He begins to speak, but I stop him. "Please let me get through this, so I can walk away with no regrets."

I take a deep breath and continue. "I saw the way you looked at Cherish tonight. It was evident that you two have a spark and I will *not* get in the way of it. But I can't leave here tonight without you knowing how amazing I think you are. You would fight an entire bar in honor of a friend. Give them the shirt off your back if they were cold. You'd even go to every store in Georgia, to make sure they had balloons on their birthday. I love how you captivate any room you walk into and how your face lights up when you talk about work.

I love the gorgeous little side smirk you give when you know you've made someone's day. Or when your eyebrows scrunch when you're overthinking things. Kind of like what you're doing now..."

He laughs and it helps release some of the seriousness of the conversation. "Bottom line, Davis... you're an incredible man and you should be with someone equally deserving."

He glances at his watch then puts his hand out. "Come with me."

"Uhhh... ok?" I say reluctantly.
He leads me to his car and I get in without question, even though I'm confused and dying to know where we're going.

As we pull onto the highway, he asks, "Did I ever tell you about the night we brought your car back?"

I'm caught off guard but go along with it. "I don't think so."

"Well, as you know, I was gone when you and Lana first walked into our lives. I'd met a girl from Nashville who had drug me to a country bar. So it wasn't until later that night, I even knew you two existed. Drew was rounding the guys up to go back and beat the shit out of your boyfriend. Which I quickly volunteered to do, but not before we took a good long joyride in that sweet little Beamer," he chuckles.

I shake my head and smile, envisioning them cruising the Strip in dad's car as he continues.

"I'm in the back seat and keep kicking something. I go to move it and see it's a purse. Lana's purse. Bored, I dig through it. Wallet, makeup, tampons, about a billion crumpled receipts. You know...normal chick shit. Then I come to a pack of pictures of a graduation party."

The second he says it, I know which photos he's talking about. They were from the party Lana's parents threw her the weekend before our trip.

"The first few were of Lana and her family. Drew had told me she was the blond, so I knew who was who. Then I flip to one of the two of you. I remember seeing you and thinking, holy shit! This chick is hot! You had the prettiest eyes and smile I'd ever seen. Of course, I couldn't dare say that out loud. I believe I went more for the 'she's fuckable' line. And being typical macho me, had to leave the snide bitch 1 and bitch 2 note when we left the car."

I nudge him in the side and call his a butthole. Still curious about where in the hell we're going

"So I knew exactly who you were when I opened the door the next day. Even with no makeup on and bumming clothes, you were just as beautiful as that picture. Unfortunately, Max had already 'called dibs' on you, so I figured being a dick was the smartest move. Not thinking for a second we'd see y'all past that weekend. But low and behold, we did. And as time went on, we slowly but surely became friends. I'd never been around a girl who made me laugh or who dished out as much shit as I did. I knew I liked you, but you were so hung up on Max and all his bullshit. I knew it wasn't the time. So I buried it.

"Then, we took our little adventure to Gatlinburg, and I got to see you in a *completely* different way." He wiggles his eyebrows and gives his infamous Davis smirk. "That night was amazing and knew right then, I was in *big* trouble. It honestly scared the living shit out of me. Which of course is why I ran off with Jenn the next day."

We drive across the Georgia state line into Alabama and park in the Walmart parking lot. The same one Lana and I had slept in so many months ago. He puts the car in park and turns towards me.

"Running off with Jenn didn't change the inevitable. I knew I was in love with you. But you had been through so much, I didn't want to put any added pressure on you. So once again, I shelved my feelings. I even tried going out with other people. After you showed up the night of my football party, I realized you needed to know." His eyes drift to the steering wheel. "Sadly, I was three sheets to the wind and couldn't even spell my name, none the less profess my love. So I made the decision to go to your apartment after my sister's wedding and tell you everything."

My head drops realizing where this is going. That was Artie's birthday weekend. The same weekend Max and I got back together.

"You can imagine my surprise when I climbed in the car that afternoon and see Max. Who spent the next two hours telling me you two were back together and how there needed to be boundaries between us moving forward. Needless to say, that railroaded my plan."

My lip quivers as I fight back tears. "I'm so sorry, Davis."

"*Then* Halloween rolls around. I think to myself… I'm a tough guy. I got this. I'm over here. We had to be around each other at some point, right? So I might as well rip off the Band-Aid. But when I saw you wearing your costume, looking hot as hell and guys hitting on you. I…I just," he stammers. "I couldn't stand it. I had never felt jealousy like that before. Oh, you know me. I tried to be the typical Davis playboy. I tried damn hard. But deep down, I was struggling. So when Max let you leave by yourself, I fucking lost it. Even though it didn't come out right, I *knew* I had to say what I did." His gaze falls to his lap. "But you walked away."

He's silent for a second and as I open my mouth to speak, he continues…

"I knew it was over. I had to let you go. I spent November trying to detox from all things Kate related. I'm sorry for lying to you at Thanksgiving. I was trying to save face. Hoping to at least salvage a friendship."
My brother's faces pop in my mind. I'll die before I admit to them they were right.

"Kevin and I went out a couple of weekends later and I met Cherish. We've been dating ever since."
The mention of her name makes me shift in my seat. He slips on his jacket and slides out of the car. He walks around to my side and opens the door. The freezing air hitting like a brick wall.

"Why are we here, Davis?" I finally ask, deflated.
He doesn't answer. Instead, he reaches his hand out to pull me from the car. I shiver and rub my hands as the bitter cold air cuts through me.

"I brought you here because it's my turn to tell you how amazing *you* are."
My head tilts, scrambling his words together.

"You're smart, ambitious, and funny as hell. I melt every time you throw your head all the way back, to laugh that big infectious laugh of yours. Or when you lick your lower lip when you're trying to concentrate on something. And if I'm being honest…I'm an ass man and you've got a fantastic one. I don't give a shit what size your boobs are."

I appreciate the joke since both of us could use the emotional break. But his face grows serious again. "You were right earlier. Cherish is beautiful and sweet and uncomplicated. And I like hanging out with her. Being with her is easy."

Oh, God. Here we go! My head drops, preparing for the inevitable rejection.

He grabs my chin, forcing my eyes to his as tears roll down my cheeks. "But she's not you, Kate. No one is you." Plumes of fog fill the air as my tears turn to sobs. "When I saw you tonight, standing there in your dress. My God, I've never seen anyone so beautiful. You took my breath away. It took every ounce of power not to run up and fling you in my arms."

"But you were so cold."

"I had to be. Max was staring right at us and I didn't want to do anything that might screw up your night.

"But you called her *your girl.*"

He chuckles. "You didn't like that, did you?"

"No, I didn't," I admit. "I wanted to rip her pretty fucking face off."

"I know. I saw it in your eyes. And that's when I knew you cared about me. And when I saw you sitting at the table alone, all I could think was how much I wished it was *you* I was dancing with. I knew I couldn't let you go without a fight."

"You did?"

"I couldn't get to you fast enough though. You ran off. I went looking, but by the time I found you, you were already talking to Max. I overheard everything."

I gasp and fall into him. Giving in to the intense need to be close. His warm body enveloping me like a blanket as I cry uncontrollably in his arms.

"As soon as you left, I explained everything to Cherish and took her home."

"Why didn't you tell me, ya big turd!?" I say, laughing through tears.

"Oh, I was enjoying hearing all the things you love about me too much to stop you."

He glances at his watch again and pulls me from his embrace. "It's time."

"Time for what?"

"Time for you to find out why the hell we're in a Walmart parking lot in the middle of the night, in the freezing cold like a couple of morons."

I wipe the tears from my cheeks. "It's about time you explained yourself."

He reaches in the car and turns up the radio as another New Year's countdown begins. Ten, Nine, Eight…"Alabama is in the central time zone. Their New Year's Eve is happening now and there is no way in hell I'm ringing the year in with anyone else, but you."

My heart explodes as the announcer on the radio yells "Happy New Year!" Davis grabs both of my cheeks in his strong hands and kisses me with more love and passion than I've ever felt in my life.

As "Auld Lang Syne" plays again, I whisper, "I love you, John. Patrick. Davis."

His eyes widen as he searches my face. "I love you, too, Kate. More than words can say."

EPILOGUE
Wedding Weekend—Current Year

The line to check-in wraps around The Sun Crest lobby and out the revolving front doors. One by one, families, friends, and couples make their way to the front desk. All in pursuit of a fun-filled week, packed with adventure and good ole R&R. Rows of gold rolling carts line up as if they're ready for battle. Each ding of the elevator is a reminder wedding *"mini-reunion"* weekend is officially here.

Shelby swipes her ID badge into the time clock. "Well, look who's all bright-eyed for her afternoon shift," I say. "I figured you'd be dragging ass after I kept you up after midnight."

"Totally worth it! There was no way in hell I was going to sleep until I knew how New Year's went," she swoons. "If the laughter and tears didn't give it away, I genuinely loved hearing it all. Even when I wanted to throw things, I felt like I was right there on the adventures with you. Thank you for sharing it."

"You're welcome!" I chuckle. "Told ya it was a long, complicated story. But it's a part of my past that made me who I am today."

"I know we ran out of time last night, but I'm dying to know what happened next. After you and Davis finally got it all out in the open."

"Um, Ms. Vines," Brad's voice blares through my two-way. "The guests in room 2240 are in the lobby requesting to speak with a manager. Evidently, the view from the twenty-second floor isn't panoramic enough.

"Gotta love peak season for the rich and bougie," Shelby snickers.

I blow out a heavy sigh. "Tell them I'll be right there, please."

Shelby throws up her hands. "Wait! Before you go. *Please* tell me what happened. I'm vested now! I *have* to know. Did Davis go back to his old ways? Did Max come back and beg you to reconsider? Were you not able to let the stoner go?" She grabs my shoulders. "Tell me! *I. Must. Know!*"

Her over-dramatic pleads cause me to chuckle. "I most certainly did *not* go back to Wayne. And as for Max… We lost touch after he got out of the Army. Last I heard he married an old flame."

"And Davis?"

I pick at a hangnail and shrug. "We had two amazing years together. He showed… *we* showed each other, what true love was for the very first time."

"Then what happened?"

I sigh, wishing I could will away the truth. "Germany happened."

Her eyes narrow. "Huh?"
I shake away my last memory of John. The one of him standing in my apartment door with tears in his eyes. Army transfer orders clutched in his hand.

"It's *another* long, complicated story." I glance at my watch. "And we are officially out of time."

I grab the doorknob. "But!" she shouts.

"Another day, Shelby. I promise. I just need to get through seeing him this weekend first."

I make my way out of the office workroom and into the grand, nautical-themed, vestibule. I pull my cell phone out of my back pocket; the little blue "F" icon begging to be tapped.

I type… John Patrick Davis in the search bar like I've done hundreds of times over the years and stare at the same profile picture he's had posted for months. His arms draped around his two boys, the sun setting behind them as they stand on the very same beach I met him at almost twenty-five years ago.

I don't regret a single moment of how my life has been. Even though Charlie and I didn't last, we've raised two beautiful daughters. I have my dream job and even managed to shed those pesky twenty pounds. But as the countdown clock to this looming weekend finally lands on zero, panic shifts to hope as my past and the years of harboring the shoulda, woulda, coulda's, finally come full circle.

Status update: One hour ago. "Just landed in Atlanta. Next stop Del Ray Island! Can't wait to see all my Army brothers!"

To be continued.

Acknowledgments

To my husband, Kyle. Even though you didn't quite understand why I needed to write this story, thank you for supporting me throughout the journey. Thank you for always being "my person."

To my son, Sam. We are so proud of you! Keep following your dreams and you'll conquer the world.

To my son and daily comic relief, Jake. The one who keeps me on my toes. The one who would ask daily, "Are you *still* not done with that book?" The one I'm proud to tell… "Mom *finally* did it!"

To my parents, Larry & Sandra. Thank you for a lifetime of unwavering love and support. Your example made me a better wife, mother, daughter, & friend. I am truly blessed to be the one who gets to call you Mom & Dad.

To my dear friend, Autumn & my sister-in-law, Julie. Thank you both for your endless support throughout this journey. For putting up with the constant questions, opinions, feedback, venting, and sometimes tears. You were both a constant rock.

To my alpha reader, Renee. This story wouldn't have seen the light of day if you hadn't seen its potential. Your initial love for the story helped solidify why I was doing this. Thank you for seeing through the mess and encouraging me to keep on digging.

To my many beta readers & book-loving friends. Thank you for your time and honest feedback. Even when it was hard to hear, I listened to every word and have a better story because of it.